I0601215

BAD
INTENT

Michael Tabman

TotalRecall Publications, Inc.
1103 Middlecreek
Friendswood, Texas 77546
281-992-3131 281-482-5390 Fax
www.totalrecallpress.com

All rights reserved. Except as permitted under the United States Copyright Act of 1976, No part of this publication may be reproduced, stored in a retrieval system, or transmitted in any form or by any means electronic or mechanical or by photocopying, recording, or otherwise without prior permission of the publisher. Exclusive worldwide content publication / distribution by TotalRecall Publications, Inc.

Copyright © 2015 by: Michael Tabman

All rights reserved
ISBN: 978-1-59095-482-9
UPC: 6-43977-48235-8

Library of Congress Control Number: 2015951450

Printed in the United States of America with simultaneous printing in Australia, Canada, and United Kingdom.

FIRST EDITION
1 2 3 4 5 6 7 8 9 10

This is a work of fiction. The characters, names, events, views, and subject matter of this book are either the author's imagination or are used fictiously. Any similarity or resemblance to any real people, real situations or actual events is purely coincidental and not intended to portray any person, place, or event in a false, disparaging or negative light.
The scanning, uploading and distribution of this book via the Internet or via any other means without the permission of the publisher is illegal and punishable by law. Please purchase only authorized electronic editions, and do not participate in or encourage electronic piracy of copyrighted materials. Your support of the author's rights is appreciated.

Dedicated to our law enforcement officers who put their lives on the line, so we don't have to. Thanks to my former partner, retired NYPD Detective Mark Zucco for the friendship, memories and inspiration.

About the Book

Cocaine was the drug of choice in America during the 1980s and 1990s. The Colombian Drug Cartels controlled drug trafficking with ruthless violence. The cartels were well organized, corrupted entire governments and had so much money, the Mob was jealous. The United States declared war on drugs. New York City was at the heart of the war. The FBI and New York City Police Department joined forces. Work the streets with FBI Agent Bob Douglas and his partner Detective Mark Zucarelli as they stumble into a drug money laundering investigation and find that they don't know who they can trust. Was there more to the drug war than met the eye. Based on the author's years as an FBI Agent assigned to the FBI-NYPD Drug Task Force, this book tells the story from someone who was in the middle of the war on drugs. Hard hitting, raw and realistic, Bad Intent will make you feel that you are right next to the FBI Agents and NYPD Detectives as they take on the cartels and their own agencies.

Foreward

Cocaine floods the streets of New York City. Drug cartels are in control. The mob wants their share. The FBI and NYPD have a drug war to fight. But, who are they fighting?

FBI Agent Bob Douglas and his partner NYPD Detective Mark Zucarelli are deep into a drug investigation. Someone is moving millions of dollars of drug money in middle of New York City under the noses of the world's best law enforcement agencies. Who is doing it? How is he getting away with it? Who is protecting him?

Can Douglas tell the truth? Will the FBI have his back?

Douglas and Zucarelli are not sure they can trust their own agencies. But can they trust each other?

Chapter 1

With my gun digging into my crotch, I squirmed restlessly trying to find a more comfortable position. That didn't work, so I slowly and carefully shifted the small suede covered holster an inch or two on my belt, hoping to not accidentally shoot my balls off. My mind replayed, and my lips silently mouthed word for word, the argument we had right before I left for work.

Frighteningly, it sounded exactly like every argument my friends described as having before their wives became their ex-wives. I never thought my marriage would even get close to heading down that road. I tried to clear my mind. Coming to work distracted was never a good idea; we all needed a clear mind focused on the mission. Tonight's mission was to conduct surveillance, make the arrest and then grab the dope and money, if and when the deal went down.

"Hey Bob, what the hell are you doing?" Detective Mark Zucarelli, my FBI-NYPD Task Force partner asked me.

"Huh? Whatta ya mean?" I responded while mindlessly looking out the window at towering apartment buildings eclipsing two-story brick faced homes of the tough, blue collar Queens neighborhood.

"You're talking to yourself."

"Oh, uh, no. I was just singing a song that's stuck in my head."

"Well, keep it in your head. You're freaking me out."

"Sorry Zook."

Zook, as he was called, was an experienced New York City Police detective, having worked undercover against the mob and in narcotics. Tall and strong, he was a confident cop, sure of himself and proud of his service. But, he was impatient. Surveillance was not his thing. When you work narcotics, if you're not the undercover agent, you're waiting around for something to happen. Drug deals never went on time.

Like the rest of squad, we sat in the car with the windows rolled up, tuning out the cold wind and the rest of the world. Even in the middle of the night, somewhere in this big city, there was cruelty and crime occurring somewhere. We could not hear the distant shrills of a woman in tears as her husband pushed her head through the thin plasterboard wall only two blocks away. Maybe some cops on patrol would be dispatched to that domestic dispute call, maybe not. For us, the possibility of a few minutes of activity on an empty gas station lot would be our only focus tonight.

"Another long night. All for what?" I muttered, not really expecting a response. "For a good bust, Bob, that's what."

"Eh, I don't know. Does anybody really care about drugs anyway?"

"Don't you think everyone would rather see us take this crap off the streets before it gets into their kids' high schools?"

"Well, when you put it like that, I guess. It just seems like everybody is so friggin' indifferent to drugs, and violence and crime in general. Of course, only until it effects them.

Then they care."

"Well, maybe not completely indifferent. They must care a little. Otherwise, we wouldn't have a job and make the big bucks, right?"

"Oh yeah, big bucks."

Silence overtook us for a few moments. Zucarelli and I got along pretty well, but we were still feeling each other out as partners. If that worked, then maybe a friendship would follow.

Gazing out the passenger window, a strong gust of wind whipped up some dirt and trash into a small whirlwind that caught my attention. The mini-tornado swirled down the sidewalk until it dissipated as it hit a random target. "Look at that poor schmuck. How do they survive this kind of cold?" I mumbled.

Saying nothing, Zucarelli looked out my window and grunted, also staring at the ragged homeless man sleeping beneath the pile of newspapers and old clothes he managed to find rummaging through the garbage.

"Problem is, they don't always survive. There's a good chance the medics will pick up his frozen corpse in the morning."

"Hmm." Then my mind drifted into oblivion, the sad plight of this homeless man leaving my thoughts as quickly as it entered.

Suddenly, my attention was brought back to the task at hand as the car radios began to crackle. FBI agents and New York City Police detectives found places to settle in and called out their locations. Engines remained on to keep warm. Steam from convenient-store coffee began to fog the windows. The wait was on.

"So what do you think, Zook?" "Think of what?"

"Of this, you think the van is going to show up?"

"Oh, it's gonna happen."

"Really. Why you so sure?"

"C'mon. Every time your star FBI agent gets assigned something, it just happens." "I know, I've seen that. Maybe he's just lucky."

"Lucky nothing. Reardon is so far up Franks' asshole, it couldn't be any more obvious. Any time a groundball case comes in, Franks assigns it to Reardon and he comes out looking like a superstar. This is a good one; it's gonna go."

"You sound pretty sure."

"Hell yeah, I'm sure. Your Miami office handed this one to us. You know they got that hot informant who infiltrated the cartel down in Colombia."

"I did know that. I didn't think you knew. I thought that was confidential information."

"Get real, Bob. Nothing is confidential. You guys leave all those secret reports right there on your desks; you talk openly on the phone. Shit, we don't know how you FBI agents keep anything confidential."

"Neither do I. Besides, what's the point of having a task force if we can't tell you everything. It's not like they're plans for a nuclear war. It's just drugs."

"Agreed. Anyway, if the snitch is right, this van is packed with coke. Once it's unloaded the dealer is gonna give them half a mil to ship back. If we do it right, we're gonna seize it all."

"Yep, and then Reardon gets a few more arrest and seizure stats and we get the privilege of backing him up."

"Now you got it, Bob."

"What I don't get, is why Reardon. There's fifteen swinging dicks on the squad, well fourteen and Julie. Why not share the wealth; that would only be fair. What's his motivation?"

"Don't be so naïve. Franks is one dumb motherfucker. Nobody can figure out how he got to be an agent, never mind a supervisor. Reardon, as the second in command, covers for Franks' screw-ups, then Franks pays Reardon back by putting him in line to get the desk when he retires in a couple of years."

"Really? You think that's his intent - you protect me from myself, and then I'll take care of you by setting you up for my desk? Is it that easy?"

"Yes it is. That is one screwed up system the Bureau has for promoting people. At least in the NYPD we got a sergeant's test to weed out some of the crap trying to move up the ranks. It ain't perfect, but it's better than the FBI way."

"The FBI way?"

"Yeah, pure friggin' politics. C'mon, don't act so surprised. That was the first thing that hit all of us when we got on this NYPD-FBI task force."

"Really, of all the things we have in the FBI, the first thing all you cops noticed was the politics?

"Pretty much. That and all the crazy rules you got. We don't know how you expect to work on the street when you need six layers of approval for everything little thing you want to do and every dollar you want to spend."

"You get used to it."

"Have you gotten used to it?"

"I don't know. I tell myself that I have, but every day I go home with my head spinning." "I gotta be honest with you Bob. Me and the rest of the cops respect the FBI and what you do with Russian spies and shit like that. But we don't really picture FBI agents as narcs. So, when we see someone like Franks leading the charge, it kinda feeds into the cop perception of the

FBI not knowing their ass from their elbow when it comes to street crimes."

Taken aback by Zucarelli's honesty, I felt my jaw drop a bit. Not that I didn't know that about the cops; we all knew how they felt. I never expected to be hit with that so bluntly. Yet, I was glad that Zucarelli was comfortable talking honestly with me.

"Really, then what made you guys decide to join an FBI task force?"

"C'mon, you kidding? We get the FBI paying our overtime, giving us rental cars and cell phones and all this other crap NYPD can't afford. Nothing like sucking from the government tit."

"I guess it is a good deal for you. Maybe we should bribe the PD to work on foreign counter intelligence task forces too."

"Good luck with that. Money can only buy you so much cooperation."

"Can't say I blame you. Those FCI guys are miserable. All they do is get breakfast, play basketball at the navy yard, go to lunch, go shopping and head home at 3:30. As long as they do one memo a day, they're good to go. What a blow job that work is."

At that moment, Franks got on the radio.

"Speaking of the dipshit..." Zucarelli chuckled.

"13-1 to all units, just a reminder of the plan. After the load is delivered and the exchange made, 13-6, 13-8 and 13-9 follow whoever takes the load and stay on them. The rest of us will follow the van for a few blocks and then jump 'em," were Franks' instructions.

"Maybe we'll get lucky and this won't go. We get home early and Reardon comes up empty handed," I said to Zucarelli, half kidding and half hoping.

"Whatever. Do we know where in Colombia the coke is coming from?" Zucarelli then asked me.

"No, we don't. It seems like things were easier to figure out before the Colombians stepped up to the plate, killing Rojas and then extraditing the Montoya brothers."

"Yeah, I know. Back then it was either the Medellin or Cali Cartel running things. With those fuckers on the run, everybody went underground. Who woulda thought the Colombians were really gonna take on the cartels like that."

"Well, they probably just pushed too far with all that violence. They would've been better off working like our mob here. I mean, look at how they whacked Catalano, the supposed boss of bosses. Right outside a restaurant, in the middle of a busy street, they take him and his bodyguard out. No one else gets hurt. It was like a friggin' work of art."

"Good point. But then look what happened. After taking over the family, Gulotti got a little too much like Rojas. He got in the government's face and backed them into a corner. They had to take him out. Crime is a funny thing. If you don't push too hard, you can get away with a lot. Like we said before, the public is pretty indifferent."

With that sobering thought, we slinked into our seat and became silent. The digital clock on the dashboard flashed 5:42 with a soft green light. The deal was supposed to go at 5:30. For drug deals, which never went on time, it was still early.

Zucarelli leaned back in his seat, closed his eyes and started rubbing his right hand over his half flexed left bicep. Even half flexed it was twice the size of my both my biceps combined. By the smile on his face, I could tell he was drifting off into his own fantasy land – whatever that was. After about fifteen minutes, I broke the uncomfortable silence.

"So, what…"

"Shut up." Zucarelli abruptly interrupted me and grabbed the radio microphone.

"13-9 to all units, I got headlights coming down 43rd street. Don't know if it's our target, stand by."

"Okay, thanks, all units hold your position and stand by," Franks responded with those obvious orders.

"Get your boney ass down," Zucarelli ordered me as if I was some rookie agent.

"Okay, but you being able to describe my ass, got me a little worried."

Zucarelli smirked and I left it at that. Jokes about my skinny physique were common. As for Zucarelli checking me out, I knew I had nothing to worry about. He was one of the most prolific players I had ever worked with. He wasn't necessarily discriminating in his choice of women, but he scored a lot.

Killing the engine, hoping the exhaust was not noticed, we sank down in our seats as the headlights slowly approached us, with Zucarelli monitoring its movement via the side view mirror. The headlights passed right by us.

"13-9 to all units, it's a van, probably our target. One male in the passenger seat. It's coming down 43rd and will hit the corner, righhht….now. And it's making a left towards the gas station, someone take the eye."

"13-2, I got it," Reardon got on the radio.

"Of course you do," Zucarelli said under his breath but loud enough for me to hear.

The timing, the van's slow pace and direction of travel

certainly led us to believe that this was the van we were waiting for. We had to move carefully. It would not be the first time everything looked right and we moved in on a car scaring the crap out of some poor bastard minding his own business, who just happened to be in the wrong place at the wrong time.

"Okay, the van is passing the gas station, stand-by," Reardon called out to the squad. "I see two Hispanic males in the front seat. This is it."

After a few moments of radio silence, Reardon was back on, "Looks like he's squaring the block, checking for a tail. Everybody stay put; let's not get burned now."

Zucarelli and I looked at each other, tilting our heads, acknowledging that this operation was falling in to place.

"He's pulling in; he's pulling in to the gas station." The excitement in Reardon's voice was getting obvious.

"All units, be on the lookout for the car with the money. We have no info on that, but not too many cars should be driving around here at this time of the morning," Franks followed up on the radio.

The van turning into the gas station was a good sign. If our information was correct, the van was packed with cocaine. The car that was supposed to meet the van was loaded with cash. In most drug buys, the cash and drugs wouldn't show up in the same place, to avoid a rip-off. This was not a drug buy; this was one drug trafficking cell collecting its own money and replenishing its inventory. If some rogue or crazy drug trafficker tried a rip-off, he knew the consequences. First, his entire family in Colombia would be killed, but only after his wife, daughter and mother were gang raped. Then, in time, he would be hunted down. Throat slit and maybe some other mutilations, his body would be stuffed in a car trunk and then the car would be set on fire. The message was always clear; very little was left to the imagination.

Within a few minutes Reardon was back on the radio.

"13-2 to all units, I got a car coming down 41st moving slowly. Dark blue two door with Jersey tags."

"Jersey tags again. Why the fuck can't they stay on their side of the bridge," I asked what I thought was a rhetorical question.

"Because they're in Jersey. Why wouldn't they come over if they had the chance to get out of that rat hole."

"How true."

It was a funny thing about FBI agents in New York. They spent all day bitching about the traffic, the high cost of everything and all the other pain-in-the-ass things about living in New York. Most of the agents who worked in Manhattan lived in Jersey and commuted for an hour or two every day. Yet, New York agents were known for their sense of superiority. Why not, we all knew that the biggest and best cases in the FBI were made in New York. Jersey was like our kid sister.

"He's circling the gas station. Stand-by," Reardon put out on the radio. "The van just blinked his headlights," Reardon followed within a minute.

"The car blinked back," Franks called in within a few seconds, the excitement in his voice now apparent, as everything seemed to be falling into place.

"13-2 to all units, I've got the eye and I'll let you know when the deal goes down."

"13-1 to all units, everyone hold their position till 13-2 gives us an update. Then stick to the plan. Follow the van or the car according to your assignment. When I give the word, we take 'em down."

"Oh shut the fuck up. How many times have we been through this?" Zucarelli mumbled, rhetorically.

We all got sick of Franks giving us detailed instructions, over and over, especially to a task force of experienced FBI agents and New York City Police Detectives. Yet, most of us knew it was necessary; that's what supervisors were supposed to do. Especially for drug deals – they just had a way of getting all fucked up. No matter how much we planned, the plan never worked.

Our task force, with the moniker C-13, was located in Jackson Heights in Queens. That was the epicenter of cocaine trafficking, rivaled only by Miami. We had a reputation as one of the most active squads in the FBI, making impressive seizures of money and drugs. We were also very good at getting the drug traffickers to flip, in other words cooperate with us by setting up the next person in the drug trafficking chain, if they knew. That's how big cases were made.

Zucarelli and I sat slumped in our seats quietly waiting for the deal to go down. The men in the van would switch with the men in the car and drive off in separate directions, neither knowing where the other guys were going; and nobody caring. If anyone got arrested and for some reason decided to cooperate, they couldn't give up the other side of the operation. For most drug deals, by the next day, the van and the car would be abandoned; one would show up in downtown Manhattan and the other would be found by the Brooklyn Bridge. Unsuspecting New York City Police patrolmen would write a ticket and have the vehicles towed to rot away at some impound lot in the Bronx. But not tonight. We were grabbing the drugs and the money. That was a rare opportunity.

"This is taking a little too long ain't it?" I asked Zucarelli.

"I think so. Whatta they doing? They usually move quickly. That's what makes a successful drug deal; you get in and get out before anything goes wrong."

"I know. Let's find out what's going on." I grabbed for the radio.

"Don't," Zucarelli told me. "You're just gonna piss off Franks for asking. He's always riding your ass for something anyway. Don't give him any more ammo. Let this play out his way. You know how he gets if he thinks someone is trying to second guess him."

Letting out a slight sigh, I realized that Zucarelli's keen insight into office politics saved me from another confrontation with Franks. Reardon got on the radio again.

"13-2 to all units, the drivers are still talking to each other. Can't be sure what's going on. Everybody hold your position."

Several more minutes passed and we could only wonder what was wrong. There were couriers for the cartel with drugs and money, hanging around a gas station in the middle of a Queens neighborhood. That didn't make sense. They should have made the exchange and been on their way. But then again, nothing in the drug world ever really made sense.

"All units hold your position. I'm gonna get a closer look. Nobody move till I give the word." Franks was about change the plans. Zucarelli and I exchanged scornful glances. That did not sound like a good idea.

"What is he doing?" Zucarelli was almost yelling at me, clearly changing his mind about being patient. "What is he trying to get a closer look at; he's gonna burn us."

"Alright, sit tight, Zook. Maybe he sees something we don't. Have a little faith."

"Faith, my ass. I told you, if it was a spy case, we would do it your way. These are street level drug dealers; not what the FBI is known for."

That was a bit much. Our squad made a lot of arrests and seizures before becoming a task force with the cops. This was not a discussion I wanted to have with him. Besides, just as FBI Agents in New York believed that they were the best FBI Agents in the country, New York City cops saw themselves as the best cops in the world. If we were going to work together successfully, egos would have to stay in check; that was not easy.

Like everyone else, we sat in the car, unsure of what Franks was hoping to see or hear and hoping we didn't get burned. Or, maybe we were burned and they were playing a waiting game with us and that was why they weren't making the exchange.

The radio was silent. Our breathing was loud. Zucarelli kept rubbing his right hand over his thick moustache. I kept brushing my hair back with both hands. We all had our own nervous habits. Then we heard a loud clang and a bang.

"What the fuck?" Zucarelli screamed at a deafening tone.

Again, we waited nervously. Then we heard the radio.

"All units move in," Franks yelled into his hand-held radio that sent out a weak, statically signal.

While I felt my heart pounding in my throat, Zucarelli put our car in gear and rushed to the gas station. We saw the car, supposedly carrying the cash, screeching out the east exit and the van turning to the west. I didn't know which vehicle we should go after. Zucarelli was focused on the rear of the gas station and drove there; from my angle, I could not see what he saw. Franks, sitting on his fat ass, smoke still coming from the shotgun barrel and debris falling on him from the part of the awning he shot out, at least had the presence of mind to give us a clue.

"I'm okay; go after the car before it disappears," he told us.

"13-1 to all units, move in stop the van. 13-9 is in pursuit of the car," Franks managed to call over the radio.

Zucarelli had quick reflexes, both physically and mentally. He heard the shot and his first instinct was to find our brother agent who might have been hurt. Who liked who, and all the office politics disappeared as soon as we sensed a threat. That's how it should be in our business. Then he quickly redirected his attention the fleeing car with Jersey tags which was now out of our sight. We turned down 45th Street after the car. Not seeing anything, Zucarelli floored the gas pedal.

"Stop," I yelled as I looked back at a row of parked cars. I saw a little puff of exhaust rising from the rear of one of them. "Zook, I think they pulled over and we just passed them."

A narrow, one-way, residential street with cars parked on both sides, there was not a lot of wiggle room. Pulling a u-turn would have been difficult and may have even left us stuck in the middle of the street. Zucarelli started to back up, slowly and carefully, allowing time to react if something unexpected was to happen.

"You'd better be right. Otherwise those motherfuckers are gonna be long gone."

"I don't know. Look four cars down on my side. I think I see some movement inside. Let me get out so I don't get boxed in, then you pull up and block the driver door, ok?"

"10-4."

I got out of our car and started approaching our suspect vehicle. Zucarelli continued to back up. Just as he got within a foot or two, the passenger door opened and one of those bastards began to run.

"I got him, call it in," I yelled to Zucarelli.

Zucarelli then rammed our car into their driver side door. He slipped out his door and snuck up from the rear as the driver tried to make his way out of the door his partner just fled from.

"Nice try." Zucarelli had his gun pointed right at his head.

Like all experienced drug couriers, he knew it was not worth a bullet to his brain. He surrendered, while his partner took off running. Zucarelli called in on the radio that I was in foot pursuit.

Foot chases were not big in the FBI; that was more of the cop thing Zucarelli was alluding to. I never had one before, and I never even knew an FBI Agent who had been in one. Trying not to slip on icy patches, I ran fast but carefully watching my steps and hoping my gun would not spring loose. Most of all, I was praying I would catch him. The ignominy of allowing a suspect to get away was not appealing and it would be hard to live through the inevitable squad room ball-busting jokes that were not really jokes, but serious slights to your FBI Agent prowess.

With the weight of my bullet proof vest, covered by my winter jacket, it took only a few hundred feet into the run before I was breathing heavily. This was not going well; that bastard seemed to be putting more distance between us. Then my luck changed. He slipped on a patch of ice and started sliding down the sidewalk. I stopped to watch the show and to make sure that

I didn't hit the same patch.

That must've been some very slick ice. He went sliding down a modest slope of street picking up speed. As he continued his descent, his body flailing in different directions as he tried to get control of himself, I stood there giggling like a little girl.

Ouch, that must've hurt, I thought to myself as he spun head first into one of two small brick columns that held little gate doors leading to the walkway of one of the attached duplexes lining the streets. Who would have thought that a drug bust would have taken such a comical turn? As I watched for a moment, bending over with my hands on my knees, trying to catch my breath, I saw the unmarked car with flashing red bulb in the windshield turn the corner onto the street where we were. I appreciated the fast response time to back me up. Don Battles, who was in my academy class came charging out the passenger door of the car, while his partner, Detective Jack Fremont continued to drive to the other side to cut off any possible escape route. That was pretty good police work. Don seemed to be moving quickly, and I tried to call out to warn him how slippery it was. He was holding his gun as he ran. Like running with scissors, that was not a good idea.

Our fleeing drug dealer held on to the brick column as he tried to regain his footing. At that moment, Battles reached him. The poor schmuck could not get his footing and was almost running in place as another hard spill on the ice appeared inevitable. Trying to break his fall, I saw both his hands reach out onto Don who could not move fast enough to get out of the way. They both began to fall in unison, like two dancers in a perfectly synched choreograph. This night was becoming even more amusing at this sight, and I was about to break out laughing. But then I saw that flash, immediately followed by that unmistakable sound. Yes, it was a gun shot.

It had just come from Battles' gun. Though I had no idea as to the bullet's trajectory, I knew to look to my left where Fremont would be coming from. There he was. And down he went.

"Officer down." Those were two words I never really expected to hear coming out of my mouth as I yelled into my hand held radio. That phrase was used so often in cop dramas that it sounded so trite – as if I was not really communicating the urgency and emotional pain of what I had just seen. First, I moved to run towards Fremont, but then I thought I had better help Battles so nobody else got hurt. *No, help Fremont* I then thought as I started going his way. *But what would I do? We needed to eliminate the threat,* was my next thought. It was probably less than a full second that those thoughts ran through my mind, yet it seemed that I was so indecisive, moving in one direction, then the other, as if I was slipping on the ice.

My decision was made and I ran towards the threat. Battles had wrestled free and slid back on his ass holding his opponent at bay, who sat there compliantly with his hands in the air. They both looked to be in shock.

"You got it, Don?"

"Yeah, I'm okay. Go help Jack."

Patting Don on the shoulder I ran off to Fremont, lying on his back. His hands were over the bleeding wound coming from his thigh area, close to his groin.

"I called it in Jack; help is on the way."

"Okay, thanks, I think I'm okay," his voice was strong. He

was coherent and aware of what had just happened.

"Go help Don," he told me.

"He's alright Jack. I'll wait here with you."

Within minutes of my distress call getting broadcast over the NYPD frequency, two patrol cars arrived. Soon, there were two more cops cars and an ambulance. Fremont spoke with one of his NYPD colleagues for a minute or two; I assume recounting the series of events.

Shootings were scary and nerve-racking, but not uncommon in New York City. These paramedics were unfazed; they knew just what to do and quickly whisked Fremont away. A couple of more cops showed up. Don was off to the side speaking to two of them. The rest of them surrounded our drug dealer friend, whom we still had no idea of who he was. Walking over there, I was stopped by two uniformed police officers.

"FBI," I told them, clearly displaying my badge and credentials.

"We understand that sir, but we are going to have to ask you to stand back."

"Stand back? This is an FBI case. You need to stand back."

"I don't think so. A New York City Police Detective has been shot. This is a police matter; now please stand back."

"Or what? You gonna fuck'n arrest me?"

"Let's not get to that point. We are going to ask you one more time; please step back."

If ever someone was completely un-intimidated by the FBI badge, it was these two cops. I was not going to win this battle of wills. They were not bluffing. I stepped back.

Redirecting myself I went over to Battles, who was clearly shaken. He was on one knee, his right arm resting over his holstered weapon, almost pushing down on it; his left hand was clenched in a fist, tucked under his chin. Two cops were hanging over him, like a tag team waiting to finish the job.

"We will need that now, Agent," one of the cops said in a demanding, if not a condescending tone.

"I'm Agent Douglas, officer, what's the problem here?"

"That's sergeant. Sergeant Collins. The problem is that we need your agent to hand his weapon over to us right now. It is evidence in a police shooting and we will take custody of it."

"I don't think so, Sergeant. This is an FBI case, and the FBI does not relinquish their weapons to local cops. Now, I just swallowed as much as shit as I going to from you guys; don't push it. This is an FBI case."

"So what are you saying? Do we have a stand-off here, Agent Douglas?"

"No, that's not what I said at all. Listen to me again. We are federal agents. You are local cops. Go back and read the constitution; there's that little thing called federal supremacy. You need to stand down now. Are we clear?" I positioned my body right between him and Battles. I would never have played that arrogant federal agent versus local cop routine if the situation had not so clearly called for it.

This time, I was on solid ground and I was not bluffing. We did not surrender our weapons to local cops. The sergeant knew this was going no further. He was not about to physically remove the weapon from our possession. I helped Battles stand up and we walked away.

As we did, I watched as what should have been our prisoner became a prisoner of the NYPD. Handcuffed, he was being led into the back of a police car. He was pushed in, but somehow he slipped and his face smashed into the car frame. The cops pulled him back and seemed to admire his bloody nose. I could not hear what they were saying, but I knew. That routine was repeated three more times. Then a cop got in the back with him. I could not see exactly what happened, but it sure looked like some more roughing up. Sergeant Collins saw me and held up his fingers like gun, pulling the trigger. There was no playful smile to accompany that gesture.

Where the hell was the rest of my squad? Why was I here by myself, having to fight off this gang of cops? were my thoughts at this troubling moment. This was an FBI case and there was plenty of work to do. Franks was probably still in a stupor over what happened back at the gas station. The cops had blocked off this crime scene. Looking around, I saw Reardon waving his arms in an apparent argument with some other cop. Finally, the cop took a step back, moved some barricades and a few more of our cars drove in. I walked Battles over to Reardon.

"Hey, you need to go to the hospital Don?" Reardon asked.

"No just get me back to the office, please."

"Sure thing."

Reardon called one of our squad's agents, Dave Richardson. "Hey, Doc, would you mind taking Don back to the office."

Doc was Richardson's nickname. It came from his initials – DR.

"No prob." Richardson put his arm around Don and walked him to the car.

Once they were in the car and out of earshot I spoke to Reardon.

"You know what happened, huh?" I asked Reardon.

"From the little I've heard, it seems like the guy went for

Don's gun and it went off, hitting Fremont."

"Well, not exactly. Look, Don is pretty shook up. He doesn't need a hospital, but he needs to talk someone; he's gonna need help."

"Don't worry. Employee Assistance will be out to see him tomorrow. That's SOP after every shooting. You know that."

"Yeah, I know. It's just seeing that look on his face; I don't know, like he was in shock or something. I guess that would make sense; I'd be in shock too."

"How did Fremont look? Was the wound serious?" Reardon asked.

"It didn't look too bad, unless there was something I couldn't see; he should be alright. I mean, I'm sure a shot near the groin is pretty painful, but he seemed to be hanging on."

"Let's hope so. Other than this, it's been a pretty good night."

"A good night? Whatta ya mean?" I was not quite sure where Reardon was going with that remark.

"We got about fifty kilos of coke off the streets and a seized a few hundred grand. That's a good haul, don't you think?"

"What I think is that we have a really bad situation here."

"Hey, I'm sorry Fremont got hurt, but he'll be okay. That doesn't wipe out our good stats.

And you, Bob, it looks like you did a really good job of chasing those scumbags and then handling this mess here. Really, all in all, C-13 should come out looking pretty good tonight."

"Really? Franks gets out of his car for no apparent reason and accidentally discharges the shotgun. Luckily no one got hurt. Then we get into this high speed pursuit only to end up having another accidental discharge. Only this time, someone does get hurt. So..."

"Hey, what Franks did or didn't do, doesn't matter. We seized the dope and the money and you caught this motherfucker who was intent on killing one of us," Reardon jumped in, cutting me off.

"Intent on killing one of us? Did you hear what I just said? There was ...."

"Yeah, yeah," Reardon quickly cut me off again, "You said Fremont's wounds were not serious; he should be fine. All's well that ends well, right?"

Before I could answer, Reardon continued, "Bob. We got two good arrests, dope and money. It's another notch on the bedpost for Squad C-13. Right?"

"Right."

"Look, Bob, go on home now. The Evidence Response Team will be here shortly, I'll wait for them and somehow we'll coordinate with NYPD. Here, take my car; I'll get a ride back."

Grabbing his keys, I walked off and got in the car. Before driving off, I called Zucarelli on his cell phone.

"What are you doing?" I asked him.

"I'm fingerprinting this asshole. Going nice and slow. By the time I get him booked, I'll have almost eight hours overtime, thanks to you feds."

"Speaking for the tax payer, our pleasure."

"Hey, I heard what happened. Your guy took a shot at Fremont, huh?" I didn't answer, not sure of what I wanted to say.

"Oh boy," Zucarelli continued without a response from me. "I know what it means when you have nothing to say. Well, I'm glad you're okay. Talk tomorrow, huh?"

"Sure, we'll talk tomorrow."

We just made a major drug bust. The informant who gave us this information was obviously well placed. But, we can't hit a drug cartel this hard without them knowing something is wrong. That snitch had a short life span. We will need to work hard and fast to bust up the distribution network here in New York. That won't be easy. In about an hour, they'll all scatter like cockroaches when the lights go on.

Then there's NYPD. They've always sent a clear message to the mobsters, drug dealers and gangs: there are lines you can't cross; when you shoot a cop, everything changes. Even though Fremont will probably be alright, the cops will be out for blood. They don't care how it happened, only that it happened.

Chapter 2

Dark clouds that unleashed the second straight day of rain over the flat, green, but sparsely populated valley in Medellin, Colombia were moving away. A distant crash of thunder appeared to announce the arrival of a black Mercedes at the front gate of the sprawling compound surrounded by rusted barbed wire and guarded by heavily armed sentries clad in camouflage. Patrolling with the discipline of a national army, their presence was frightening and intimidating – just as it was meant to be.

Though the sentry knew who sat on the passenger side, behind the darkened window, he also knew to follow established protocol as he walked around the front of the car, remaining in constant view of its occupants. A breach of protocol was a security risk. It was also a sign of impending danger. Nobody was completely trusted; everybody was expendable.

"Good day, Senor Rojas," the guard answered respectfully, with a small tremble in his voice, revealing the fear all employees at the compound felt when Diego Rojas arrived.

"Any visitors today?"

"No sir." The guard knew what Rojas was really asking. No military, no police, no rival drug traffickers to be concerned with, at least not today.

Heavy fortified front gates marked with small peep holes for looking out or for shooting back, slowly opened to allow Rojas' car in to the former training compound of the Colombian military; it had been sold to the Rojas family more than thirty years ago. Most of the guards were former Colombian cops and military. They used to be on the government payroll, but since the military gunned down family patriarch Juan Rojas, things had changed. The trust and cooperation were gone. Now they had to choose one side or the other. Many came to the Rojas side.

"Number two," Rojas told his driver who then headed to the center building, renovated from its previous life as a military munitions factory. Patrolling around the muddy grounds, armed with military-grade automatic weapons and magazines with hundreds of rounds of ammunition hanging from their belts, Rojas' security forces stood at attention as he drove by, though nobody could actually see him behind the car's blackened windows.

Within moments of Rojas' arrival, guards began pointing, screaming and scrambling as a small plane was spotted flying over the compound. Some guards took cover and trained their weapons on the plane. Others ran to designated elevated posts around the fence ready to defend the citadel in an epic encounter. Spitting up mud balls, spinning tires sped Rojas' car into opening garage doors to take cover. Silent, tense moments passed as the fear of a government raid subsided. Sometimes a plane is just a plane.

On each side, mustachioed, huge men, dressed in black business suits escorted Rojas as he slowly toured one of his three old factories on the compound, renovated to package and export consumer products. At five foot seven and of thin build, Rojas' unintimidating appearance belied the pain and suffering he was capable of inflicting. Lifeless black hair naturally parted in the middle, fell flat on his head, slightly curling at the top of his ears. Wearing a black suit with a white shirt and black tie sent an appropriate and deliberate message. Business was black and white – either you were with him or were against him. He inherited his father's cocaine empire, built on the blood of rivals, police, soldiers and innocent civilians. He also learned where to draw the line, having watched the kings of cocaine die by the same violence they relied upon for their success.

One factory packaged stuffed animals, another was used for textiles and one, where he stood now was heavily engaged in filling cans of coffee to be shipped to a caffeine-addicted America. Actually, all his products were shipped to the United States. Different products with little in common, except for their high demand in the States. The coffee, stuffed animals and colorful fabrics themselves were not in demand, and were of no particular quality to differentiate them from the competition. They did not command top dollar prices and were not even all that profitable. Their value was what they were able to provide for Rojas – cover for the real product that Americans demanded. That was Colombian cocaine.

Conveyor belts moved steadily, in cadence with the robotic movements of the workers standing on opposite sides every three feet. Rojas' attention was drawn to the belt where each can of coffee was loaded with small packages of cocaine and then moved to the next station where coffee would be poured over the cocaine. Each can held only a little less than half a pound of the white powder. The numbers still added up in Rojas' favor. A kilogram was 2.2 pounds. The dealers in Miami and New York would cut the cocaine with adulterants like baking soda, exponentially increasing the cocaine to dealer-size amounts. A kilo of coke would bring in over $30,000. Broken down into smaller units for the individual user snorting the poison up his nose, the coke was even more profitable, and less risky than getting caught with kilo weight.

Long black hair ran down her shoulders, covering the beauty of her smooth olive skin and emerald eyes as she stood at the conveyor belt, not looking up and not looking away from her work. Carmen's thin, white gown with no pockets and no buttons, belts or any way to close it, barely covered her 20 year old body of long, sleek legs, thin waist and round, firm breasts. While Carmen was only one of many young women dressed in nothing but this skimpy and revealing attire designed to dehumanize these women and assure that no one could furtively walk away with some of Rojas' treasured cocaine, she was the one to catch his eye.

Rojas walked up behind Carmen. Her gaze never diverted from her work, yet she sensed his approach and hoped that by ignoring what was happening, it would not happen. Leaning into her and moving his hands under her gown, Rojas brought himself cheek to cheek with Carmen. Repulsed by his heavy breath, Carmen knew she could not react. For if she did, at best, she would lose the best paying job she could find to support her and her young siblings who lost their parents three years ago, killed by an exploding car they innocently walked by while shopping. At worst, she could lose a whole lot more than the job.

"What is your name, dear?" Rojas asked.

Closing her eyes, praying that speaking with Rojas was all she would have to endure, but inside, knowing differently, she softly told him her name.

"Well, Carmen. I see you do fine work. Why not take a rest. Allow me to bring you upstairs to my room where we can relax."

"Thank you, senor. I am appreciative. But there is so much work to do. I should stay and help the others."

With Rojas kissing her neck and pawing every part of her, Carmen froze, knowing there was nothing to do. Rojas, with no humility, and for the entertainment of his security entourage continued to probe her body.

In an instance, Rojas screamed and Carmen's muscles tightened to rigidity as she stood erect.

"What?" an enraged Rojas yelled as he stepped back, gritting his stained teeth and clenching both his fists, trembling with anger and frustration. He then moved forward toward Carmen, grabbing her by the hair and threw her to the ground. Her seductive body, now fully exposed, sprawling by his feet, did not distract him.

"Ramon, Ramon," Rojas yelled to the compound's chief security officer as he pointed to Carmen. Ramon knew the drill as did the rest of the security entourage. Instinctively, Carmen tried to retreat to a fetal position, which proved futile. As Ramon grabbed Carmen's arms, two burly security guards grabbed her by the ankles and spread her legs apart.

Rojas kneeled down between her legs. He methodically inserted his thumb and forefinger into her, as if performing gynecological surgery, and not for the first time. He removed exactly what he knew he would find – two packets of his cocaine.

"I treat you like gold and you steal from me," he roared.

"Please senor. I didn't want to, I ..."

"Shut up." Rojas yelled even louder as he stood up and

looked at the gawking workers; they all diverted their stares and got back to work. Yet, Rojas wanted them to see this.

"Stand her up," he ordered.

"What shall we do senor? Perhaps slit her throat and dump her on the road for her village to see what happens when you steal from Diego Rojas."

"No, Ramon," Rojas responded in a now composed whisper.

"We must learn our lesson. Look at my father and uncles; where are they now? And my brother and cousins; blown to bits with them. Too much violence only brings us trouble. Have your men take her to the back and show her what that small piece of real estate between her legs is really good for," Rojas continued as smiles sprung on the faces of the men holding Carmen.

"Then Senor?" Ramon asked.

"Then let her clean up and get back to work. After all, are we not forgiving people?" "Yes, we are."

Held at the elbows, Carmen's feet slid along the floor's dirty wooden planks as her limp body, devoid of any will to fight, accepting the inevitable, was dragged away. The work at hand continued as if nothing happened; because for all the workers who would live through another day, nothing of any consequence did happen – at least not for them.

Ramon escorted Rojas as he walked out the door and looked over to a flatbed truck being loaded with crates of coffee. He ordered the work to stop and for the palette about to be loaded on to the truck, to be laid on the ground.

"What is the count today, Ramon?" Rojas asked.

"Forty-six by three and one third." Ramon replied with confidence.

Rojas turned to his security detail, snapped his fingers and pointed to the palette. No words were necessary. They knew what they needed to do simply by watching Rojas. Those who could not follow his orders without being told, did not earn the privilege of personally serving him. Working closely to Rojas had its benefits, but also had its dangers. Disappointing Rojas usually proved deadly.

The cryptic numbers given by Ramon held a specific meaning known only to Rojas' inner circle; two particular cans of coffee were taken from the palette and cut open by switchblades carried by Rojas' men. Tearing the cans open, packets of cocaine fell to the ground. Ramon silently breathed a sigh of relief.

"At least something is working correctly around here." Rojas mumbled clearly enough to be understood. Just as Rojas was about to relax, he saw his driver wave to him holding up the car phone. Only trouble could be on the other end of that call. There was no reason to call the boss if all went as planned. Also obtained from the military, this phone was one of the few methods of secure communications.

"Senor, I am sorry, we lost sixteen last night," was the opening line to Rojas.

"Policia?"

"Si senor."

"Which way?" "Both ways?"

"Both? How did that happen?"

"Not sure yet. But if we need extermination, we will get it." "Have we cleaned up?"

"Yes. Apartment was cleaned. Phones dumped, papers destroyed. "That is the second loss this month."

"I am sorry sir. We will figure this out."

Rojas waved to Ramon to join him in the car. The car drove off.

"Ramon, we have lost a lot of cash in the last few weeks up in the States."

"Yes, senor, we have. We have had some bad luck lately."

"It is not bad luck my friend. And it is not just us. The Moldonado's lost a few million in Los Angeles last week and Miami the week before."

"Really? The brothers? We know they won't take that easily. Blood will spill."

"Losing product is one thing, there is always plenty more. But losing cash is dangerous. A lot of our friends expect to get paid on time. Losing both is inexcusable."

"The Americans are getting very aggressive these days. They have been able to turn our own people against us."

"Yes, they have. We've gotten sloppy. We've tried to rush and cut corners to avoid them and all we managed to do is lose more than usual."

"Maybe then we need to get more aggressive ourselves. Perhaps a few feds lying in the streets will send a message."

"No Ramon. As I said before, we must learn from the mistakes of our predecessors. Even Escobar did not see that it was time to change the way we do business. You are not going to find me running across the rooftops trying to outrun gunfire from our own government; not after all the money my family has given them over the years."

"Then what Senor?"

"It's time for a new way to do business. I've been giving this some thought for a while. Ramon, you have always been a good businessman. You know how to make things work."

"Thank you, Senor. I am honored to serve you." "Ramon, I want you in New York."

"New York?" "Yes."

"For how long senor."

"I don't know. It may become home for you. We will see."

"Very well, Senor. I will tell Camille to start packing and tell the children that we are going on a journey. When do we leave?"

"You leave tomorrow. Your family will stay. I love you like a brother, Ramon, but this is how our business is run. You know that, yes?"

"Yes, Senor. I will leave tomorrow."

"Good, let's discuss our plans on the way to dinner."

Ramon knew the rules. His wife and children would stay in Colombia. If he was to dare cross Rojas, he knew their fate. They would pay a painful price.

Studious, diligent and loyal, Ramon did his homework. He knew what Rojas expected of him. Not forgetting the threat to his family, Ramon did not want to disappoint Rojas for other reasons. After all, had it not been for Senor Rojas, Ramon would still be a laborer, and a poor laborer for that matter. Rojas brought him money, security and respect. As he feared Rojas, others feared him. The line between fear and respect was a blurred one, if it existed at all in a country controlled by drug lords.

Within a week of arriving in New York with his new marching orders, he stalked his prey and planned his attack. There were no green pastures or dirt roads that Ramon was used to as he walked down the unyielding concrete sidewalks, surrounded by high risers. He was a bit overwhelmed by an unforgiving swarm of New Yorkers speedily walking to their offices and meetings. Heads down, tightly clutching their jacket collars to block out the cold wind blowing light flakey snow into their hair, they were oblivious to anything not on their agenda, including Ramon.   The bodily bumps and nudges seemed to rattle only him. Nobody feared him, nobody respected him; nobody even noticed him.

There was no time to admire the decorations hanging from streetlamp to streetlamp, or the Christmas trees and menorahs in the shop windows. Everyone had somewhere else they would rather be and something else they would rather be doing.

To the passer-by strolling down 47th Street in Manhattan, they sounded more like peanut vendors at the baseball game than merchants of the world's finest jewelry. Against the backdrop of glistening diamonds and beautiful jewels, hustlers and con men neatly dressed and well manicured lined up outside their shops and booths with a special deal, for you, and you and you. The smartest shopper, the savviest bargainer was no match for them. The dealers of Manhattan's famous Diamond District were members of a fraternity with their own jargon and ways of doing business, fiercely competitive but mutually guarding against anything or anybody that would threaten their stranglehold on New York's diamond market. Anybody could be casing their next score or could be New York's undercover anti-crime cops ready to pounce on the next young thug who grabbed a purse, picked a pocket or ran off with Santa's kettle of cash.

Licking the bear claw's brown flakes of frosting off stout fingers with dirty nails, Tony Scarlotta washed it down with his light coffee with three sugars. Looking at his huge, sagging gut, Scarlotta knew that his six foot, three inch frame had long strayed from the tall, slim physique of his high school basketball days. A starting forward, he played a good game, but the scholarship he hoped for never came. That was alright. Scarlotta was nobody's fool. Growing up in Brooklyn, neither strong enough nor tough enough to be an enforcer, he worked for bookmakers, dealt in swag and arranged for cars to be stolen for those preferring to make an insurance claim instead of trying to sell. He never dabbled in drugs; not because of any moral opposition, just the reality of the situation. Drugs were too risky – rip-offs, violence and jail time. It was not worth it. His coffee break was interrupted by the ringing of his doorbell. Looking through the glass door and seeing two husky white guys, he buzzed them in.

Tony looked over to his pal Danny D'Albote and nodded his head in the direction of the small back office. Danny took the hint and as he opened the door, papers and bills strewn across the metallic desks were sent airborne, some falling on the floor. Ignoring the papers, Danny left the door to the office partially open so he could see and hear Tony, without being right there. Then he looked at the back door which led to the ground floor of the office building of jewelers, brokers, import/export agents and a slew of cash only businesses. Danny knew that if shit hit the fan, that back door was his escape route.

"How you doin' Tony?" the first one said, as he unzipped his brown leather jacket.

"Okay. Wassup?"

"You know, it's that time of year. We gotta spread a little holiday cheer if we're gonna get a little spreading in return. You know what I mean?"

"I know what you mean, Vinny." Tony answered to a choir of boyish laughter.

"So whatta ya got?"

"Well, look at this bracelet here." Tony handed it over for inspection.

"Whatta ya think?"

"That depends, Tony. What are you charging your old friends here? You know we gotta take care of each other."

"I know, I know. Look, this would go 10 C notes easy. How about five hundred, and I'm taking it up the ass at that price."

"Tony, something tells me that you never take it up the ass, at least not when it comes to jewelry. As for what you do on your personal time, I don't know." Vinny laughed, turning to his partner who then gave a supportive chuckle.

"That's pretty funny. And what about you sarge, what are you looking for?" Tony directed his attention to the taller cop who was running his fingers over his hairy chest exposed by a shirt open three buttons down from the collar.

"That looks pretty good. You got another one?" "Right here." Tony handed him an identical bracelet. "How much, Tony?" Sergeant Gilroy asked Tony.

Knowing he had just told Officer Vincent Parente it was five hundred, Tony stared for a moment, knowing he must have missed something.

"Oh, right, I'm sorry. A little off for each stripe on the arm. That is if you were wearing a uniform. Okay, how about 4?"

"You know, Tony, for all that protection you've been getting, this should be on the arm."

"What, but I..."

"Look at poor Goldbloom over there," the sergeant continued. "How unfortunate that there were no cops on the block the other night when those naughty burglars broke in and blew his safe. Nobody heard nothin' and nobody saw nothin'. He got cleaned out, right Vinny?"

"Yea, that's right, sarge. That poor Jew bastard got nothing left to sell during the busiest shopping time of the year. What bad timing."

"You guys kidding?' Insurance is gonna cover him, you know that." Tony responded almost defensively.

"I don't think so, not this time. It was his third claim this year. The way the police report reads, this one stinks of an inside job. The insurance company is going be looking at this really hard; they ain't paying out so fast. Goldbloom is done."

"Wow. I see you guys have really come a long way in the shakedown business. What did Goldbloom do to deserve that?"

"He didn't do anything, Tony. Absolutely nothing. Where do you come off accusing us of a shaking someone down? That's very offensive, ya know. Why would you assume we have such dishonest intentions?" Sergeant Gilroy answered and then asked a rhetorical question.

"Then what are we talking about here?" Tony wanted to get the conversation over with.

"We're just talking, that's all."

"And this discount that you're looking for is what – just honest negotiations?"

"C'mon Tony, you know that cops are terribly underpaid. At this time of year, we count on the generosity of our good citizens so we can get our wives and kids some nice Christmas gifts.

Is that too much to ask?"

"No, I guess not. Alright. I get it. Just take the fuck'n things, no charge. Okay?"

"Well, we would never ask for so much generosity, but have it your way. Happy holidays, Tony."

Tony stared as the two cops left his store, slipping the bracelets into their pockets. He had always worked with the cops - a little give and take - but this was much more taking than he was used to. As they left, Danny came out from the back room. He waited for the door to close behind them before he began to speak.

Hey, Tony, what the fuck? You're the best fence around. Half your business comes from the family. Do you really gotta take shit from those guys?"

"Unfortunately, Danny, I do. It's all part of the game. But it ain't so bad."

"Not so bad? Whatta ya mean? In five minutes, you just let a thousand bucks walk out the front door. You call that good business?"

"C'mon. You know me better than that. How long have I been doing this? I knew they'd be coming around. I was ready for them. I just laid off on them, genuine, 24 karat crap. That shit wasn't worth five bucks."

"Oh, great idea, Tony. Then when their wives skin starts turning green from wearing that bogus shit, they'll be back with a fuck'n vengeance."

"Danny, Danny, don't be so naive. Those bracelets aren't for any wives. They're gonna give 'em to some strippers who suck their dicks when they're working midnights and shaking down night clubs. Then, the strippers sell the bracelets for whatever coke they can shove up their noses. And that's the end of that."

"Well, I'm glad you have this all figured out. I hope you know what you're doing." "Yeah, me too."

Within a few minutes, the doorbell rang again.

"Well, now what can this be about?" Tony looked out to see a man wearing a full length herring bone coat partially open, revealing a dark olive suit with matching tie. Short, but standing straight and motionless with a polite smile on his face, exuding an almost eerie sense of confidence. He had the look of customer ready to do business. Tony let him in.

"Hello, Mr. Scarlotta."

"Who are you and how the fuck do you know who I am?" Tony asked, shaken by this stranger with a strong South American accent, who appeared to be armed with more information than he should have. Though Tony towered over him, Tony found himself a bit scared.

"You are well known, Mr. Scarlotta. You have a very good reputation and provide excellent service from what I am told." The gentleman removed his hat to reveal thick black hair slicked back exposing a small scar at the hairline on his forehead.

"And just who in Mexico would tell you that?"

Smiling, then breaking out in a laugh, the man responded, "I am not from Mexico, Mr. Scarlotta. I am from Colombia."

"Colombia, like drug cartel Colombia?"

"Yes. Unfortunately, that is the only thing you Americans know of our beautiful country. But yes, I am from that Colombia."

"Well, I'm just a jeweler. I don't get mixed up with cocaine or any drugs for that matter. You got the wrong guy." While

Tony wasn't quite sure where this conversation could possibly be heading, he knew that a slick Colombian showing up from nowhere could only be about one thing.

"Let's not jump to conclusions as to my intentions. Isn't that what you people call profiling?"

"That's very funny. Can we stop dancing here?"

"I am not here to discuss drugs with you, Mr. Scarlotta. I am here to see if you would like to engage in a mutually beneficial business arrangement. Can we talk privately?"

"We can talk right here. This is my partner. You talk to me, you talk to him."

Danny recognized that this quick change from being rushed off to the back when the cops were there meant he was seeing something that he rarely witnessed. With a six inch and 200 pound advantage over this rather meek man, Tony could have simply pounced all over him. But, Tony's street smarts warned him against that. Tony was afraid and did not want to be alone.

Neither Tony nor Danny knew what was unfolding, but they both knew it was something big.

"Okay, then, "Ramon continued, "My employer would like to buy gold from you at various times."

"Your employer? Who would that be?" "That is not really important, is it?" "Well, ya know…"

"Mr. Scarlotta, we will pay you the London spot in cash, with no negotiation. We will be buying anywhere from several hundred thousand to one million dollars worth at a time. Can you accommodate us?"

"Cash? Spot? Really?" "Yes, really."

"Is this a fuck'n joke; whatta you a cop or fed or something?"

"Look at me, Mr. Scarlotta. Do you really believe that?"

"No, but this sounds way to easy. What's the catch?"

"No catch, but after we buy your gold with cash we will need you to buy it back from us through a wire transfer."

"Buy it back. Oh, no catch huh? What am I buying it back at; your cost plus a premium or something? Why would I want to do that?"

"Because, Mr. Scarlotta, when we ask you to, you will buy it back from us at the same price minus a convenience fee for you of, shall we say, seven percent."

"Seven percent? You're going to pay me seven percent just for doing that?"

"That's right. Just make sure you have invoices to cover the sale, and bank accounts set up to accommodate the transfers. We don't want to attract any attention of your government. Of course, not that we are doing anything illegal, we just value our privacy."

"I'm sure you do."

"You have our offer Mr. Scarlotta. How does it sound?"

"It sounds good. Sounds very good. Almost too good." Tony paused expecting Ramon to fill in the silence. He did not. After a few moments of awkward silence, Tony continued, "What do I gotta do now?"

"Just wait. In a few weeks you will get a visit from friends of mine. They will give you cash. You take it and an hour or two after that, someone will call you with wire transfer instructions."

"Okay, how will I know they work for you?"

"You will know."

"Which leads back to my earlier question; just who the fuck are you?" Turning around, walking towards the door, he replied, "My name is Ramon."

"Okay Ramon. How do you know that I won't just take your money and not transfer you a friggin penny?"

Ramon, now with a wide smile on his face, laughed a few times and then turned back to face Tony while still reaching for the door.

"Oh, I think you know the answer to that question."

"Yes, I think I do." Tony resigned himself to the realities of his new business partners. Tony and Danny stared at each other with a bit of amazement on their faces.

"Fuck, I get a visit from the cops and the cartel in the same day, and I almost can't tell them apart. What does that tell ya?"

"I don't know Tony, but either one big opportunity just walked in the door or we just stepped into some deep shit."

Chapter 3

Driving to work under gray skies, through littered streets and surrounded by thousands of disaffected commuters, I was once again overwhelmed by the inevitable doldrums and near depression of the day's reality. The feigned exuberance and ridiculous expectations that after one particular midnight, life was going to change, was nothing more than pure fantasy. It always was. My life plan seemed to have been written in stone.

Despite this feeling, New Year's Eve came and went without a hitch. Elaine and I went to a party with some old friends. We managed to have a good time without any of the stupid arguments we'd been having lately, giving me hope that our marriage of only two and half years could possibly survive. Maybe not drinking helped, though that was not by choice. I couldn't have any alcohol because the FBI put all personnel on stand-by, in case of the big one striking at the stroke of midnight when the new millennium would begin. At least I was not one of the unlucky schmucks, who had to spend New Year's Eve in our hyped-up command post in Manhattan. To the public, a command post sounded like FBI Agents watching simultaneous satellite feeds from around the world, secretly monitoring thousands of conversations and tracking movements of suspicious individuals on electronic maps that reached from floor to ceiling. In reality, a command post was just a bunch of agents sitting by phones and watching ball-drops from around the world via cable news channels. There was absolutely no intelligence that anything was going to happen. Even worse, we had no idea of what was expected to happen and no plan of action on how to respond. But, we had a command post and that made the public feel safer. Allowing the public to feel safe was almost as important as actually keeping them safe. The only cost for that warm, fuzzy feeling was screwing some FBI agents out of an exciting New Year's Eve – they did not even get paid overtime.

The office seemed quiet this morning. The normal buzz of activity and banter was absent. Franks was at his desk reading the paper. Reardon was in deep conversation with Richardson and Battles. A few of the cops were huddled together in the back, having a quiet, yet animated conversation. Ray Simone, the most senior of the detectives appeared to be holding court.

"Hey, how was your New Year's, Zook?" I asked Zucarelli as I placed my coffee down on my 1999 calendar blotter, stained with many circles of coffee from the past year.

"Pretty good. A couple of the guys I used to work vice with came over with their wives. We all used to go out together quite a bit. It was fun to reconnect. How about you?"

"Not bad. Just went to a party. Normal crap, but we had a good time. Not only did we not fight, we actually did a little bit of the nasty – in the car."

"Good man. I hope things work out for you guys."

"How about the two of you? I mean, you're the only divorced couple I know still living together."

"Well, that wasn't the original plan. After we split, we realized the kids were really having a hard time, so we thought we could keep it civil for their sake. So, I moved back in."

"I gotta tell ya, that seems kinda strange to me. You don't think the kids would be better off just having to accept the truth."

"Come see me when you have kids. You'll see; you'll feel differently. It's one of those things that you can't judge until you are in the situation yourself."

"Fair enough. And I'm sorry; I didn't mean to sound like I was judging you." I meant that.

I hated when someone decided what was right for someone else. That was extremely arrogant.

"I know; it's alright. Besides, I ain't that sensitive. If I was, I would definitely be in the wrong business."

There was nothing meaningful to add, and I let the conversation drop. As I picked up my coffee, I noticed that I had placed the cup on top of a sticky-note, which I grabbed and read.

"Oh shit, the PLA, my old buddy Jerry French, wants to see me at 10 o'clock." I moaned. "PLA, what's that?" Zucarelli asked.

"Oh, that's the Principal Legal Adviser. Every office has one. Basically, it's the FBI lawyer for that office."

"Oh. So I guess you gotta get into Manhattan, huh?"

"Of course. Too bad they don't make Queens its own field office instead of being a Resident Agency out of Manhattan. But, I ain't complaining. At least I don't have to drive to that shit hole every day. Just every now and then, and this is one of those times.

"Well, it's about 8:30. So, if you leave now, you may just make it," Zucarelli laughed.

"This sucks. Anything and everything that involves a lawyer

is either a major pain in the ass or costs a lot of money. Or both. At least, this lawyer can't charge me. He can screw me, but on the taxpayer's dime. I know Jerry from when we were first office rookies. He's a good guy, but no matter what, this can't be good. "

Zucarelli just nodded with a smile.

"I wonder what he wants with me. I hate driving all the way there not knowing what's up. You know me; I'm paranoid about getting in trouble."

"Want me to drive you in? Then you don't have to worry about parking and being late." "Gee, Zook, that's a pretty generous offer. What are you gonna do while I'm meeting?" "No problem. I got things to do, people to see. I'll be okay."

I was not going to refuse that offer. I gathered my things and checked in with Franks to let him know where I was heading. He didn't seem to care. Actually, he seemed to already know.

As we walked out, I noticed Zucarelli turn back and look at Simone. They appeared to nod at each other. That seemed odd. I wasn't sure why, but I didn't like it.

I thought I'd grab a quick nap as Zucarelli drove. That was not the politest thing to do, but Zucarelli rarely cared about social niceties. Almost immediately into the drive as we got on the Long Island Expressway, Zucarelli began the conversation.

"So, you can't imagine why your legal beagle wants to see you, huh?"

"I don't know," I answered with my eyes still closed and the seat reclined.

"No idea?" Zucarelli followed up on his own question.

At that point I opened my eyes and looked at Zucarelli; he kept his stare on the road. Bringing the seat back up, I readied myself for the conversation I knew Zucarelli was trying to start.

"Why, you've heard something?" I asked him, though I kind of knew the answer. "Just rumors, you know."

"Rumors my ass, what's up?" I knew he heard something more than rumor. He had an agenda.

"It's probably about Hernandez." "Who?"

"Hernandez, you know that fuck'n Colombian who shot Fremont with Battles' gun."

"Shot Fremont? He didn't shoot Fremont, he sli…"

"That's the point, Bob." Zucarelli appeared ready for that, and let out his response like a warning shot. "He did shoot Fremont. The bullet did more damage than it first appeared. Now Fremont is partially paralyzed; they're gonna retire him."

"I know; I heard that. That's unfortunate, and I really feel bad about it, but the truth is…"

It was clear that I was not going to finish a sentence.

"The truth is that this drug dealing, Colombian scumbucket shot a cop. Now he's got to pay. If he gets off, for any reason, then we are sending the wrong message." Zucarelli had his right finger pointing right at me.

"Message?"

"Yeah, message. And that message is that you do not get away with shooting a cop. Not in New York City you don't. Those are the rules; even the mob knows that. You got a problem with that?"

"No, that's not it. You know that. But Zook, look I saw what I saw."

"That's just it, Bob. You only saw what you think you saw. You don't know for sure. You were several yards away. Battles said Hernandez tried to grab his gun, that's how it when off and that's why Fremont got shot. How do you know any different?"

"He wasn't grabbing…."

"You're not hearing me Bob. Battles said he went for the gun. Fremont said he went for the gun. Before this thing is over, there's gonna be a lot of evidence that Hernandez went for the gun. You're gonna be the only one saying that it was an accident; except for Hernandez, of course. Is that the side you want to be on Bob, you and Hernandez versus NYPD and your own agents?"

"I don't want to be on any side. I just want to tell the truth. Are you telling me I should lie?"

"Hey, don't even go there – making this about me telling you to do something wrong.

I'm trying to be your friend here. I've been a cop a long time and I know where this is heading." "Yeah, well I'm a cop too, you know."

"No Bob, you are not a cop. You're an FBI Agent. Maybe you can call it law enforcement, but don't kid yourself; you and all your other anal FBI agents are not cops."

"What the fuck does that mean?"

"Bob, that's really a conversation for another day. For right now, please listen to what I'm telling you. You better think about what you know as compared to what you think you know.

There are gonna be some really serious consequences for you if you go down the wrong path."

"What? Serious consequences? Are you threatening me?"

"C'mon Bob, that's a stupid question. Of course, I'm not threatening you. I'm just being painfully honest with you. I know you don't see it now, but I really am trying to be your friend here. Before you go up there and give a final statement, just think things out. That's all."

At that moment, Zucarelli was maintaining his composure as I became unwound. With the conversation over, that would have been a good time to grab that nap. But after that exchange, I was not closing my eyes.

Fortunately, with the holidays over, and the throngs of shoppers gone, traffic was rather light heading into the city; though the streets in Manhattan would be jammed just because it was Manhattan. We made it through the Midtown Tunnel and got down to 26 Federal Plaza, which we simply called 26, in plenty of time. Zucarelli took off and I went to the 3rd floor cafeteria for a cup of watered-down coffee and some intense thinking before making my way up another 25 floors.

The FBI was just one of many federal offices in this tall, bland, gray federal building. Located at the lower end of Manhattan, near City Hall, Little Italy and Chinatown, 26 Federal Plaza was surrounded by filthy streets, fast food joints and pizzerias serving the throngs of downtrodden government workers walking around lost in their thoughts and consumed by their troubles and the struggle to get through the day. A huge and strange metal structure, once referred to as art, sat in the middle of the plaza area that led to the courthouse, and seemed to serve no purpose other than to disrupt pedestrian traffic and provide an additional eye-sore. Long lines of immigrants circled the building, as did those in need of other federal services. Inside 26 Federal Plaza were federal police officers – well-paid security guards monitoring metal detectors. Above it all, was an inescapable sense of drudgery which permeated every nook and cranny of the building.

The silver doors of the elevator opened to the FBI Wall of Honor of decorative wood and metal. It was an impressive display of photographs and little blurbs that told the stories of FBI Agents killed in the line of duty. Besides being just plain sad, it had significant historical value. FBI Agents had been killed in a gun battle with Baby Face Nelson, others killed in an ambush or by a crazed gunman. Two of the agents, I had known. That felt surreal. To my left was the main entrance – a solid wall of bullet-proof glass with the FBI seal engraved on one side, and a small opening on the other leading to the metal detector and two uniformed FBI Police Officers. There was something ironic about the FBI having uniformed cops.

"Bob Douglas here to see Jerry French," I introduced myself to the receptionist, holding out my badge and credentials; she appeared to be expecting me, quickly pointing me to the next door as she buzzed me in. I sat down in the waiting area of the Administrative Section of the office.

There was the ADIC's office – the Assistant Director in Charge. Most offices were run by a Special Agent in Charge, known as SAC. But, New York was New York, and the ADIC was "the man" with SACs running the various sections – Foreign Counter Intelligence, Criminal, and Administrative.

To my right I saw the depressed faces of the agents assigned to the Applicant Squad, whose sole responsibility was to conduct background checks by calling a lot of people and asking the same stupid questions over and over again. It was the most demoralizing work in the FBI. Management assigned you there if you were being unofficially punished, or if they just wanted to screw with you. I should know; I spent a year on that squad after making the mistake of asking to be transferred from the Organized Crime squad to the Drug Squad in Queens where I was now assigned. Supervisors got insulted when you asked for a transfer. I got my transfer, but had to do my time in the "penalty box" on the infamous Applicant Squad. Every day was a fight to not eat my gun. It was friggin' miserable.

Jerry French and I were in the Oklahoma City office together, our first assignments after graduating the FBI Academy about three months apart. After a couple of years in a small office, the Bureau transferred rookie agents to a large office; nine times out of ten, that was New York.

Jerry was a smart guy and a pretty good agent. He was probably a little too smart though; management didn't like when he questioned their decisions, so they transferred him to the Legal Unit. That was the risk you took when you applied to the FBI as a lawyer. Given our mutual tendency to question authority, Jerry and I got along pretty well, and shared the hardships of constantly raising the ire of our superiors. While we were friendly, he was still a lawyer for the FBI. I did not know what to expect.

"Hey Bob," Jerry startled me as he peeked around the wall from his office to greet me. "Hey, Jer, wassup?" I returned the greeting as we shook hands. I tried not to be too obvious as I focused on his increasingly receding hair line. Everyone from our rookie days was approaching that age. Subconsciously, I rubbed my forehead, fluffing up my brown, coarse hair to assure all spots were covered.

In a white shirt and black suit, hanging loosely off his slightly overweight body, shirt collar unbuttoned and tie knot brought down an inch or two, Jerry slapped me on the back as he led me to his office, making some small talk.

"Good to see ya Bob. Sorry to bring you all the way into Manhattan. We just needed to talk to you for a little bit."

We? Who was we?

Having picked up on "we" I should not have been so surprised when I walked in and saw two people I did not know, though one looked familiar. Yet, that rattled me a bit. The female sat behind Jerry's desk with a short, balding and bespectacled male to her right. The dark clouds forming outside the window behind them echoed my foreboding.

The female stood up, short and stout, with short black hair, wearing a black pant suit with a white blouse; that must be the FBI lawyer uniform. Chomping on an unlit cigar, she introduced herself.

"Agent Douglas, I am Valerie Caroleo, Bureau Legal Counsel. I am here from Headquarters representing the Director."

"Really? All the way from Headquarters?" I was focused on the cigar more than the issues at hand.

"Yes." Then she remained silent. I had nothing else to say.

I turned to the gentleman sitting next to her. He did not move and this uncomfortable silence continued, though I could not understand why.

"And you are?" I asked him.

He began to stand up, when Caroleo began speaking for him.

"This is John Browning. He is Legal Counsel for the New York City Police Department." "Nice to meet you, Agent Douglas." Browning extended his hand. I took a strong grip and squeezed. Why? I don't know, but it made me feel better.

When we were done shaking hands, again, nobody said anything.

"Well, why don't we get started," Jerry said as he walked over to the couch facing his desk which had been seized by these lawyers representing their agencies' top brass. Just as Jerry's ass was about to land on the couch, Valerie spoke up.

"Uh, Jerry, can you excuse us please. We would like to speak to Agent Douglas alone." "But, this is..."

"Jerry, this is coming straight from the Director." Caroleo looked up over her reading glasses, from the papers she was holding.

French had to place his hand on the couch to stop his downward motion, not expecting to be thrown out of his own office. He hesitated for a second, gathering his thoughts, ultimately realizing that once the word "Director" was invoked; there was nothing left to say. A bit flustered and embarrassed, French just walked out, choosing not to shut the door behind him, in a meek display of defiance after such an obvious, professional snub.

"Have a seat, Agent Douglas." Caroleo directed me, while gesturing for me to shut the door. Like an autonomic response, I complied by pushing the door closed, wondering why I did that. I should have told her to close the door herself, though I could not imagine that would have helped the situation – whatever the situation was.

"Agent Douglas, may I call you Bob?" Caroleo asked.

"Of course."

"Great, please call me Valerie and my colleague, John."

Browning and I exchanged nods.

"Bob, we wanted to talk you about the shooting of Detective Jack Fremont. You were a witness to that event, correct?"

"Correct."

"And you recall what happened that night?"

"Yeah, of course I do. But, Inspections hasn't asked me for my statement yet, do you want that now? I was…"

"Hold up, Bob. We don't want your statement now. You have to give that to the Inspection Division's Shooting Team first."

"That's what I thought. So why haven't I been interviewed yet?"

"Well, Bob, it was very apparent from we've heard that you weren't quite sure about what you saw."

"I wasn't? Who told you that?"

"Other people have been interviewed. According to their statements you were unsure as to what you saw. You had been running after this guy and he got away from you, so you didn't really have a clear view of what happened."

"Other people? What other people said that?"

"Bob, you know these statements are confidential. But who said what, is not the point. We are here to decide a prosecutorial strategy and we need to know if you think you're ready to give your statement, you know, if you have cleared up any questions you had in your own mind."

"I don't think…"

"You see Bob," Caroleo was not letting me finish; she was aggressive. "If there are any questions as to what happened out there, we may not be able to prosecute Hernandez for shooting a police officer. Then, if he goes free, who knows what could happen with a wannabe cop killer out there. We wouldn't want…"

"Wannabe cop…" This was my turn to interrupt.

"Yes, wannabe cop killer," she interrupted me again, leaning forward on the desk, the unlit cigar resting between her middle and index fingers. "He was a drug dealer, sent to our country from the Colombian Cartels. He had every intention of getting back to Colombia no matter what. Even if that meant killing a cop. He's one of the bad guys, Bob. We're in the business of putting away bad guys, isn't that right?"

Not sure where to go with this, I changed course a bit.

"Why is he here? I nodded my head towards Browning. "Isn't this Bureau business?" "John is here representing our partners at the NYPD. We are in this together. They have a lot at stake here too, you know. Cops don't like when other cops get shot. And they look to the FBI to stand with them. Isn't that right John?"

"That's right Valerie."

I was a little startled just hearing him speak; I thought for sure Caroleo had him under a gag order.

"That is the whole reason for these task forces; so we can work together as partners and count on each other. If we don't work together, who knows what would happen," Browning continued.

What would happen? What did that mean? That sounded just like Zucarelli in the car on the ride in. This was getting ugly.

"Alright, what do you want from me?

"It's not a matter of us wanting anything. We're just trying to figure out whether we want to prosecute this federally, because Detective Fremont was deputized as a federal marshal. Or, we can defer and let NYPD pursue this on the state level. We can go either way."

"That's uh great, that you're coordinating so closely. But that's really an issue for you legal people. Where do I figure in to that decision making?"

"You don't Bob. And we're not asking for your opinion."

"Okay, Valerie, then I'm back to my original question, why am I here?'

"We need to start planning our prosecutorial strategy. We just want to know if you are ready to give your statement to the Inspection Division about how Hernandez grabbed Agent Battles' gun and shot Detective Fremont. Or..."

"Or nothing. You tell Inspections to send the Shooting Team and I'll answer their questions. Fair enough?" I stood up from my seat, clearly indicating that I was ready to leave before I was forced into saying something I did not want to say.

"Okay, Agent Douglas. I guess we are done here." "I guess so."

As I walked out the door I almost walked right into the ADIC.

"Oops, excuse me sir," I politely said as I looked up; he was about three inches taller than me.

"Oh no problem, Bob. Good to see you over here in Manhattan. Keep up the good work out there in Queens." He tapped my shoulder with his fist and walked away.

I had been assigned to the New York Office for more than five years. I never said two words to the ADIC. He never knew my name. He wouldn't know me if I spit in his face. Now, he just happens to be outside the door, calls me Bob and gives me a two second pep talk. That just smelled of crap.

After the slow elevator ride down, I left the building, turning south on Broadway heading to City Hall. I knew where Zucarelli would be parked, right near a small post manned by NYPD uniformed officers to protect City Hall. I was a little more than a block away when I saw what I knew was Zucarelli's figure by the car. He seemed to be pushing someone up against the car.

Was he making an arrest? That seemed unlikely; there were no other cops there and no activity going on. I picked up my pace and got close to Zucarelli. With his back to me, he didn't see me or hear me coming. He kept doing what he was doing.

"Uh, excuse me officer. This is my car." I was trying to be a bit funny.

A little shocked by my voice, Zucarelli turned around quickly. While I surprised him, he was completely unfazed by me presence.

"Hey partner. What's goin' on?" Zucarelli asked me.

"Uhh, that is an excellent question. Why don't you answer that one for me."

"Oh, you mean Cheryl here? Cheryl, this is my partner Bob Douglas. He's a real live FBI Agent."

"FBI? Cool," Cheryl's response was kind of what I expected, based solely on what I was seeing. With nothing to say in return, I shook my head in disbelief and turned both palms up, trying to express a "what the fuck?" response. Zucarelli got it and turned to Cheryl.

"Hey, listen, I'll call ya. I think my partner here wants to go back to work."

"Okay, Markie, call me soon," were Cheryl's parting words. I joined Zucarelli, staring as she walked away. Indiscreet maybe; but that was a nice tight ass Zucarelli chose to grab.

"Okay Markie, can we get back to work now?"

"You got it," Zucarelli answered, completely ignoring my sarcasm.

We got in the car, neither one of us short of fodder for conversation.

"So, how did it go?" he asked me.

"Okay. Ya know, all these conversations with the legal folk are confidential, so..." "No prob, I get it."

"And you?" I asked.

"Me? I got nothing to talk about."

"Really. I find you humping some blonde on my car in the middle of the street, and you got nothing to talk about?"

"Eh, c'mon. It was nothin'. Just a little kissing, a little bumping and grinding. She's an old girlfriend; we just ran into each other, so I figured what the fuck, why not?"

"Why not? Didn't you just move back in with your wife?" "Yeah, well ..."

"Look, I don't care if you screw around or not, that's your business. But right in the middle of the street, daylight, I mean..."

"Stop worrying. First of all, she's my ex-wife, not my wife. We're living together for the kids. I can do whatever I want to whomever I want."

"So, if you come home and she's sucking some guy's dick?"

"Hey, I tell you what; if I catch her sucking some guy's dick, those are two bodies that won't ever be found."

"Okay then."

A few seconds later, as we headed north to the Midtown Tunnel, the radio began to crackle. "13-4 to all units, we got the car stopped at 47th and 7th. Start back-up this way."

"Shit, that's Doc. He's up by the Diamond District. What the hell is he doing there?" I found that surprising; almost all our work was in Queens. We rarely had shit happening in Manhattan.

"Probably that wiretap he's been working on. Must've finally paid off. We're close, let's help out."

"Fuck'n A. Let's go."

The Diamond District was north, which was the direction we were heading, back to the Midtown Tunnel, but a little further, just past the Times Square Station. I put that little red flashing light on the car dashboard and Zucarelli put the pedal to the metal. That didn't really help much; Manhattan had too much traffic and everybody was inured to sirens and red flashing lights. Doc had a wiretap up for three months now and was waiting for just the right moment to strike; like we did with Reardon's case. That was the nature of drug work – you had to hit 'em at just the right time. You either walked away with drugs or money, or holding nothing but your dick in your hands. Those were the only options.

The car was still moving as I managed to jump the curb and land two wheels on the sidewalk, when Zucarelli opened the door, got out and shouted, "Hey Doc, whatta ya got?"

Doc and Simone had two Colombians spread-eagle over the car as frenetic Manhattan pedestrians managed to find time out of their busy day to watch a little cop action. Even in the heart of New York City, a first row seat to a drug bust was a rare treat. Two uniformed patrol cops walked over, partially to help out, but more out of sheer curiosity. Simone flashed his NYPD detective badge. I overhead him explain to the cops that he was on an FBI Task Force. The cops then stepped back to start watching the crowd and make sure nobody was going to sneak up on us; either someone trying to free the Colombians or someone just being an asshole.

Zucarelli walked over to talk to Simone, got the Colombians

handcuffed and put one in the back of our car and the other in the patrol car, while I spoke to Doc. We all worked together as a Task Force and tried to be friendly, but when it came down to it, the cops preferred to talk to their fellow cops. The FBI agents stuck together more because the cops wouldn't let them in their tightly knit circle.

"We heard over the wire that a load was getting picked up at a bodega just a few blocks from the office, so we were able to jump on it," Doc told me.

"And?"

"And we saw them put two filled duffel bags in the car. We figured that had to be a major load of cocaine."

"So how much did you get?" "Cocaine? We didn't get any cocaine" "What?"

"Take a look."

Doc walked me over to the trunk of his car and opened one of the duffel bags.

"Fuck, that is a lot of cash." I had never seen so many twenty dollar bills before. "How much is that?" I asked.

"No clue. It's gotta be several hundred thousand. Looks like more than we got from Reardon's bust, ya think?"

"I guess."

"Look, Bob, can you and Zook bring this cash back to the office, get it counted and sealed while we book these fuckers?"

"Yeah Doc, of course."

Zucarelli and I took the money and as we drove back to the office, joked about what we could do with all that money. Just harmless jokes.

"Something doesn't make sense, Bob"

"Whatta ya mean?"

"Well, we got two Colombians with a shitload of cash driving around the Diamond District. That's not right."

"Not right how?" I asked, not liking that Zucarelli was figuring something out, which was getting by me.

"C'mon Bob, this is mob territory. The Morelli Crew has been squeezing the shit out the district for years. How the hell do two Colombians with all that money find their way here?"

"I don't know, Zook. Whatta ya think it means?"

"Not sure, but something tells me, that whatever is going on, we better get a mop."

"A mop?"

"Oh yeah, there's gonna be plenty of blood to clean up."

Chapter 4

Gazing out the corner window of the 28th floor office of the Federal Building, FBI Assistant Director in Charge, J. Peter Gunn looked over the rooftops, beyond the construction and past the stand-still traffic, towards Little Italy. He reflected back on the FBI's famous Commission Trial which finally cut off the heads of the New York mob families. Gunn never forgot how lucky he was to be eating lunch at his desk that day when Jimmy Gianello walked into the FBI office offering to inform on his mob family. Gianello, with the wits of a veteran mobster, knew his time had come; he was about to be whacked. Getting the protection of the FBI seemed like a smart move. All he had to do was talk and wear a wire. That was a bit risky, but with a small army of FBI Agents always tucked away nearby, he felt bullet proof. It was no secret on the streets that the FBI relied heavily upon informants, and paid good money for the right information. Great things can happen when motive meets opportunity. Just as Gianello saw an opportunity, so did Gunn. With the wits of a veteran street agent looking to move up the ranks quickly, he seized the moment.

Within minutes of interviewing Gianello, Gunn walked into his supervisor's office, armed with the required pile of FBI forms and paperwork and opened Gianello as an informant. What an informant he proved to be; bringing the FBI its biggest success against the leadership of La Cosa Nostra that for years had appeared to be beyond the grasp of the law. Gunn rode that success. Speeches, presentations, interviews and talk about writing a book – after retirement of course, kept him in the Bureau limelight. In less than 15 years, he rose from a street agent to the coveted position of Assistant Director in Charge of the FBI New York Office, known as the NYO. The fact that the federal prosecutor of that case was later named FBI Director did not hurt either. Life in the Bureau had been good to J. Peter Gunn.

Born John Peter Gunn, his name went through two changes. At about 10 years old, he asked his parents to start calling him by his middle name so he could model himself after the popular, fictional private eye. Reaching adulthood, he officially changed his name to J. Peter Gunn in deference to his new hero, J. Edgar Hoover. Yes, J. Peter Gunn's stellar career in the FBI seemed pre-ordained.

Gunn enjoyed the nickname "Pistol Pete" which his college teammates bestowed upon him - a reference to his ball hogging on the basketball court. Very few young FBI agents knew of the real basketball legend Pistol Pete, who died so tragically at 40 years of age. Now, as a big boss in the FBI, Gunn's nickname was a reference to his willingness to shoot the legs out of anybody who stood in his way of success. He had a plan – he would be the next Director of the FBI.

"Mr. Gunn, Director Mullins is on the line." His secretary's meek voice over the intercom interrupted his daydream. Letting out a small grunt, Gunn slid his right hand down his blue striped tie and ran his left hand over his gaunt cheeks as he walked back to his desk and sat down in the black leather chair.

"Thanks, Mary." Then hitting the next button, Gunn was on line with the director at his office in FBI Headquarters in Washington, DC.

"Good morning Bill."

"Good morning Pete. How's the Big Apple today?" "Same as always. What's the latest at HQ?"

"Same crap here too. I heard from Valerie about her discussion with that agent of yours out there. She was not happy. This could be a pretty high profile prosecution for us."

"Oh yeah, Bob Douglas. Yep, he's something else. One of his task force cops gets shot right in front of him and he can't figure out what he wants to say."

"Maybe we should transfer him back to Manhattan and let him rot on an FCI squad. That will give him a little time to think about things."

"Easy, Bill. That would send a very strong message; but if we did that now, it would be way too obvious. Just give it time. Every agent needs his back covered some time in his career. We'll just put Agent Douglas on our little mental blacklist of those who haven't learned how to be a team player. We'll get the last laugh, you'll see."

"I hope so. I'm getting tired of everyone having their own opinions about how we need to do things. The FBI way of doing things has worked just fine for close to a hundred years."

"Okay Bill, what's up? You seem more stressed than usual."

"You know I had to appear on the Hill yesterday. They called me at five, just when all the analysts were heading home and told me to be there at six. What a pain in the ass it was trying to get all those stats last second."

"I can imagine. That'll do it. Those congressional hearings usually give you a migraine. How did it go?"

"Those friggin' congressmen. They're not all that bright, but give 'em that bully pulpit and they can put a beating on you. Ya know, they sit there in those high chairs and yell stupid questions at you."

"Kinda like going from being the prosecutor to being the defendant, huh?"

"Just like it. I like being the prosecutor better. It's easy to sound like you know what you're talking about when you get to frame the conversation and ask all the questions."

"So, what was the upshot?"

"They really beat us up on this drug war thing."

"For what? Our stats are probably twice what they were last year."

"Maybe so, but they're only about half of what DEA got. Drugs, money – they are kicking our ass in seizures."

"True, but that's because they rely on the old buy and bust routine. Those are easy stats but don't accomplish anything. Did you explain to them how we're attacking this from the criminal enterprise approach like we did the mob, and we've started task forces with the cops and all that other good stuff?"

"I think we've played that card as much as we can; they're starting to see through that. Look, all they know is numbers. How much dope, how much money seized. They don't understand our statistical reports. Potential economic loss prevented? I don't even know what that means. You think a bunch of jerk-off congressmen get it?"

"Probably not. So, I guess it was not time to present your plan, huh?"

"No, suggesting we take over DEA at that moment did not seem wise. I don't know Pete; we tried this once before and we know how well that worked out. It lasted for what...one day and then DEA told us to shove it up our ass."

"I wouldn't be thinking about that. That was almost twenty years ago. It was a different director and a different time."

"Yeah, yeah, I know. But once I open this Pandora's Box, I gotta win."

"I know, but we can't keep letting DEA get in the way of what we want to achieve. These drug cartels are our biggest threats to American security."

Director Mullins chuckled softly. "Biggest threat to our security...I remember when we made that same argument about the mob, how they intended to rule our country through violence and intimidation and we needed more money for informants and wiretaps, and..."

"And we were right. Look, we did what we had to do and now the mob is like a beaten up puppy, sitting in the corner licking its wounds, with its tail between its legs."

"Pete, that was great how we did that. It put you and me in our respective seats. But, we never coulda gotten that far if we hadn't made peace with the NYPD by throwing all that money their way. We can't do that with DEA; they're dishing out just as much federal dollars as we are, if not more. They're pushing hard to take control of this drug war thing and they got a lot of congressmen behind them."

"I know Bill, but we have to get them outta the way. They're a pain in the ass and we spend more time arguing and bumping heads with them than we do investigating. We can't have DEA on the forefront of this drug war; it's too high profile. It's gotta be us, Bill. I mean, we're the FBI and that's that."

"Pete, you're right. But I gotta be careful. I can't piss off congress anymore than I already have. I can't go through another grilling by them. Word is that they plan on cutting our budget and we'll have to slash agent positions, probably right out of the drug program."

"Great. Take agent positions away, then we'll never be able to compete with DEA." "That's another thing. They're getting kinda tired hearing about our constant turf wars.

There's rumors going around that a few congressmen want us out of the drug enforcement business altogether just to avoid the infighting, never mind us taking over the whole damn thing. I can't have that happen under my watch. I mean, the FBI losing investigative authority cannot be my legacy as FBI Director. " His voice quivered, knowing that successful FBI Directors built empires, and did not cede jurisdiction to anybody.

"So whatta we do, Bill? We can't get cut out of all that money. I mean, if DEA gets to outspend us, they'll clean our clock and we will get pushed aside."

"We'll have to be creative. DEA has been ramping up their money laundering program; you know trying to seize any money or assets that the dopers touch. They're seizing bank accounts, expensive cars, even homes. It's working pretty well for them; they're getting some good press and Congress is taking notice. Do you have anything like that going on in New York?"

"Well, just the other day, our drug squad seized several hundred thousand up by the Diamond District ."

"Really? So, we just seized a big chunk of drug money; that's good news. Having a press conference?"

"No, we're not. We're not sure it is drug money. We got some intel off a wire that led us there, but we can't really prove shit. Not to mention, it was in the Diamond District, not where you'd expect to find the Colombians."

"Alright Pete. Listen, things are changing. These other agencies are all trying to grow at our expense. It's not just DEA. Customs, and even the IRS are trying to get into the drug wars, money laundering, even kiddy porn. This is all the stuff the FBI always controlled. We've got to protect FBI primacy, but it ain't easy. Look, New York is our flagship office; you are the FBI. You know what I mean?"

"I know what you mean, Bill. Don't worry, I got your back."

"I hope so. I'm starting to worry that I can't fend off the dogs much longer."

After hanging up the phone, Gunn sat for a moment reflecting what the director had just told him; it wasn't the director's back that Gunn was worried about.

That's why we call him Director Muffins. He doesn't have the backbone to stand up to Congress or the DEA. When pressured, he breaks into crumbs, like a muffin. Those thoughts threatened Gunn – at least his plans for his career. Like it or not, Gunn knew his success was hitched to the director.

Gunn also knew things were changing. The FBI was never known for being nimble and changing with the times. Nobody could stay on top forever. The director was right about one thing: if the FBI did not move quickly, the FBI would not be J. Edgar Hoover's FBI much longer. Gunn knew what his next move had to be. He picked up the phone.

✱✱✱✱✱

At 4:30 on a Friday afternoon, slipping out the backdoor and heading home while things were quiet seemed tempting. But then I glanced out the window overlooking the Long Island Expressway heading eastbound. While that heavy traffic was the norm, just looking at it made the thought of my usual 75 minute ride to my small apartment in Nassau County seem all that more unbearable. Leaving early or coming in late was never a big issue in the New York Office. If you didn't overdo it and you were there when the bell rang, most supervisors didn't care what you did when it wasn't busy, as long as you didn't get in any trouble. Some agents did not know where to draw the line - like using their down time to sell Amway out of the Bureau car. The public probably could never imagine that even the busiest and most active squads in the FBI had quiet times. That was just the nature of the business. You never knew when the shit would hit and you were working around the clock.

Reardon was on the phone, laughing and enjoying himself. Facing the corner, speaking softly, he was desperately trying not to be overheard, which was hard to do in the bullpen – as the squad room was known with all the desks pushed together and all of us working on top of each other. Reardon's attempt at privacy was so unnecessary. When speaking with his wife, he would blankly stare out the window or signal for Franks to call him with an emergency. We all knew that when he was smiling and laughing on the telephone, he was speaking with Special Agent Carol Gardner.

A single gal, with an average looking face, Gardner was a bit of a loner, never hanging out with the other female agents, not dating the male agents and never discussing a significant other. That was a puzzle for the guys and fodder for a lot of speculation, until her clandestine relationship with Reardon was finally figured out. They could never acknowledge their relationship; our squad had a few parties a year with our spouses, and a slip of the lip could be deadly. All-in-all nobody really cared, but cops and FBI agents were entertained by office gossip as much as anyone else. Doc was busy typing away at the computer; he always found some work to do. Battles, leaning back in his chair, his feet hoisted up on the desk, was chatting with some of the younger agents, regaling them with stories that even in their inexperience, they knew to be pure bullshit and fantasy.

Zucarelli was sitting on a desk in the back of the bullpen with the rest of the cops. Behind him, on the wall of blue, peeling paint was a poster of two topless babes sitting on a beach together. That probably violated some law or rule, but nobody seemed to care. As always, Simone was holding court - standing up, sitting down, waving his hands or pointing his finger; he was the center of attention. Julie was the only agent sitting with them. She loved the attention - sexual innuendos and all - that the cops gave her. They were a little less concerned about appropriate office conduct than were the agents. There were rumors about her and Detective Dwayne Banks – known simply as D, but, if true, they were much more discreet than Gardner and Reardon. Julie was engaged, and I didn't believe that she would be carrying on with D; just enjoying the attention. The long blonde hair was all Julie needed to get that kind of attention. Short, slim and flat-chested, she was nothing special, but she held it together well. Given the choice, I'd rather slip it to Gardner. Of course, I was never given such a choice.

Zucarelli looked over at me and gave me a small smile and nod of the head. He knew that I wished I was welcome to sit with them too. Of course, if I did walk over, nobody would say anything, but there would be a chill. I wasn't sure why, but the cops didn't like me much. Trying to figure out how to kill the rest of the day, I was almost relieved when I heard Franks call out to the squad.

"Hey everybody, let's have a quick squad meeting before the weekend and just kinda plan out next week," was Franks' announcement.

Slowly, while letting out a few grunts and groans, everybody got up and walked back to their desks, Zucarelli slapping me on the shoulder as he slipped behind me to get into his chair. Reardon hung up the phone and walked to the front to take his place next to Franks as he stood outside his office's doorway.

"Okay, listen up. It's been a little quiet around here the last couple of days. Come Monday, we need to start beating the bushes again. Talk to your informants and get things rolling. In the meantime, before we break for the weekend, I figured we'd get some updates. First, we'll start with Steve's case, then Doc, and then Bob."

Franks turned to Reardon to get the briefings started.

"Hey guys," Reardon started the first briefing. "Again, thanks for all your help on that seizure the other week. We're all real sorry about Fremont having to retire. D and I were at his house the other day and spoke to him for a long time. He loves being a cop and will miss it, but I think he'll be okay."

The squad broke out in spontaneous applauds. I kept my stare straight at Reardon, without looking around.

Reardon explained how we tried to round up a few drug dealers since the arrests and seizure at the gas station, but as we expected, they were long gone. Word moved fast in the drug trade. When we took that loaded van down, there were probably a couple of Colombians watching the whole thing through binoculars from one of the hundreds of windows overlooking that gas station. Once we made a move, a few phone calls followed and apartments were quickly cleaned out.

Doc gave a similar presentation. After taking down those two Colombians in the Diamond District, the wiretap went dead. It's not hard to figure out that you're phone is tapped when as soon as you say something suspicious, the cops and FBI are all over you.

Franks then looked at me to present the case Zucarelli and I had been working but was getting a little cold from inactivity.

"Thanks Larry." I saw no harm in being polite to my supervisor. My doubts about his competence, and his dislike for me were well known on the squad, but there was rarely a need to hang out our dirty laundry.

"As you guys know, Zook and I opened a case on Roberto Sanchez. The case is a spin-off from an undercover operation in Detroit. That operation is still going on, so we can't use any of its information for probable cause, so we've got to build a parallel case." I was about to continue when Zucarelli piped in.

"What Bob is saying is exactly right. Detroit has Sanchez on a wire talking about moving a lot of coke. But since we can't use that right now, we don't have squat for a wiretap and no informants."

"So then what are you doing?" Reardon asked, masking his sarcasm as an honest question. "We've got SOG on him eight hours a day for the last two weeks."

"And?" Reardon asked.

"And nothing. That's just the point. Sanchez has no job and no visible source of income. But SOG has him at buildings he owns, buying crap, meeting people on street corners and on his cell every waking moment. If that ain't drug trafficking, I don't know what is."

"That's all well and good," Franks said, "but we can't tie up the Surveillance Operations Group on one case like this much longer. If they think we're wasting their time, we'll have a hard time getting them again."

Franks was right. Getting full-time surveillance for any case was a luxury. Every other squad wanted them too. There weren't many agents willing to do nothing but surveillance - all day, every day. They must've been one burned out group of malcontents.

When do you think you'll have something?"

Zucarelli and I looked at each other. There was no way to answer that question.

"I uh, I don't know Larry. I mean, it's surveillance. We'll get something when we get something. We can't make it happen."

"Well, it better happen quickly or I'm pulling the plug. Undercover op or not, if we can't get up on a wire or develop informants, we're pissing in the wind. We got better things for our surveillance guys to do."

When neither Zucarelli nor I had a response, Franks finished up, "Alright; everyone have a good weekend and we'll get a fresh start early Monday." Of course, for the drug squad, early meant before 10 a.m..

We all headed out, only a few stayed back, deciding what bar to hit before going home. Zucarelli was one of them. I was not a drinker and wanted to do what I could to save my eroding marriage.

"SOG-9 to 13-8. SOG 9 to 13-8," I heard come over the radio, but it did not register that it was directed to me."

"SOG-9 to 13-8," came over again with a little more desperation in his voice and I realized that SOG was calling me.

"This is 13-8, go," I responded.

"13-8, we have Sanchez at LaGuardia Airport. He came with another male and they met two other unsub males who arrived on a flight from Miami. Copy?"

"10-4, I copy. Do you want me to respond?"

"That's 10-4, 13-8, head to airport."

SOG explained that Sanchez and the unknown male subject just met with two unknown subjects, which we called unsubs, who flew in from Miami with four suitcases. Sanchez and his partner split up, each pairing with one of the unsubs. Then, each pair took two of the suitcases and placed them into two different cars.

"We only have three units and can follow only one car. What do you advise, 13-8?" SOG asked me on the radio.

I didn't know what to advise, but had to guess very quickly. The two unsubs flying in from Miami and handing off suitcases could only mean one thing.

"SOG-9, maintain surveillance on Sanchez, I'll head out and try to catch up to the unknown male, but call out a full description of the car."

I could not imagine that SOG would try to keep a surveillance of a drug dealer with only three cars. A really good surveillance needed six cars, but four at a minimum. Following a surveillance-conscious drug dealer was harder than it sounded. Given what they had, SOG-9 was correct to stay on one car, but they had to first tell me what the other car looked like in the unlikely event I could actually catch up and find it before it disappeared into New York traffic. I quickly called

Zucarelli, who fortunately, was still in the office with a few of the guys.

SOG kept their surveillance on Sanchez. I headed towards LaGuardia Airport planning to go in and then out to the exit road, hoping to find the vehicle that according to SOG had two unsubs. One had been with Sanchez and then left with one of the guys from Miami, taking two of the suitcases with them.

"We're heading out right now 13-8. We have the car description and we'll try to intercept them leaving the airport," Zucarelli called out on the radio.

"Okay, SOG continue with Sanchez and C-13 units will take the unsubs. Do not stop Sanchez without checking with me first."

"Got it, 13-8. Good luck," the SOG Team Leader responded.

Luck was right. The odds of finding this car were not in our favor. Then we would be stuck making a move on Sanchez. At that point, we would be all in; either we hit him with a load or we walk away with that infamous nothing but your dick in your hands walk. That was worse than the long walk back to the bar after a girl turned you down for a dance. With that mental image, something told me that I would be back in that scene sooner than I thought. But, that was a thought for another day.

Without hearing anything on the radio, I knew everyone was scrambling. When action was breaking, we were all there – we lived for this stuff. With each passing minute, the window of opportunity for finding this vehicle was closing.

"I got it. I think I got the car." Zucarelli could not hide his excitement in that radio transmission. If he was right, he was saving the day.

"Where are you Zook, what direction?" Now my excitement

was becoming apparent. "We're on the Grand Central heading towards the Whitestone Expressway."

"I'll be with you in one minute," Doc yelled into the radio, over the blare of his siren. "We're on the Expressway, I think he's heading for the bridge," Zucarelli called out.

At that moment, the SOG Team Leader got on the radio to tell me that Sanchez just crossed the Throgs Neck Bridge en route to the Bronx. The Bronx was a tough borough of New York City.

The Whitestone Expressway led to the Whitestone Bridge which also fed into the Bronx. Both cars going to the Bronx, but taking two different bridges was no coincidence; that was a planned out, counter-surveillance route.

"Okay, SOG, you maintain surveillance. Do not stop Sanchez. We're gonna stop the other vehicle here."

"That's 10-4," SOG responded.

"Zook, try to wait for back-up if you can, but do not let that car get on the bridge. We can't let them hook up in the Bronx."

"Well, you better move it. They're about to get on now. I'm pulling them over." Then I heard Zucarelli blasting his siren.

I stepped on the gas as I was sure everyone else was. While Zucarelli was a highly experienced and capable cop, car stops were dangerous, especially of drug dealers, and especially two against one.

Doc pulled up a few seconds before I did. Guns drawn, with a slow, deliberate and tactical approach to the car, Zucarelli walked towards the driver side. Doc walked around the passenger side. Staying back, out of the line of fire, I was watching them carefully, while also watching the traffic zipping by. Brake lights came on as soon as the motorists saw there were cops in action. You always had to worry about some idiot forgetting he was driving while trying to watch what was happening, and then would drive right into you. Zucarelli and Doc got them outside the car and off to the far side of the highway shoulder, for all of our safety.

The driver held out his identification, which I took, remaining at arm's length, and then stepped back. The passenger, claiming to barely speak English, had no identification on him. How convenient.

"This your car?" I asked the skinny, short driver who showed no signs of being intimidated by the cops surrounding him.

"No, some guy paid me a few bucks to take this car and pick this guy up. That's all I'm saying."

"Then you don't mind if we search the car, huh?" Zucarelli asked him, while keeping his gun pointed at the driver.

"It's not my car. I'm not agreeing to anything or saying anything else. What happened to my right to remain silent?"

Looking at Zucarelli's face, it wasn't hard to see his thoughts about that smart-ass response. Something told me that if we were not in the middle of the street, and it was just Zucarelli and some cops – no FBI Agents – the driver would've had Zucarelli's fist down his throat and another cop's boot up his ass.

These two weren't talking. We had experienced cops up against experienced drug traffickers. We had a stand-off.

"What do you want to do?" Zucarelli asked me.

I thought for a second. There was only one answer.

"Open the trunk," I said.

Zucarelli impishly smiled with obvious approval. Waving

his left hand, he signaled for me to cover him as he quickly holstered his weapon and then gave the driver a very strong body slam against the car, handcuffing him behind his back. I couldn't hear the clicks, but as the driver closed his eyes and grit his teeth, I knew that Zucarelli clamped those handcuffs pretty tightly. He then pulled up on the cuffs and positioned the driver in front of him as he walked to take the car keys out of the ignition. Zucarelli then led the driver over to the trunk. Standing behind him, Zucarelli unlocked the trunk and moved them both backwards. As the trunk door swung open, a sudden but dim flash of light came from inside and we all paused for one second. We looked at each other and I moved cautiously to the trunk. Inside, sat two plain, black suitcases amongst empty soda cans, a jack, oily rags and a bunch of crap. With the setting sun behind me, my shadow dulled the reflection of the light against one of the paper-thin locks securing a suitcase.

While staring at the suitcases, knowing what I was ultimately going to do, SOG called me on the radio. Sanchez and his companion arrived at a residential building. They were met by three bodyguard types who escorted them and the two suitcases into the building.

"Okay, be sure to see exactly where those suitcases go to. Stand-by."

I wasn't sure how SOG was going to safely do that, but that was their problem; I had my own issues at hand.

As the rest of the squad showed up, Zucarelli gave custody of the driver to Simone and Battles and then walked over to me.

"Now what? We gotta do something. We can't just sit out here," Zucarelli told me. "I know. We should probably get a search warrant to play it safe."

"That ain't safe, Bob. We got units hanging out in the Bronx. We may be under counter-surveillance right now. It's gonna take hours to get a warrant."

"I know. Don't worry; I haven't forgotten my academy law classes. This is a classic Caroll Doctrine search." Zucarelli was not impressed with my recall of that landmark law case that allowed police to search a vehicle without a warrant under these circumstances, at least in my opinion. He sensed my hesitation.

"And?" he asked me.

"You know what's gonna happen if we hit something. The first thing their attorneys are gonna do is move to quash, ya know, challenge the probable cause."

"So, let 'em challenge. That's what you got prosecutors for; let them worry about it." "Yea, but it's not the prosecutor getting his ass beat up on the witness stand."

"Bob, it ain't safe just sitting out here like this. You've gotta make a fuck'n decision, now."

Zucarelli was right.

With only a slight tug, that little lock easily broke apart. I then unzipped the suitcase.

"Holy shit." Zucarelli and I spoke in harmony.

Then I repeated the same process on the next suitcase.

"Well, fuck me. We hit it." Zucarelli was happy and smacked me on the back. "Good job."

"That's a lot of coke, Zook, isn't it?"

"Oh yeah, looks like almost a hundred kilos. Nice, very nice."

I immediately called out to SOG, telling them what we found. Now, we had probable cause to go into that apartment and grab those suitcases. But that apartment was not a car. I needed to get a search warrant. I told SOG to stay on that apartment until we got a warrant. They didn't like that plan; they considered themselves an 8 hour per day squad, despite the fact that FBI Agents were paid to work as many hours as it took.

"What if someone leaves with a suitcase?" the SOG Team Leader asked me.

"Then follow them away and out of view, then jump 'em. Do not lose those suitcases; we can't let that much coke get into the population."

Doc called me as he put his prisoner into his car.

"Hey Bob, look at this. I found it tucked into this scumbag's sock."

I didn't appreciate handling this folded envelope, damp from our drug courier's sweat, but had no choice at the moment.

"You gonna open it?" Zucarelli asked.

"I've come this far."

I slowly peeled open the envelope, trying to use only the tips of my fingers. I pulled out a note, hand written in Spanish and read the only words I could figure out.

"Hmm. El Gordo? I wonder who that is," I said to Zucarelli.

"Yeah, but more importantly look at that address. You know where that is?" "Looks like Manhattan."

"Not just Manhattan, it's the Diamond District, about one block away from where we stopped Doc's guys who had all that money."

"The Diamond District again? Whatta ya think?" I asked Zucarelli.

"I think we need to go find out who El Gordo in the Diamond District is."

"No problem. We'll just go ask; right?"

"Yeah, that should do it. We have someone called El Gordo working the drug business in the Diamond District. Someone is gonna have a problem with that."

"I assume you're talking about the mob."

"Who else?"

"But we knocked the shit out of those bastards years ago. Is anybody really afraid of them anymore?"

"Hey, that Commission Trial was like, uh, what, fifteen years ago. Don't kid yourself; they're still here. They just learned their lesson, you know, keeping things quiet and low key, staying under the radar."

"So, your point is…?"

"Remember what I told you when we grabbed that money."

"You mean your thing about needing a mop."

"Yep. Make that one big fuck'n mop."

Chapter 5

"**S**hit, why is there so much traffic going in to Manhattan this time of the evening? Seems like no matter what we do, we get stuck in this crap." Zucarelli's impatience with traffic was out of character for him.

"Whoa, you sound like me now. I thought I'm the one with the patience of a two year old?" I said, hoping to engage him in some more discussion.

"Well, that's correct; you are. I'm just a little nervous." "You? Nervous? Wassup?"

"I don't know. It's, uh, just, you know, I don't like the idea of our squad hanging out in the Bronx watching this stash house. I mean, the Colombians ain't stupid. Like I said, they could be watching us watching them. If they feel threatened, ya know, like trapped rats, they're gonna come out shooting. And usually they out-gun us. Let's just get this warrant signed and get up there."

'Okay, okay. I'm not used to seeing you this much on edge."

I glanced over at Zucarelli, waiting for a response, but he just stared straight ahead, once again, slowly stroking the edges of his moustache with this thumb and forefinger.

The drive in to Manhattan was slow, but seemed much slower knowing we had our squad sitting on the streets of the Bronx. Despite being in street clothes and experienced at surveillance, it was not likely that a small cadre of cops and FBI Agents outside of a stash house would remain unnoticed for very long. Zucarelli's concern had me more uneasy than usual.

With government workers heading home, the shops and fast food joints closing up, there were several open parking spots on the street. Putting my Police placard in the windshield, which never spared us parking tickets anyway, we slammed the car doors shut and walked over to the United States Attorney's Office. The US Attorney was the head prosecutor for the district.

Appointed by the president, it was a highly political position. Each new president brought a new US Attorney and the offices' entire hierarchy would be restructured. I could not imagine an FBI field office routinely going through such gyrations. Each prosecutor was known as an Assistant United States Attorney, or simply AUSA.

"Do you know which AUSA is on duty tonight?" Zucarelli asked me. "No. Does it really matter?"

"Yes, it does; some are dicks, and some aren't."

"Can't argue that." And I couldn't; it was a simple and straightforward statement of fact. Opening the door to the US Attorney's Office, we saw a short, blonde in a tight fitting skirt and blouse taking out some papers from her mailbox at the reception desk. She was a little stocky for such tight clothes but left that one extra button open to reveal just enough cleavage to distract wandering and judgmental eyes.

"You two looking for me?" she asked staring at me and Zucarelli.

Then she quickly turned around with the papers she had just grabbed. Without waiting for our answer, she kept walking towards her office, we assumed. The narrow hallway of plain tan carpet circled the 9th floor, with windowed offices every few feet that overlooked the FDR Drive, the Brooklyn or Manhattan bridges – or both, and then on to Brooklyn itself. Now getting dark, the view was mostly lights.

Her ass was a bit too wide to be considered really hot, but it was very round which did give it some eye appeal; that tight dress highlighted each sideways sway as she continued to walk.

After a quick look-over, Zucarelli and I looked at each other, raising our eyebrows and tilting our heads which was our non-verbal acknowledgement that she would do in a pinch – not first choice, but not bad.

"Umm, we were looking for the on-call AUSA," I called out to her.

She didn't turn around or reply, other than to hold up her forefinger and give us the "follow me" finger wave. Zucarelli and I looked at each other again and broke out in small and quiet laughter. Something about that response was surprising and entertaining as well. So, we followed her, eyes on the ass – she knew it, and liked it, I suspected. Turning to the right and walking in to her small, cluttered office, she walked around the desk and sat down. Without waiting for Zucarelli and me to get seated, she began talking.

"So…"

Grabbing our badges and credentials, I responded, "Well, I'm Agent Douglas, FBI and this is my partner, NYPD Detective Zucarelli."

She did not take notice of our badges. "Yes, I got a call you were coming."

Then there was a bit of that strange silence as she looked at me, while leaning back in her chair.

"Douglas? Is that Agent *Bob* Douglas?" with a big stress on the Bob. "Yes, Bob Douglas."

"Out of the Queens office, right?" "

Yes, that's right."

"Okay, good."

Zucarelli and I then looked at each other again, this time with a squint of our eyes - the non-verbal for "What was that about?"

"I don't think we've met before. Your name is…?"

"I am AUSA Allison Brevard. So, what do we got?"

"Well, we just seized a boatload of coke in two suitcases, and there are two more suitcases in the Bronx now, which have either the same amount of coke, or a lot of money."

"Which is it Agent Douglas, coke or money?" "I can make an argument either way."

"That's just great, because probable cause for a search warrant requires specificity and a compelling argument. Can you argue specifically one way or the other or do you want to argue your case out of both sides of your mouth?"

"Uh, look, Ms. Brevard, I know all about probable cause and specificity, and I'm not sure what I said to deserve that kind of response. But, there is either money or drugs in those suitcases – instrumentalities and practices of the drug trade. It's not a complicated matter. I've used it several times before to get a search warrant; kinda boilerplate, ya know?"

"Yes, and I know all about boilerplates and crappy affidavits. You come in here after hours, and we have a judge standing by; you're gonna need something more than boilerplate."

"We have plenty. Based on everything that happened leading up to us coming here, we have probable cause. It's …"

Picking up my sarcasm, Zucarelli slightly tapped my leg.

Looking down, I saw his hand waving back and forth. That was another non-verbal for "Back off." He was right. You can't piss off an AUSA you are trying to get to write a warrant and bring to a judge for authorization after hours.

"It just needs to be spelled our chronologically. I think if we do that, you and I can get on the same sheet of music. Fair enough?" I toned it down.

"Okay then, Agent Douglas, why don't you give me all the facts leading up to this."

So I did, explaining how the case unfolded from an undercover investigation that we were still working and could not be burned. All the probable cause about Sanchez and this operation had to start with what we saw today.

"I don't know, Bob. May I call you Bob?"

"Please."

"Well, Bob. This may be shaky."

"Whatta ya mean, shaky. This is solid; we had probable cause up the ass. And we were right, we found the coke. And a lot of it."

"I'm sure you learned in the FBI Academy that being right doesn't mean you had probable cause. Evidence is thrown out all the time. And talking about asses, it's gonna be mine on the line when their attorneys move to quash the evidence."

"No, it will be my ass on the witness stand defending this, and I'm willing to do that..." "Well good for you," she interrupted, "but it is my reputation as a prosecutor that I need to think about. Judges don't..."

"Hey," now I was interrupting, "this is not about what a judge or jury may say months down the road. Right now, we're sitting on maybe one hundred kilos of coke and we got agents and cops sitting on a stash house in the Bronx."

"Yes, you have one hundred kilos of cocaine that you seized from two guys who did nothing illegal and did not give you permission to search the car. Now you want a search warrant for a residence when you have no idea of what is in there. Is that what you're saying?"

'What I'm saying is that I made a legal Carroll Doctrine search on a vehicle. I'm sure you learned that in AUSA School."

"I don't appreciate your sarcasm. You're attitude is not going…"

"Well, I think you…"

"Hey, hey, hey," now Zucarelli was interrupting. "This is worse than cops and district attorneys, which I thought was bad enough. Now c'mon, both of you. Let's tone it down and get back to business, which is getting drugs off the streets and the drug dealers in jail. Can we do that?"

I took the lead.

"Okay, Allison, I apologize. But, I think the probable cause is pretty clear. I am comfortable going before the judge and swearing to that."

"You know, Bob, probable cause is rarely black and white, it can be a very gray area." Then she stopped and did that staring thing again. Remembering my meeting with Bureau Legal Counsel Valerie Caroleo, I wondered if there was a class on strategic staring in law school. Or was this a female power play taught to them from their mommas.

"Okay…and…?"

"And probable cause is in the eyes of the beholder, is it not?"

Before I could answer, though I didn't have one, Zucarelli jumped in.

"I gotta take this call," Zucarelli grabbed his cell phone, making some indiscernible hand gesture at me, as he stepped out of the doorway, holding his cell phone against his ear. I could not tell if that raised or lowered the tension.

"Yea, whatta ya got?" He whispered in the phone as he continued to walk away.

Getting back to Brevard's comment about probable cause being in the eye of the beholder, I responded.

"Yes, probable cause is subject to interpretation. Look, Allison, this was a good stop and search. The coke was legally obtained and if you consider everything that SOG observed, there is p.c. especially from the perspective of an FBI Agent and New York City detective working on the street."

Silent, she continued to stare at me, when Zucarelli poked his head back in the doorway.

"That was Simone," Zucarelli said. "They stopped someone leaving the stash house."

My heart pounded heavily for a moment. Stopping someone at this critical stage could be dangerous and unravel the entire investigation. Or, it could yield some good intelligence.

"They did? Why? What happened?' Did they…?"

Zucarelli held up his hand, for me to stop talking and he started walking back out the door.

"What's that? Are you sure?" was all I could hear him say.

Brevard and I looked at each other; now we both had "holy shit?" looks on our faces; this was the first time we appeared to be in concurrence. We both chose to remain silent and await Zucarelli's return. You never know when one tidbit of information could change everything.

"Whatta ya got, Zook?" I jumped at Zucarelli as soon as he

re-appeared in the doorway, not allowing an extra second to pass.

"You're not going to believe this." Then he hesitated looking at me first, then Brevard. "What, what?" I was yelling at him, my high pitch revealing my excitement, and nerves. "The guy they stopped is wanted for killing a cop out on the west coast. This is getting bad.

We gotta get in there." Zucarelli stared Brevard down.

"Well, I guess that does add to the urgency of the situation. Can you get me more information on that?" she asked Zucarelli.

"No," he barked out in response. "We don't have time for that.   We think we can get this mother-fuck'n cop killer to cooperate, so we can't risk that by putting his name in the affidavit. Now, please, you know we have p.c. from everything that happened. We need that search warrant, right fuck'n now." Zucarelli was in control.

Frozen for a moment by Zucarelli's strong words, I had to consciously shift my gaze from him to Brevard. I looked at her looking at me. Zucarelli had thrown her off balance and now she and I both knew where this was heading. The balance of power had just shifted and I loved it.

"Okay, let's get this warrant written. Judge Sweetley is standing by. We don't want to leave him waiting."

"Let's do it."

As she swung her chair around to face the computer, with her back turned to us. I turned my head towards Zucarelli. He gave me a wink and small smile. He then nodded his head towards Brevard, signaling that I should turn my attention away from him and to her. Before doing that, I had to give him a second look. I was not sure why.

*****

Law book upon law book stacked the mahogany shelves lining the walls in this dimly lit, decorative yet refined room filled with a dour silence, known as the judge's chamber. Judge Sweetley read each page of the affidavit under the desk lamp, as we sat there watching him, looking for non-verbal cues as to whether he believed we had probable cause to search that apartment in the Bronx. When all is said and done, only the opinion of the judge mattered.

Judge Sweetley finished the last page and gently placed the affidavit on to the table. He sat back and tucked his right hand in his waistband. Sighing, he began rubbing his fingers of his left hand along his left brow. With no expression, Judge Sweetley turned to me.

"I signed a search warrant affidavit for you about six months ago, didn't I Agent Douglas?"

"Yes, your honor, you did." I wasn't sure where he was heading.

"Stop making me think so much."

Then he gave me a wink and smile. That was his style and we all let out a cathartic chuckle. He signed the warrant and handed it to me.

"Thank you, your honor."

"Okay Agent, now I gave you no-knock service because I have seen how dangerous these drug raids can be. I'm not sure the danger is worth it, but I respect what you do. Please be careful."

"We will, your honor. Thank you very much for your patience, sir."

I shook hands with Judge Sweetley. More than seventy years

of age, he had one strong grip – both literally and figuratively. He was one of the more cerebral judges. An outspoken critic of the war on drugs, he often spoke of the wasted time, money and resources we spent trying to keep something out of the hands of consenting adults, not unlike Prohibition. He did not support the strict sentencing guidelines. But, he was a man of the law. His rulings were rarely overturned if even challenged.

As he said, he supported the efforts of law enforcement. No-knock warrants were not granted easily. Usually, police had to knock and announce before making entry. In a dangerous situation, a judge could authorize us to enter without notice. In other words, we broke down the door and stormed in. We tried to exercise that power cautiously; if we abused it, we would lose it.

I took that warrant and Zucarelli and I hurried down the hall and in to the elevator. No words were exchanged with Brevard; there was nothing more to say.

"Okay, let's get up to the Bronx and get this warrant served. Can you drive like a real cop?"

Zucarelli asked with a hint of busting my balls.

"Sure can." I handed him the red flashing bubble and I stepped on the gas.

"So what about this cop killer? Think he'll cooperate? I mean, there isn't much we can negotiate."

Though I was looking straight ahead as I sped up to the Bronx, form the corner of my eye, I could see Zucarelli turn to me with that self-satisfied smile of his.

"Cop killer? What cop killer?"

"What cop killer? You kidding me? The one they jumped and Simone called you about."

"Oh yeah, about that." "About what, Zook?"

"Ya see, there really wasn't any cop killer."

"But that call from Simone."

"Ehh, yeah, there wasn't really any call from Simone either. That was just great acting on my part. There was no jumping a guy, there was no cop killer, and everyone is still just sitting out there waiting for this friggin' warrant."

"Zook, what the hell are you talking about? You told an AUSA that we had a cop killer. She based the p.c. for the warrant on that. That's how we got this thing."

"I know. And you're welcome."

"Uhh, and you know, there's this little thing called perjury; have you heard of that."

"Bob, I never swore to anything. There is nothing in the affidavit about a cop killer. This bad boy is based on everything SOG saw and our seizing that coke. That's it. Exactly as you tried to explain it to that stupid cunt."

"You're right. We didn't use any of that info, did we? It's not in the affidavit. How'd you do that? Why…"

"Look, she was not giving you that warrant, no matter how much p.c. you had. I had to make her nervous and light a fire under her slight rotund, but suitable ass. Ya know?"

"Yeah, her ass was…"

"Bob, I'm not really asking you about her ass…wait, did I just say that? Anyway, what I mean is, did you realize that you were not getting that warrant without something dramatic? We had to have her thinking that she had something to lose."

"I guess you're right."

"You guess? Of course I'm right."

"Okay, then tell me why was she so against the warrant?

Why wouldn't she want to grab the drugs and all those scumbags? Wouldn't that be good for her too?"

"You are so naive, Bob."

"What?"

"This wasn't about probable cause, it wasn't about drugs. It was about you." "Me? Why was this about me?"

"Didn't it surprise you that she knew your first name when the two of you never met? Remember how she asked if you were *Bob* Douglas?"

"Uh, yeah, That was a bit strange, but I didn't give it much thought. So, where you heading with this?"

"Bob, she was sending you a message."

"A message about what?"

"Damn, you're one of the stupidest smart guys I know. It was about Hernandez." "Hernandez? What?"

"Bob, our world is a small world. Everyone knows that you haven't taken a stand on the Hernandez shooting. A cop on a federal task force gets shot and the successful prosecution rests in your hands – what you are willing to say on the stand. The US Attorney's Office and the District Attorney are in bed together on this one. You got the feds and locals pissed at you. They talk. Everybody talks."

"Oh. Now I get it. Her comment about probable cause being in the eyes of the beholder.

Not the best analogy, but now it makes sense. Man, I really can be slow on the take."

"Well, take it easy on yourself. You're only an FBI Agent. That's why they gave you a real detective to watch after you. I got your back."

He did. At least I hoped he did. My back needed some cover.

*****

"Okay, we got an ETA of two." Zucarelli called on the radio, arranging to meet up with Simone and Doc so we could get quickly briefed and then get the warrant served.

We drove over to a small parking lot on the side of a bodega next to a small apartment building with windows overlooking us. Some neighbors were watching us; white guys with nice haircuts only meant one thing. The jeans, sneakers and attempts to fit in were useless. Even our undercover cars were obvious. A few of the neighbors glanced at us and then went back about their business. A pending police action was neither new nor exciting to them.

"Could you guys have taken any longer?" We got our asses hanging out here."

"C'mon Ray. You know this takes time. We moved as fast as we could." Zucarelli answered, probably thinking that I would start an argument with Simone.

"How's it looking?" Zucarelli asked.

"Not good. The apartment is on the top floor, three stories up. It's a high security door, fortified with a reinforced frame. There are three deadbolt locks. We gonna have to move quickly if we're gonna surprise them, assuming we're not burnt already." Simone described the situation.

"Did you get no-knock service?" Doc asked.

"Of course we did, Doc. Whatta ya think, we're a couple of rookies?" "Sorry, Bob. I didn't mean anything by it."

"Nah, I'm sorry Doc. I'm just kinda jumpy. That AUSA really pissed me off and..." "Forget it; let's just get back to business." Doc was right.

"Is Franks up here yet?" I asked.

"Of course; and speaking of the devil."

We all looked over as Franks and Reardon pulled up with Reardon at the wheel.

Franks was a little slow getting out of the passenger seat as Reardon waited for him at the front of the car. Then they walked over together.

"So, we got the warrant, right?" "Yes, Larry, we do," I answered. "Okay, then, what's the plan?"

"That's what we were just discussing. It's a tough one. Three flights up and then we gotta breach a fortified door really quickly. We don't know if we've been burned or not. We've been out here for a while."

"Well then, I guess it's time to call out our SWAT team, huh?" Franks turned to Reardon for his concurrence. Reardon was a member of the SWAT team.

"Yep, I'll call it in."

"Wait a second," I interrupted. "SWAT is great, but think about it, the team leader and most of the team are probably already in their pajamas in Jersey. It'll take hours to get them mobilized. We can't sit out here that long."

Franks and Reardon did not respond, and could not hide the glance they gave each other. They knew I was right but did not have a ready response.

"Hey," Zucarelli spoke up, "Let me call our Emergency Services Unit. They can get here in twenty minutes. They're the best SWAT team in the country, if not the world. I'll call HQ."

As he started pulling out his cell phone, Franks stopped him.

"Hold it a second, Mark." Franks sounded uncharacteristically authoritative. "I gotta make a call."

Franks signaled for Reardon to come with him and they

walked back to the car.

"A phone call? Now? Is this for real?" Zucarelli blurted this out, knowing that none of us would respond. We didn't have to. For Franks, doing the unexpected, was rarely unexpected.

Franks and Reardon had a brief discussion and then Franks made his call. Reardon turned his back on Franks momentarily, in what I thought was a small sign of disagreement. Franks' call didn't last long. He then spoke to Reardon who nodded his head in agreement but Reardon still did not appear to truly be in agreement with what Franks was telling him. Side by side and in cadence, they walked back to us.

"Okay, we don't want to wait, not even for ESU. We got three SWAT team members on our squad, Steve, Doc and Vic. They can handle it."

"Larry, we all appreciate that you have SWAT trained guys, but this is an inner city counter drug assault. This is exactly what ESU does. I think it's worth the wait." Simone spoke his mind clearly.

"He's right, Larry. We should go with ESU. No disrespect to the Bureau, but ESU really is better equipped for this." Zucarelli knew that supporting Simone sounded like an NYPD versus FBI moment. That was not his intent. Both he and Simone felt strongly that waiting for ESU was the right move.

"I appreciate what you're saying. But look, from the moment I got here, you all told me how dangerous waiting around has been. I think we need to do this now."

Without waiting for any other input, he turned to Reardon and asked, "You have all your equipment and everything?"

"Yes, we do. We got our uniforms, gear and we even got the rabbit. We're ready, right here, right now."

Franks knew that would be Reardon's answer and Reardon was ready to be asked.

"Steve will take the lead, followed by Doc and Vic. After they make entry and secure the scene, Bob and Mark will enter. Ray, you and I will cover the doorway. The rest of the squad will watch the perimeter and the vehicles. Then we'll search and make the arrests and seizures as necessary. Any questions?"

There weren't any questions. From their body language, it was clear that Zucarelli and Simone were the most frustrated at Franks not waiting for NYPD's ESU. We all went to our cars and prepared for the entry.

"By the way, what the hell is a rabbit?"

"Oh, that's a great tool. It works on air pressure. It's got these two long tongs, kinda like rabbit ears I guess. You shove those tongs into the door jam and start pumping. Usually within a couple of seconds, the door frame spreads out and the door pops open."

"Cool."

"Let's just hope they're not sitting there waiting for us and we get in and out without a problem."

"I still think we should've waited for ESU. At this point, what's another twenty minutes?"

"I agree, Zook. I don't know who Franks called, but I gotta think that whoever it was had something to do with this decision. Not to mention, even though Reardon didn't seem happy about something, I'm sure he doesn't mind leading this informal SWAT assault."

"Informal and SWAT don't go together. It can't be both."

"I know."

"I didn't know that Candelaria was a SWAT guy. He's seems

a little too scrawny for that." "Vic? Eh, he's a good guy. He ain't too big, and he's got that baby face, but I think underneath it all, he's one tough m.f. He grew up in the South Bronx; that says something." "I guess."

"Okay, everyone stand by, we are about to move." Reardon came on the radio. A few seconds of silence followed, and then he was on the radio again.

"Three, two, one; execute, execute, execute."

At that moment, Reardon, Candelaria and Doc, dressed in their black SWAT jump suits, helmets and all, jumped out of the car and ran up the stairs to the hallway, holding their automatic weapons. Two young teenage boys, who had been sitting on the edge of the stairs, quickly got u up and began jumping up and down, enjoying the excitement.

Zucarelli and I began to follow from about 10 feet behind and up to the third floor landing. Franks and Simone stopped at the second floor landing to stop anyone from walking up the steps. The rest of the squad started taking up their positions to secure the outer perimeter. We always had to be sure that nobody entered the scene behind us. That could be deadly.

From behind a wall in the hallway, Zucarelli and I watched Doc shove that rabbit in the doorframe and then stand back to train his weapon on the door itself along with Reardon. Candelaria began pumping the rabbit with the foot pedal, holding his weapon in the same manner. We heard a few creaks, saw the doorframe spread, and then the door popped open. Our SWAT boys made entry.

Immediately, before finishing yelling, "Police" one, then two shots were heard. Small chips of wood and plaster came flying from the doorway. Then a third and fourth shot. From where we were, Zucarelli and I had no idea who shot who. We knew we couldn't go running in to an active shooting scene blind, but we also knew that we could not just stand there, safely behind the wall while our squad-mates came under fire. Staying low and hugging the wall we crept over to opposite sides of the doorway. No more shots were heard. Peeking in, we saw Reardon on the left holding one suspect at gunpoint. Opposite him was Candelaria holding another suspect at gunpoint. Towards the rear of the apartment, we saw Doc slowly and cautiously turn down a hallway. Hearing heavy breathing, I turned to see Franks make it up the steps, kneeling down trying to catch his breath. Simone made sure that Franks was not having a heart attack. I could not be concerned with Franks at that moment.

"Psst, Steve. We're here, what should we do?" I asked Reardon as he held his position. "Bob, Mark, go straight to back of apartment and assist Doc. 10-4?" Reardon spoke loudly so we could all hear his directions.

"We're coming in, Doc," I called to him.

"10-4. Move it, move it." Doc responded.

Trusting the scene was secured, Zucarelli and I came in and ran to the hallway to where we saw Doc go. He held up his hand, signaling for us to stop as he leaned against the wall, his automatic weapon pointing at a closed door, leading to what we assumed was a bedroom. Doc then held up one finger and pointed to the door to warn us. We nodded that we understood. Slowly, he moved back to speak with us, his gun never taken off target. A narrow hallway, we were clustered close together – not a safe situation.

"Zook, I'll kick in the door and enter sweeping left. You stay low in the hall and cover center," Doc whispered.

Zucarelli acknowledged.

"Bob, stay low and as soon as the door swings open, make sure it does not swing back on us. You make entry and clear that side of the room. You gotta move fast."

I acknowledged.

"Okay, on three," Doc directed us.

Doc held up one, then two, then three fingers and he kicked the door. Before the door had a chance to swing back, I saw muzzle flashes out of the corner of my eye and heard two, maybe three shots; maybe more. Turning to the sound, the door hit me in the back, reminding me that I had not cleared my side of the room. Afraid of what might be behind me I quickly spun around to find an empty room with only one old wooded end table that had been knocked down. Grateful that I had not turned my back on an armed threat I looked back at Doc. Still pointing his gun, he ran forward to the body of the jerk who chose to shoot it out, now wedged in the panel wall - his head and upper torso hanging halfway through to the neighboring apartment. I got closer and saw the blood from two large holes in his chest.

That was pretty good shooting, I thought to myself. *And what kinda cheap- ass walls are these?* was my next thought.

Zucarelli was not in the room. I turned around to the doorway and saw Zucarelli laying on the floor. Running over, I fell to my knees to see what happened. His eyes were open and there was a long, raw and bloody scratch above his left brow.

"Zook, Zook, are you alright?"

"Yeah, yeah, I think so." He remained motionless and stared at the ceiling.

"Can you move? Can you get up?"

"Yeah, I think I'm alright."

Zucarelli struggled to get up on his elbows and then I helped him sit up, and lean against the wall.

"Fuck, it looks like you got grazed. Are you hit anywhere?"

"I don' think so. I think I'm okay."

I got closer, almost nose to nose, to make an inspection of his wound. It did not look serious; at least not for a gun shot. Without thinking, I grabbed his head and pulled it towards my chest, giving him a very awkward man hug.

"Bob, Bob. I'm okay. You're weirding me out here." He pushed himself off me and against the wall.

"Sorry, man. Just glad you're okay."

"I know. Thanks. But go see how Doc and the guys are doing; give me a moment."

I helped him to his feet when I heard a shriek come from the building hallway. I hesitated and Zucarelli looked at me.

"Go, go," he yelled, waving his hand.

As Candelaria and Reardon were securing their prisoners with Simone and Franks, I ran through the apartment and out the door in to the building hallway. Following the screams, I turned to my right and saw a tall, thin woman in her late twenties, wearing a long gray night shirt standing in the doorway of the next apartment down from where we were. Incoherent and running in small circles, she was pointing in to her apartment. I ran in to a narrow hallway that had two doors; this looked as if one apartment had been rigged into two. Through the doorway on the right, I caught a glimpse of Julie, already inside, go in to a bedroom. I followed a few seconds behind. When I got in, she just looked at me and then stepped aside. There was Doc. He apparently came in through the hole in the panel wall where the body of the man he shot had fallen completely through the wall. Doc was down on his knees, holding on to the crib. With his other hand over his eyes, he was sobbing silently.

Walking over to the crib, I looked over the top and saw the only thing that could make sense of Doc's behavior. There was this tiny baby in a pink and flowery footed pajama. Not moving and not crying, but blood oozing from a pronounced hole in its little, bald head. The story was clear; there was nothing to say.

*****

The next few weeks were slow and quiet. No new work was getting assigned to our squad. The squad room bullpen had little frivolity and no ball busting banter that was hallmark of our existence. Doc was not back to work. He was cleared administratively; despite the incredible tragedy, it was a good shoot – he acted in self defense. Would he ever come back? How does someone live with that hanging over his head?

Sitting at my desk, trying to appear busy, Zucarelli put his hands on my shoulders.

"I'm going out for a smoke. Wanna take a break?"

Zucarelli knew I hated cigarette smoke. Then I realized he wanted me to walk out with him. Down the elevator and out the front door, we turned on to Queens Boulevard and started walking towards the Queens Mall. Zucarelli lit up his cigarette and took a long and deliberate drag, followed by a slow exhale as we walked along the busy street.

"You know," he said, clearly having something on his mind, "word at NYPD is that we really fucked this thing up."

"By this thing, you mean…?"

"You know what I mean. That little baby getting shot. It didn't have to happen."

"Of course it didn't have to happen. But, we can't blame Doc. He had to shoot. How about blaming that mother fucker for shooting at us? Getting killed was too good for him."

"Nobody is blaming Doc."

"Then who? Who are they blaming for this gigantic clusterfuck?" "They're blaming us."

"Us? As in me and you, us?"

"Not exactly. Kinda just the squad in general. But mostly the FBI." "What for?"

"Bob, we should've waited for ESU. If we did, this wouldn't have happened."

"How do you know that? We didn't know that these apartments were illegal, rigged with fake walls and makeshift everything."

"That's just it, Bob. ESU would've known." "Really? How would they know that?"

"C'mon, think about it. We're the NYPD. We're the size of small army. Whatta ya think, we don't collect intel; we don't have blueprints and inside info on what's happening on our city? Yeah, ESU would have known that and they wouldn't have gone in there with those high powered weapons and ammo."

"Well that's just fuck'n great. All we do is try to work a case and look what happened. A baby gets killed. The NYPD blames the FBI. All for what? For nothing."

"Not exactly nothing. We got another hundred kilos of coke, a small cache of weapons and three violent cocksuckers off the street."

"C'mon Zook. Look at the price we paid. What about Doc? He's one of the nicest guys you could know, and he'll probably go psycho. Hardly worth it."

"I know. I know."

We walked in silence to the corner, and instinctively we turned around in unison and headed back to the office.

I was usually one of the first ones out of the office to head home. With things at home getting tense again, this seemed like the perfect time to stay late. Reardon was always the one to turn off the lights. When the office was empty except for me and him, I looked over at him as he spoke on the phone, smiling and laughing, probably talking to Carol Gardner again. He saw me looking at him, and must've known that I wanted to talk to him, but swung around in his chair to face the window. So, I walked over to the seat next to him and sat down. That could not get any more obvious.

"Uh, I'll have to call you back. Something just came up."

He hung up the phone.

"Okay, Bob, what's up?"

"Look Steve, there's always been a lot of tension between you and I. Can we put that aside for a moment? I mean, this is about Doc. We all consider him a friend."

Invoking Doc appeared to work. Reardon took a deep breath and settled more comfortably in to his seat.

"Alright, Bob. What's on your mind?"

"Steve, I know you're tight with Franks, I really appreciate that, but not calling in ESU for that raid, was, I don't know, just wrong. I mean, look what happened. Who knows what will happen to Doc."

"Okay. So yes, it turned to shit. Larry had no way of knowing that would happen. What's done is done Bob. Where are you going with this?"

"It was a bad decision. And this is hardly his first bad decision. We can't keep risking our lives like this. Yes, you're usually here to bring him back to earth, but look what happened this time. I didn't get the impression that you liked the idea of going in with just a few SWAT guys."

"Bob, look, I'm not agreeing or disagreeing with you. But, just for the sake of argument, what do you propose? Where do you go in the FBI if you don't like your supervisor?"

"Steve, this isn't a matter of not liking him. It's literally a matter of life and death."

"So, back to my question. What do you propose?"

"I don't know. Let's go to the AD. Let him know we got a supervisor who may get us hurt. Maybe they could move him somewhere less dangerous, like FCI or something."

"Gunn? You wanna go to The Pistol? Not a good idea, Bob." He was almost laughing at my suggestion.

"Why not? What's going on?"

Reardon hesitated looking down at his desk. He fumbled with a rubber band and then a paper clip. Then he looked up.

"I'm gonna tell you something, but this can't go further than you and me. Do I have your word, Bob?"

"Yes, you do. You know I keep my word."

"I do know that, Bob. Whew. Okay. It wasn't Larry." "Whatta ya mean it wasn't Larry?"

"It was Gunn's call not to wait for ESU. He was on the phone with Larry and insisted that we use our people." "What? Why was the AD so in the weeds on a case like this?"

"I don't know. But he knew everything that was going on and was calling all the shots. He knew we were on to something big and he wanted to make sure it was the FBI up front. He didn't want us getting overshadowed by the PD."

"You're kidding. Tell me you're fuck'n kidding. That's what drove this whole thing? Who got top billing. Fuck."

"That's it, Bob. It was all Gunn. Whatta ya want to do now? Go to the director."

"The director? Oh yeah, Director Muffins. That'll work. He can't stand up to Gunn. The Pistol will shoot him right down. Everyone knows that."

"That's right, and you know The Pistol. If you keep pushing this, and he thinks you're pointing the finger at him, he'll shoot your legs right out from under you. You wanna take on Gunn? Go ahead."

Reardon was right. Zucarelli was right. Was I the only one not seeing what was going on around me?

Chapter 6

"**S**tart getting comfortable my friend. We may be here for a while."

Slowly driving down the one-way Manhattan street, Zucarelli was looking for that one strategic spot to set up our surveillance. As always, traffic inched along and my impatience had my gut churning, though I did not know why. We were in no rush and on no particular time schedule. As Zucarelli said, we were in for a long day, or week or even months. Surveillance was unpredictable and uneventful most of the time. Many hours were spent waiting for that one exciting moment.

"That's great. Nothing else I'd rather be doing," I replied to Zucarelli, with no attempt to hide my sarcasm and lack of enthusiasm.

"Well, Bob, that's what the drug business is all about. Sitting and waiting and waiting some more. Haven't you learned that lesson already?"

"Say what? You're teaching me about patience? Aren't you the hyper half of this partnership?"

"Perhaps. But, I'm maturing."

"Maturing? Not exactly the word I would use, but okay, this is the new and matured Detective Mark Zucarelli."

"Yes it is"

"Anyway," I continued, "I wonder how many hours we've actually spent sitting in the car or sitting on a wire."

"Really? You wonder about that?"

"Not literally. But, not a whole lot else to think about out here."

"No? Nothing else to think about at in midtown Manhattan in this nice weather? Try thinking about that." As soon as Zucarelli pointed his finger, he redirected his gaze. "And look at that." Zucarelli nodded towards a couple of smartly dressed, attractive businesswomen walking by. They were deeply engaged in conversation, hands moving and acting as if they did not notice the stares they were getting. Suddenly, my body was thrust forward as Zucarelli slammed on the brakes, just short of rear-ending the white Toyota in front of us.

"Well, brakes work," he said to me laughing at his near miss.

"C'mon, watch what you're doing, Zook."

"Oh, I'm watching, my friend. Watching pussy that is; you can never go wrong admiring some good looking pussy. If I teach you nothing else, please remember that," Zucarelli went on with this lesson.

While not bad advice, I thought Zucarelli's reference to teaching me something was a bit condescending. Then again, I did pick up a lot of life's little lessons since partnering up with him. Street smarts were probably a lot more valuable than anything I could learn in school or even at the FBI Academy; especially working drugs.

"Is this the best we can do?" I asked Zucarelli as he parked on the street right across from the address we had for the mysterious El Gordo in the Diamond District .

"You got a better idea?"

Looking at the crowded sidewalk of street vendors, diamond dealers, patrol cops in sloppy uniforms and would-be crooks and pickpockets stalking their prey, there seemed to be no logical position to take for a discreet, stationary surveillance.

"No, I guess not."

"Okay then; sit back and let's make the best of it. Surveillance sucks, but ultimately, it's what makes the case. There's nothing like seeing something with your own eyes." Before I could respond Zucarelli started again.

"Hey, talk about seeing it with your own eyes, look at that. Now, that is one set of titties, huh?" Zucarelli asked me nodding towards a tall, thin pretty blond walking down the street. She was holding on to her purse's black leather strap hanging from her shoulder with one hand and pushing back her long straight hair with her other hand. She was not moving quickly, as her tight skirt and high heels kept her strides short. That gave us a few more minutes to look.

"No bad; not bad at all. That silk blouse really lets those things bounce."

"C'mon, Bob, those babies are definitely better than not bad. They got shape and I don't know, personality even. Oh yeah, look at that, now she's doing a little window shopping. There you go, take a closer look, bend over baby. C'mon, just a little more…there we go. Nice tits complemented by a tight, thin ass. I'd like to walk right up there and stick …"

"Whoa, Zook please, that's enough."

"What? We can't talk about our raunchy fantasies? Is that some kinda FBI rule or something? Seems like the "FBI's got a rule for everything""

"Well, yes it does. I don't think talking about raunchy fantasies is one of them. Wait, actually, that's not true. I guess we can have them; we just can't talk about 'em. At least not in the office and especially not in earshot of a female with an attitude."

"Like Gordon?"

"Gordon? Oh yeah, Julie. For some reason I don't think of females by their last name. I don't know, I think Julie's alright. I can't see her making an EEO complaint or nothing. Why, Zook, you think differently?"

"I don't know. She just seems like she's got her radar up; like she's on the lookout for something."

"Well, whatever. But getting back to our fantasies, mine don't include you sticking anything to anybody. That is definitely not a picture I want to visualize."

"I'll take that as a good sign, 'cause ya know, every once in a while, I do catch you checking me out."

"Yeah, very funny."

"Anyway, wait till the summer heat really hits. Short shirts, tank tops and no bras - there'll be a lot of skin walking around here. We'll have plenty of eye candy to fantasize about. And I like to verbalize my fantasies."

"Hopefully, we'll get lucky and be outta here before then. There will be plenty of skin all over the city. I don't want to be stuck in this car with you all summer."

"There could be worse things, ya know." Zucarelli gave me one of his sarcastic smiles. Then he reached for the newspaper he had tucked between the coffee stained, brown car seat spotted cigarette burns. He then closed the ash tray; he had to push a couple of time because it was stuffed with cigarette butts. I hated cigarette smoke and Zucarelli was trying to respect my wishes.

As much as I hated the smoke, Zucarelli hated not smoking when out in the car. That was another odd cultural difference.

Almost all the cops smoked. Almost none of the FBI Agents smoked. Smoking in federal buildings had been banned years ago. The cops didn't care. Their smoke filled the office bullpen and hovered near the low, false ceiling like a dense fog. Franks didn't have the balls to take on the cops. He dismissed it as too small an issue to waste his time on. To the cops, it was just another sign of FBI Agents having no backbone. Smoking was nothing more than another territorial grab; trying to explain that to anybody would only make me come off as a whiney bitch.

I settled in and began staring at everything and seeing nothing. I cleared my mind of all the trivia Zucarelli and I were taking about and started to wonder how we would figure out who El Gordo was.

"So, ya wanna hear what your boss had to say about Doc's shooting?" Zucarelli asked me as he looked at the newspaper now spread open across the steering wheel.

"Huh, whatta ya mean? When did he...?" I turned to Zucarelli and quickly removed my hand from the black center console as it hit something sticky. I didn't know what I landed my hand in and didn't ask.

"Right here, page two of the News. And the headline reads, FBI answers questions as citizens express outrage over shooting death of Bronx infant." Zucarelli stopped and looked up at me.

"Okay, so read it already." I wasn't sure what kind of reaction he was expecting from me.

"Let's see," Zucarelli looked back down at the newspaper, running his forefinger side to side and downwards on the page, trying to find the best place to start reading. "Shit I'm gonna need reading glasses soon," as he began to squint a bit. I had to chuckle watching this six-foot-two, muscular tough guy show any kind of weakness. In my late thirties, and Zucarelli a few years older, we were both well beyond our rookie years, desperately clinging to our youth.

"Here it is," he continued. "The head of the FBI New York Office expressed deep regret yesterday for the accidental shooting of an infant in the Bronx last week, during a drug raid by the FBI and New York City Police. According to Assistant Director J. Peter Gunn, 'This was a terrible tragedy; that a beautiful little baby should become victim to this dangerous drug war. I ask all of you to please keep in mind that our agent returned fire against an armed drug dealer who initiated a gun battle with law enforcement officers. Our agent did everything correctly, defending himself and killing the suspect. He could not have foreseen that a bullet would penetrate a wall and enter into a neighboring apartment. We are deeply sorry and certainly wish this never happened, but I must point out that the walls within that apartment building were illegally constructed and did not meet code standards.' Wow, that was a mouthful of damage control. He must be a lawyer."

"Actually, I think he is."

"He sure sounds like all those other windbag lawyers in the Bureau."

There was Zucarelli taking another pot-shot at the FBI. He loved doing that.

"Oh, and here's a little more you might like," Zucarelli continued, "According to Gunn, and I quote, 'The Colombian Drug Cartels are the greatest threat to our American way of life. They seek to destroy our youth, our economy and our security by trafficking this poison to our children. They funnel millions of dollars into the underground and out of our country. We will fight them at every turn and with every resource at our disposal. Unfortunately, there will be casualties along the way. Make no mistake, this is a war.' There you have it. He is one slick politician, huh?"

"Sure seems that way. He's running for something," I conceded.

"He really plays on this being a war and a threat to our American way of life and blah, blah, blah." Zucarelli started flapping his thumb against his fingers, almost subconsciously.

"Why not? That fear card really works. Just look at history. Focus on what scares us and then find someone to blame. Ya know what I mean? He points to the drug cartels and shifts attention away from the shooting."

"You know what I think about that shooting. If only we had..."

"Zook, please," I held up my hand interrupting him. "I do know what you think, and I'm not trying to be an asshole about it, but the whole thing really bothers me. Can we just drop it? Please."

Zucarelli looked me in the eye.

"Sure, no problem." But, he stared for that extra second, with a forced smirk that told me that he knew I was holding something back.

"Is there something you wanna tell me, Bob?" His eyebrows scrunching together just enough to relay a message that he wasn't really asking a question; he knew the answer.

The next few seconds dragged on for what seemed so long, I thought I would crack.

"No." The quick diversion of my eyes away from Zucarelli's stare was a dead give-away.

Zucarelli continued to stare and once again started rubbing his thumb and forefinger down each side of his moustache. I wanted to share what I knew with my partner; that's what partners do. But I gave Reardon my word not to give up that it was Gunn's decision not to wait for ESU. I wasn't the most popular guy on the squad, but at least everyone knew they could trust me. I couldn't lose that. Besides, if Gunn learned that we were bad-mouthing him, who knew what hell he would bring down upon us.

We sat there quietly, as all the busy people walking up and down 47th street in the heart of the Diamond District appeared to be absorbed in their own lives. Yet, our mission involved almost no activity; just sitting and looking and looking again.

"Besides us not knowing who El Gordo is, what do you think he's doing? I mean, how does he figure into this whole scheme of things?" I asked.

"Well, look; we already seized all that money right around here on Reardon's case. It had to be drug money. So, the only thing I can think of is that El Gordo launders their money."

"How's that work?"

"I'm not really sure, Bob. I'm guessing that he's probably some jeweler that we're looking at right now. Not sure how he does it, but I guess he launders the drug money through his business, avoiding CTRs and SARs and all that other reporting crap I don't understand, I guess."

The Currency Transaction Reports and Suspicious Activity Reports were all started by the federal government as a tool to fight money laundering.

"If we're working drugs, we should really understand that stuff better, don't you think?"

"Yes, I do. A friend of mine I was on patrol with is on a DEA task force now. He told me that DEA has really been working on the money side of drugs. They got a good handle on this shit."

"Well, we better figure out what we're doing. Remember Dave Scotto?"

"Yeah, of course I remember him; he got promoted to your HQ not too long ago. Why?"

"I spoke to him a few weeks ago. He told me that the Drug Section was freaking out 'cause the director had to explain to Congress why DEA has been kicking our ass on stats. They're killing us on arrests and seizures. When the director gets stressed, you don't want to be in HQ; the shit rolls downhill fast."

"Same with us. When the commish gets beat up by the mayor, every division at 1 PP starts writing new rules. Anyway, we gonna have figure this out. It's all about the money. Follow the money, right?"

"Absolutely."

"You do know what 1 PP is, right?"

"Yes, your Headquarters at 1 Police Plaza. I have been around a while, you know."

Then we sat there quietly. Zucarelli would look around and then take a glance at the newspaper. I kept my eyes on the street. I was going to find El Gordo.

"What are you doing?" I asked Zucarelli as he put the Police plaque in the windshield.

"Whatta ya mean?"

"I mean, why would you put that plaque in the windshield and let everyone know who we are?"

"Bob, seriously, do you really believe that everyone doesn't already know who we are? What two jerks would be sitting in this stupid car all day except two idiot cops. By not trying to be so sneaky, we may fit in better; everyone will just ignore us."

"Then, how the hell we gonna find El Gordo? If everyone knows we're here, nobody is gonna do anything."

"We'll figure it out. Something, somewhere, somehow will be out of place."

"And?"

"And, being the highly trained observers that we are, we'll see it and that'll be our break."

"You think so? Just being observant can get us over the hump."

"That's all it takes; just one break."

"One break, that's all, huh?" I said that somewhat under my breath, slightly nodding my head up and down.

Zucarelli ignored me. He knew I was frustrated, not challenging his street cop expertise.

Returning to quietly staring mindlessly, I carefully watched the crowd and saw nothing of interest. Zucarelli kept his routine of reading a few sentences in the newspaper, then looking up and scanning the street. He did that several times before his stare locked on something down the street.

"Whatta we got? Some good t and a comin' our way?"

"Not exactly."

"Then what?'

Look at those schvartzes over there." Zucarelli pointed over the steering wheel, though that did not help me home in on the target. I tried to follow his stare instead.

"Schvartzes? Did you just say schvartzes?"

"Yeah, you know, black people, its.."

"Yes, Zook, I know what it means, but you using that word, is just, uh, I don't know."

"Well, we are in the Diamond District . When in Rome, do like the Romans. When in the Diamond District , do like the sids."

"Sids? What's a sid?"

"You know, the Hassidic Jews, those guys with the crazy curls. They own half this place."

"Oh, sids for Hassidic; I get it. Well, what about those two kids anyway?"

"This is exactly what I was talking about. They're out of place. Nothing to do with El Gordo of course, but they're up to something."

"You know that how?"

"C'mon Bob. This is exactly what I mean about FBI Agents not being cops. Look around this place. You got your Jews and you got your Italians. The only blacks here are either homeless or dressed in business suits. That's pretty much it. What are two young black kids doing walking down the street. Actually any kids should be in school right now anyway? They ain't buying anything here. They're up to something."

"Okay, so now what?"

"We sit here and watch them. That's about all we can do right now."

"Whatta ya think they're doing?"

"Not sure yet. Right now, they're looking around."

"They'll see us, won't they?"

"I doubt it. Whatever they're up to, they're new at this. They're probably on the look-out for uniforms, but let's play it safe." Zucarelli slowly moved the police plaque from the windshield to the floor and sunk himself a little deeper in to the seat. I took the hint and did the same.

Not sure what to do next, I sat there watching Zucarelli watching the boys. I was more interested in learning from his powers of observation than whatever those kids were up to, because whatever it was, it was probably not an FBI thing.

"Okay, look, they've got their sights on something or someone. They're looking down this way."

"So what do we do now?"

"We sit here until they make a move. Make sure you're ready to respond quickly."

"I guess I just got deputized as an honorary NYPD cop, huh?"

"You are so anointed, my child." Zucarelli raised his hand and tapped my shoulders and head – I was knighted by King Zucarelli.

"Look, they're starting to make their move now. And... they're off, running right in our direction. Get ready."

They ran right passed us and then they hit; about ten yards down the block one of them body slammed the blonde we had just been ogling and the other wrestled her purse away. We heard her shriek and they were off as she stood there screaming, pointing and jumping up and down in complete hysteria.

"Move, move," Zucarelli yelled to me and he was out the car door, pulling on the small chain necklace holding his badge, bringing it out from beneath his shirt. I was right behind him.

As they ran, they knocked in to some pedestrians and ran around others. Nobody stopped them. They turned the corner, and probably did not even realize that Zucarelli and I were in pursuit.

"The subway, they're going for the subway. We'll lose them in there."

Zucarelli's words were clear. We had to stop these little pricks in the next few seconds. The one holding the purse was in front. It was more important to catch him with the evidence. I didn't have to be a street cop to know that. Zucarelli was a few strides ahead of me. As he got close, he laid a heavy hand on the shoulder of the kid running behind and dragged him down.

"Go, go," he yelled at me as he struggled with this scraggly kid who was no match for Zucarelli.

I kept running. As the kid with the purse hit the stairs to the subway, he slowed down just a bit to grab the railing. I wasn't ready for that and my momentum carried me right into him as I continued to fly down the stairs. I was not going alone. Managing to grab the collar of my fleeing purse snatcher and dragged him with me. He too was a skinny one and I easily pulled him in front of me. When we fell, he hit the floor first and I fell on top of him. Not a bad apprehension. The purse sprung loose from his hands and I quickly grabbed it to make sure some passing pedestrian didn't scoop it up and run off.

"Turn over on your face, motherfucker." It was fun to yell at someone with that kind of hostility and authority. Like most FBI Agents, I fantasized about being a tough street cop and doing the things FBI Agents didn't get to do. Trouble starts when an FBI Agent cannot separate that fantasy from reality and starts making arrests for street crimes, and traffic infractions whether on or off duty. It doesn't happen often, but it does happen – usually with young rookie agents. That is when the FBI shows them the door and a promising career comes to a screeching halt.

My badge was still clipped on my belt and my gun was still holstered. While I thought this was pretty exciting, for New Yorker commuters, this was nothing new. Some stopped briefly to watch, and probably assumed I was a plain clothes cop making an arrest for something like fare jumping. Then they went on with their day. Half dazed from the fall, my arrestee was compliant. I got his arms behind his back, handcuffed him and pulled him to his feet by grabbing on to his elbow.

"Rodney King," some passerby called out, trying to stir up trouble, especially seeing a white cop was arresting a black kid. He was met with a few grunts and groans from the small crowd, but most of the busy commuters had their heads up their asses; they probably did not even remember the Rodney King incident. The anti-police rally cry used to be "Attica" but I was sure not one young punk in a business suit would know what that meant.

I was alone and not sure as to what to do. Street arrests were not an FBI thing. So, I took my prisoner by the wrist and started heading back up the stairs. I was glad to see Zucarelli and a uniformed patrol officer at the top of the stairs. Zucarelli, with a big smile, was jokingly applauding me.

✳✳✳✳✳

"Come in, come in," Tony Scarlotta whispered under his breath, as he hit the buzzer to unlock the glass door to his jewelry shop. His expression made clear he was not pleased to see the visitor.

"Good to see you, Tony, thought I don't think you feel the same," was Ramon's greeting. Then he continued, "Did you see those idiots the cops grabbed just down the block?"

"No, I didn't. What happened? Who'd they grab?" Tony's nerves were apparent.

"Easy Tony, everything is alright. I think it was just some plainclothes cops; they probably caught some punk who mugged someone or jumped the toll. Didn't look like anything big. Let's not get paranoid."

"Yeah, easy for you say. How are things in Colombia, Ramon?"

"All is good."

"When do I get to meet your boss, this El Tigre?"

"Tony, what is your obsessive interest in meeting El Tigre?"

"I don't know. Maybe I just like knowing who I'm doing business with."

"Well Tony, you're doing business with me. That is all you need to know."

"Oh yeah? Maybe I'll just hold up your money one day and make El Tigre come get it himself. Then we'll meet."

After a hearty laugh, Ramon refocused his stare from the ceiling to directly and Tony and slid his right hand down his silk red tie.

"Tony, I wouldn't recommend that. You'll hear from El Tigre, but you won't meet him. You won't like the message he sends. But, I think you already know that, don't you."

"You know, Ramon, I belong to a family too, and they don't get pushed around easy. You screw with me and…"

"Tony, Tony, easy. Why are we even talking like this? Is something wrong?"

"Well, it seems like I'm taking an awful risk. Like you just said, I got plain clothes cops walking around and I got Colombians with briefcases walking in and out of my office.

Even these asshole cops are gonna notice something's wrong."

"What do you mean, Tony?"

"C'mon Ramon, look out the window. How many Colombians do you see walking around the Diamond District ? Everybody's either a fuck'n kike or one of my goombas. No Colombians."

"I see. Tipping off the police is not exactly what we want to do, is it?"

"No, we don't want to tip off anybody to anything. That is not smart business."

Ramon hesitated to respond. He had a hard believing that Tony was really that afraid on the police. He wanted to ask Tony just exactly who else he was afraid of. The Russians? The Mexicans? Either of those can get pretty feisty. If they started encroaching on Colombian Cartel territory, a very stern message would have to be sent. Territory was to be respected.

"So, what is it you want Tony?"

"Money, Ramon. I think I deserve a bigger cut. The bigger the risk, the bigger the pay-off. That's how it's supposed to work here in America, ya know."

"Yes, I know all about it. Tony, I think we offered you a very reasonable deal. You seemed pretty satisfied with the terms. I don't think that you trying to push us into a corner is good business for either one of us. Do you?"

Scarlotta read Ramon's tone accurately. He wasn't outright threatening him, but Scarlotta knew that the cartel did not shun violence. At times, their brand of retribution made the mob look like choir boys. Would the cartel hit an Italian with mob connections in the states, right there in New York City? That would be bad business. Or would it? Maybe it would send a message. Scarlotta didn't know if it was worth finding out.

"Look Ramon, we got a good thing going here. But, like I said, I think it's getting a bit risky. Maybe a little more money for my troubles? I'm just saying, not pushing. Fair enough?"

"Fair enough Tony. I will talk to El Tigre."

"Oh yeah? You heading back to Colombia soon, or talking to him on the phone?"

Ramon started to laugh again.

"Tony, I don't ask your business. You know better than to ask mine."

*****

"So what now?" I asked Zucarelli as we walked back to the car.

"Nothing much. Patrol will get them booked into juvie. Their parents will pick 'em up, call the NAACP, complain that this was racial profiling and try to make a lot of noise hoping the DA drops the case.

"And then what?"

"Probably not much. Maybe we'll have to testify for a few minutes and that'll be that. If we didn't have a victim and this was something where it was our word against theirs, the DA may let it go. But, we go parading a good looking bitch like Melanie in there and she's talks about getting her purse snatched, we'll get a conviction. "

"Melanie?"

"Yeah Melanie, the babe they grabbed the purse from. You know, we were watching her and…"

"I know, I know. I didn't forget; it was only a few minutes ago. But you're calling her Melanie like you've known her forever."

"Not forever, but long enough. I mean, she get's robbed, then a good looking cop like me comes to her rescue, takes her statement, gets her phone number...ya know what I'm talking about?"

"Yes, I know what you're talking about. You are unbelievable."

"Yes I am, my friend, yes I am."

"Alright, so now what do we do?"

"I just told you," Zucarelli sounded exasperated by my question, "The DA gets..."

"No, Zook, not about these two dipshits. About our case, you know, El Gordo and all that stuff; or did you forget? Maybe got Melanie on your mind."

"Oh, I'm gonna have Melanie on more than my mind. I'm gonna..."

"Okay, Zook, I got it. But what are we going to do now that everybody's seen us? I mean, if by some miracle they didn't see the police plaque in the windshield, they saw us make the arrest. They know we're cops and they know exactly what we look like. How do we go back to surveillance now?"

"We don't."

"We don't? Then how the hell are we gonna work this case?"

"Easy, my man. We'll go back. Just not right now. Let things cool down a bit. Memories are short. Our little escapade will be forgotten by tomorrow. Besides, who knows who saw what. There's so much crap going on there, nobody gives a flying fuck about anything anyway. Let's give it a few days, maybe a week and then we set up again."

"A week? How could we wait a week? We'll miss a lot of

shit happening. This case..."

"Bob, Bob, you gotta ease up, man. The drug business has been around a long time and it ain't going anywhere. Just like those kilos we seized. It was a great job; but there is plenty more to replace 'em. We can only do what we can do. El Gordo will still be here, whoever the scumbag is. Okay?"

"Okay."

Zucarelli heard the disappointment in my answer. "Hey, we got plenty of stuff we need to do anyway."

"Like what?"

"Let's see. We got Sanchez's suppression hearing coming up."

"And we got that DEA surveillance training too," I reminded him.

"Whoa, where did we come from? That was something the FBI agreed to do with DEA, not the NYPD."

"Yeah, but you're my partner. Wherever I go, you go, right?"

Zucarelli's response to that was to give me the finger. That meant he agreed.

"Also, Reardon needs some help on that wire; that case from Miami is still going on." We should probably volunteer to take a shift or two. We're gonna need some help soon too; so you know, we gotta be team players."

"Yes, we do." I answered him.

We pulled into the parking garage where we were greeted by Manny who had been operating the gate and managing the garage for ten years. This was not an FBI building; we just rented office space like every other tenant, though we did employ some extra security measures. Manny knew each one of us and each car we drove. He knew when we came and went. He got to know each one of us personally – where we lived, our families and friends. Manny had become one of the guys.

"Hey Zook, Bob, how you guys doing?" Manny asked from his booth that was just wide enough and tall enough for one average sized person.

"Doing good, Manny, how about you?" Zucarelli answered.

"Okay, I guess. What where you guys out doing?"

"Just fighting the fight, Manny."

"Yeah, I heard you guys jumped a couple of punks doing a mugging. Nice going. Hey, Bob, I didn't know FBI Agents did stuff like that."

Zucarelli looked at me. "Yeah, Bob, I didn't know FBI Agent did stuff like that." He was smiling, enjoying that moment.

"I am never going to hear the end of this, am I?"

"No, you're not."

Chapter 7

"Congratulations to the newest New York City Police Detective, our very own Bob Douglas. His baptism by fire came the other day when he and partner Detective Zucarelli arrested two heavily armed and extremely dangerous teenage purse snatchers. Word on the street was that the perpetrators were in possession of a stick of gum and a very sharp number two pencil. Let's congratulate them," Franks could hardly control his laughter as he started wrapping up our squad meeting.

The squad was applauding and getting a good laugh at our expense. While I felt a little self-conscious, Zucarelli loved being at the center of attention. After all, nabbing purse snatchers is what cops do and was certainly worth of an atta-boy. For an FBI Agent, this was definitely some ball-busting; yet nothing I wouldn't do had it been someone else. Zucarelli and I looked at each other and knew what we had to do next; we stepped in front of the squad and took a bow to join in the fun.

"Thank you everyone, thank you. But if you will excuse us, Detective Zucarelli and I have to get to court for Sanchez's suppression hearing. I'm sure you all remember Mr. Sanchez. We need to keep his ass in jail." I thought that was a good pivot. I did not want to sound as if I was gloating – which I deserved to do, based on the drugs we seized – but with a little baby dead, and the unspoken rift between the NYPD and FBI that developed, I had to be careful.

As usual, when going to the courthouse, Zucarelli drove so he could drop me off and then go find parking, so I would not be late. I loosened my tie and unbuttoned my collar; court appearances were the only times drug squad agents wore a suit. Opening the car's rear passenger door, I took off my black, pin striped suit jacket and folded it in half before I placed on the car back seat, but not before wiping off the crumbs and other crap.

"I hate to admit it, Zook, but I'm a little nervous about testifying."

"Really, why?"

"Well, I haven't testified a whole lot. Most of our cases in the FBI get pled out before trial. I mean, with wiretaps, videos and all the shit we do before we make the arrest, it usually doesn't leave much for the defense."

"I can see that. It's not like being a cop on the street and having to make decisions in a few split seconds, then lawyers and judges argue on how it should have been done."

"Absolutely. Hey, I respect what street cops face. Even our little purse snatch arrest was good police work. That was fast thinking. Maybe I didn't say it, but I was impressed. You're a good cop. You did good."

"You did good too. Well, for an FBI Agent that is."

"Of course. I should've seen that coming."

"Look, don't worry about this hearing; you'll do fine. Just don't let an asshole attorney get you flustered or upset or anything like that. He's gonna make it sound like we didn't have probable cause to search the car and then try to get all the evidence suppressed."

"Ah, c'mon. We had p.c. up the ass."

"There you go; that's the attitude you need. Now don't get

cocky or hostile or nuthin', but tell it like it is, or like it was."

"That's the plan, man."

"It's not always that easy. These lawyers are pretty slick. They'll try to confuse you, ask you four or five questions at one time and then press you for a quick answer."

"Well, that's what we got an AUSA for; do all that objecting and stuff and keep it clean."

"I wouldn't count on that, Bob. Once you're up there, you're kinda on your own. You gotta really think about everything before you answer. I mean, if the attorney says things like 'isn't it true?' or 'wouldn't you agree?' don't rush your answer and say yes. He could be trying to trap you. Think about the question."

"Okay. I got it. Thanks."

"Oh yeah, and if he asks you to guess or speculate about something, don't do it. Just say..." Zucarelli's voice was getting a bit high in pitch and he was talking a little quicker than usual. He seemed uncharacteristically worked up over this. We had a pretty solid case, or so we thought. I hoped it was just professional concern, not a lack of confidence in my ability to be a good witness for the prosecution. I had just as much at stake as he did, if not more.

"Zook, okay, I understand. Look, I appreciate the advice, really. But it's not like I'm some virgin here. I only said that I haven't testified a whole lot, but I have testified. It's just that this one seems like it might be a little more combative than most. So, I'm a little nervous, that's all."

Zucarelli let out a big sigh and continued to drive as I leaned back a little further in to the passenger seat and closed my eyes as I usually did on these drives. Even with my eyes closed, I knew that he had taken one hand off the steering wheel to rub his fingers along his moustache. The silence did not last very long.

"And remember, Bob, confidence. It's all about confidence. You gotta let this scumbag lawyer know that he can't shake you. He's gonna hit you with a lot of stuff real quickly. I mean like bang, bang; he's gonna keep shooting bullshit at you hoping you say something stupid. Just be cool."

"Okay Zook, I will, I promise." At this point, I was starting to laugh. Our one-sided conversation was approaching ridiculous.

"Ya know Bob, really, you're one of the smarter guys on the squad. I mean it. We all kinda think that."

"Well, thank you. I'm pretty confident about this, Zook. The facts are on our side."

"Yeah, they are. But unfortunately, the facts aren't always enough."

"Ain't that the truth."

As we approached the courthouse, I turned around to grab my suit jacket off the back seat. Zucarelli pulled up in front of the courthouse and I got out of the car with it barely coming to a full stop; off he went to grab a parking spot. I jogged up the concrete steps, passing pairs of mismatched people – defendants and their attorneys – skirting away from the court; the defendant hoping not to return and the attorney amassing billable hours.

Inside the doorway, I moved to the left of the line being herded by the U.S. Marshals through the metal detectors. I flashed my badge and creds and began walking towards the U.S. Marshal's Office to begin the routine.

"Check in at our office, Agent," a young Marshall verbally directed me. I gave him a nod.

There was a reason that I flashed my creds and began walking to their office instead of the courtrooms via the metal detectors. I knew the drill; he knew I knew the drill. But, he had to get that fleeting moment of exercising power over me. Checking x-ray monitors and looking through ladies' handbags didn't cut it as a law enforcement officer. Flexing muscle over other federal agents and cops filled that void. Pushing open the grey steel door marked Marshals Office with peeling white paint, I was met by another Marshal sitting on a three legged wooden stool who placed his left hand on his back and grimaced as he stood up. With his white, thinning hair, sagging belly, and apparent resignation of sitting in this small room all day, I could only think to myself, *this poor fuck needs to retire.* He pulled my creds out of my hand and looked at them carefully as if he had never seen one before. He stared at me, stared at the photo that was overlapped by the letters FBI and looked at me again. Then he nodded, grunted and handed me back my creds. I nodded back. He was just doing his job; I knew that, but I get impatient when challenged while simply trying to do my job. Back on the stool he went.

Lifting up my pant leg, I unsnapped my Sig Sauer P226 from my ankle holster. Ankle holsters were uncomfortable, awkward and not the best option if you needed to draw your weapon quickly. When walking around in a suit and not expecting a confrontation, it made sense. Mostly, I wanted to be able to take my suit jacket off when eating without exposing my gun. I locked my gun in one the lockers mounted on the wall and secured the small key in my pocket. Then I went through the back door, coming out of the other side of the metal detectors and walked up the one flight of stairs, making my way to Judge Sweetley's courtroom. I stopped in the bathroom, not only to assure of no sudden urges during testimony, but for the last minute checks. As I often did, I tried manipulating my slightly wavy brown hair to cover the thinning spots on my forehead. On my way out, coming in was a short, bald guy. He passed by quickly and there was something familiar about him. I was not going to go back in to the bathroom to get a second look. Then again, I knew a lot of short, bald guys. When I entered the courtroom I was greeted - more like accosted, by a tall, slim young man in a sharp olive green business suit extending his hand for a shake.

"Agent Douglas…"

"Yes, may I help you?" I asked, obviously and deliberately withholding my handshake until I knew who this was.

"Yes, I'm First Assistant United States Attorney Louis Wheeler. I'm going to be representing the government today in this proceeding."

"Okay." I grabbed his hand to return the shake. "Excuse my surprise, but I was kinda expecting Allison. What hap…"

"Well, nothing happened. Allison is just very busy, so the United States Attorney asked me to step in."

"Really? The First Assistant? There weren't any other line prosecutors available?"

"Well, Agent Douglas, this is a pretty big case. You seized a lot of drugs and we want to make sure nothing gets suppressed. You did a great job out there and my job is to assure that your good work does not get undone by some underhanded defense chicanery."

"Well, thank you Mr. Wheeler. Nobody likes underhanded defense chicanery."

"Please, call me Louis."

"Great, and please call me Bob."

'Thank you. Of course, while you are on the stand, we will be more formal. I will refer to you as Agent Douglas. You should simply answer my questions with no superfluous conversation. Same goes for the defense attorney. Just answer what he asks. Don't get into debate or discussion with him. Okay?"

"Okay. I will be formal, not superfluous, and neither debate nor discuss. Sound good?"

"Sounds good." Wheeler smirked as he titled his head, acknowledging my semi-sarcasm at his choice of words, but glad that I seemed to have gotten his message. Strangely, his message was fairly similar to Zucarelli's. "Take a seat at the prosecutor's table and I'll be there in a minute." Wheeler gave me a friendly pat on the shoulder as he walked off. I found that a bit condescending mostly because of Wheeler's baby face that made him look fresh out of law school. Of course, even at such a high rank in the United States Attorney's Office, that may not have been too far from the truth. Appointments were political.

Before sitting down at the table, I looked around the courtroom. Standing to the side of the door was a tall man with a military bearing. No facial expressions, he stood nearly at attention. The door next to him opened and Zucarelli walked in. Zucarelli noticed this man, gave him a second look, and then stopped to shake his hand. The body language was clear; Zucarelli may as well have kissed his ring. He was an important person in the NYPD brass. Zucarelli spoke with him for only a few minutes and then took a seat near the back of the courtroom.   He looked at me and gave me a thumbs up. Wheeler joined me at the table, and as I was about to turn my attention to him, I saw, in the front row of seats, the man I had noticed in the bathroom as he sat down. My memory was jolted by my shock as he was joined by FBI Legal Counsel Valerie Caroleo. Here she is again, all the way from HQ and joining up with the NYPD Legal Counsel. Last time, they tag-teamed me in Jerry French's office. Today, they snuck up on me in court. *What the fuck were they doing here?*

"All rise," the Marshal yelled out, "The Honorable Robert J. Sweetley presiding."

Wheeler had to nudge me to rise for the judge. Sitting at the table staring out the window, I was engrossed in my thoughts, wondering why Browning and Caroleo were there. I was not ignoring the judge's grand entrance, but my true feelings, which I never shared, were that I resented this custom. I respected a judge, and I respected Judge Sweetley, but no one in this country had the right to demand this type of reverence – they could expect it or request it, but not demand it under penalty of law.

"We are here on a motion to suppress evidence, namely 92 kilograms of cocaine seized without a warrant during a car stop. The defense claims that the warrantless search was without probable cause. The motion also seeks to suppress all evidence seized as a result of a search warrant that was premised upon the seizure of drugs under the fruits of the poisonous tree doctrine. Let's proceed."

Both attorneys stood up immediately.

"First Assistant United States Attorney Louis Wheeler for government your honor."

"Frederick Bryant for the defense your honor."

"Very good. Mr. Wheeler."

"Yes, your honor, the Government calls FBI Agent Robert Douglas."

"Agent Douglas, take the stand please."

I quickly stood up, got sworn in and took my seat on the witness stand, remaining cognizant of every move I made. Then I quickly scanned the crowd for any more surprises."

"Agent Douglas, how long have you been a Special Agent with the FBI."

"Twelve years."

"And in those twelve years, how many arrests have you been involved in?"

"Well, I don't have a count and can only estimate, but I could comfortably say that in my twelve years, I have been involved in several hundred arrests."

"Several hundred. Would that be more than two or three hundred? Closer to a thousand?"

"I would say closer to a thousand."

"Very good. And what is your experience specifically in drug investigations and drug arrests."

"Specifically, I have been assigned to the FBI-NYPD Drug Task Force for seven years. During that time, as a squad, we make an average of two or three arrests per week, which include the arrests of several people for one investigation."

"Do those arrests usually include obtaining arrest and search warrants and executing those warrants."

"Yes, most of the time our arrests also involve the execution of search warrants for drugs, money, paraphernalia, and, uh, other evidence of drug trafficking."

"During the course of these arrests and search warrants, do you sometimes find weapons?"

"Yes, we do."

"You find drugs, money, weapons....all in all, do you consider drug investigations as dangerous?"

"Yes, drug work is considered one of the more dangerous assignments in the FBI."

"Because it is so dangerous, do you and your fellow FBI Agents take extreme precautions when affecting an arrest or executing a search warrant."

"Yes, we along with the NYPD, who are on our task force, use extreme caution when we are out there doing our job."

Wheeler stood there for a moment, just staring at me. I did not think he was pulling that remaining silent stunt – hoping that I would fill the void and say something stupid – as defense attorneys do. We were on the same side. He did appear to honestly be in thought.

"One more thing Agent Douglas. How do you determine probable cause when deciding whether or not to make an arrest or seize evidence without a warrant?"

That was an excellent question obviously designed to fend off the impending defense attorney attack that probable cause did not exist for Zucarelli and me to stop the car and seize the drugs. It was imperative that the judge ruled in our favor. If that seizure was thrown out for lack of probable cause, then everything we did in the Bronx, which was based on seizing those drugs, would also be thrown out as the fruits of the poisonous tree. A little baby would be dead for nothing – although there was, and never would, be a fair balance here. The drug wars would go on forever. That baby was not coming back and that poor mother would never be the same. Nor would Doc, who was only doing his job. A lot hinged on this one hearing. I waited to collect my thoughts and took a deep breath.

"Probable cause is the facts and circumstances, in toto, that lead a law enforcement officer to believe that a crime has occurred or that criminal activity is afoot." That was as about "text book" as an answer could be.

"What about training, Agent Douglas? Have you received specific training in probable cause?"

"Yes, I have."

Wheeler looked at me. It was obvious that he wanted me to expound upon that answer, but I was sticking to my plan – answer only the question asked.

"Can you please explain the nature of that training?" Wheeler smiled, almost chuckling that I was forcing him to ask for more information.

"I, as do all FBI Agents, go through extensive legal training in the FBI Academy which includes instruction on probable cause. We also all attend in-service training during the year which often discusses probable cause and relevant case law."

"So, combined with your formal instruction and years of experience applying the concept of probable cause to a variety of fast breaking situations, is it fair to say that you possess a reasonable amount of expertise in probable cause."

"Yes, based on my training and years of experience, that is a fair statement."

"Very good. Thank you Agent Douglas."

"Thank you, sir."

"Mr. Bryant," Judge Sweetley called to the defense attorney

with a hand gesture indicating that it was his turn to take some shots at me.

"Thank you, your honor."

Bryant stood up and ran his hands down his suit jacket sleeves, picked up his yellow, legal sized notepads to review what he had been scribbling and then cleared his throat. His dark grey kinky hair reminded of the term we used as kids, "Brillo head."

"Agent Douglas, you just stated that you are an expert in probable cause."

"No, I did not state that."

"You didn't? You just said..."

"I said that based on my experience and training I possess expertise, not that I am an expert. That is not the same." As I finished that sentence I realized that I cut him off, not allowing him to finish his question. That was just what I was trying to avoid. Jumping the gun can screw up testimony. Fortunately, I think I came out of this one unharmed.

"Okay, then. Let's approach this from your expertise. Let's see if you appropriately applied probable cause in the matter before us today." Bryant then pulled the stop and stare routine. I knew what I wanted to say in response to his cheap sarcasm, but I remained silent.

"Agent, you stated in your affidavit that Mr. Sanchez had been under surveillance by the FBI Surveillance Team for a number of weeks prior to the seizure in question. Is that correct?"

"That is correct." I did not address him as "sir" as I did Wheeler. That was my attempt at sending a subliminal message that the prosecutor was more worthy of respect than the defense attorney. I would never know if that worked, or even made a bit of sense.

"Why is that? Why did you have Mr. Sanchez under surveillance?"

"We had information that Mr. Sanchez was involved in drug trafficking."

"Oh really, information? What kind of information?"

"Just information."

"Just information, really?" Bryant was annoyed at that vague answer.

"We are dealing with probable cause here, not to mention my client's civil rights. Now I ask you again, explain exactly what information you had that gave the FBI the right to launch an investigation of my client." Bryant raised his voice and started waving his finger at me. I was amused watching him play the part of outraged defense attorney.

I waited a moment to see if Wheeler wanted to object, or throw in some conditions. He did not.

"We had confidential source information that Mr. Sanchez was involved in drug trafficking, so we started a surveillance to see if we could corroborate that information."

"So, you get information about a supposed drug trafficker and you run out and start doing an investigation. Do you do this every time you get a bit of information? You send out teams of FBI Agents to follow them?"

"No, that is not correct. We received specific information about Mr. Sanchez from a reliable source. Based on that information, we initiated a surveillance."

"Oh, a reliable source. Now we're getting somewhere. Who is this *reliable* source?" Bryant heavily stressed the word "reliable" signaling his intent to question the informant's reliability.

I knew that he knew we were not going to reveal our source. I also knew that Wheeler knew that. I didn't answer and waited for Wheeler's objection. When it didn't come within a few, but very long seconds, I looked over to Wheeler. He was studiously looking at his blank pad; he knew I'd be looking at him. He was avoiding eye contact. I was on my own.

"I cannot reveal that information."

"Agent, the entire premise of your case against my client obviously starts with this supposedly reliable, confidential source. If you cannot reveal who that is, then we cannot establish probable cause, can we?"

Again, I waited for Wheeler. Nothing. I waited for Judge Sweetley. He sat in his bench, head resting on his left hand, looking at me and waiting for my answer. I realized that it was not for the judge to object; that was up to the prosecutor.

"The confidential source had provided reliable information in the past."

"So that's it? We're supposed to just believe you? Mr. Sanchez should go to jail just because FBI Agent Douglas has a confidential source. Is that what you're telling this court?"

I had to think this one out. Knowing that Wheeler was not going to help me, I wondered what the right approach would be. Tempted to play in to Bryant's showboating, I was thinking of a good smart-ass answer, but backed off that idea.

"I am simply saying that we had reliable information and we initiated a surveillance based on that information." I stopped.

"Well then Agent Douglas, I am asking you right now, while you are under oath, to tell the court who your source was and how your source had such information."

"I cannot reveal the identity of a confidential source." That was my answer; I was ready and confident – we learned that one in the Academy.

"Your honor, the identity of this confidential source is critical to determining whether or not Agent Douglas had probable cause to search my client's vehicle. I move that either the court direct Agent Douglas to disclose his source or our motion to quash be granted."

At this point, there was no question that Wheeler would have to look up from his phony stare at his notepad and argue in my defense. If he did not, I was sure Judge Sweetley would ask him to. Wheeler did not need to be prodded. Up he stood.

"Your honor, the defense argument has no grounds and the court should neither direct Agent Douglas to reveal his source nor quash the subpoena. The precedent is clear your honor; there is no compelling reason for the FBI to reveal a confidential source who simply provided general information. The search conducted by Agent Douglas and his team was not based on informant information; it was based on the surveillance."

"Exactly, your honor." Bryant exclaimed raising his right hand in the air towards Judge Sweetley. "That surveillance was based on informant information, and.."

Wheeler interrupted, "And probable cause is not required to initiate surveillance, your honor. The defense may not like that, but that is the law. The FBI..,"

"The FBI," now Bryant pulled a counter-interruption, "…cannot just start a surveillance of any civilian…"

"Okay, let's settle down here." Now Judge Sweetley gave the final interruption – at least for the moment. "This is not a complicated matter. Mr. Bryant, if you wish to argue that the FBI did not have probable cause to search the car, then you should continue along those lines. But, I am not going to direct Agent Douglas to reveal the identity of his confidential source. The government is correct, probable cause is not necessary for the FBI to conduct a surveillance. If they want to follow someone around all day based solely on an allegation that they believe is credible, that's their business. Now, no more questions about this informant; let's move on."

"Thank you, your honor," Wheeler sated with an upbeat tone.

"Yes, your honor," Bryant responded with a sigh of resignation.

"Agent Douglas, for how long were you following my client?"

"Oh, I am not sure of the exact number of days, but I can safely say two weeks, give or take."

"Two weeks. Hmm. Was that all day, every day? As you would say, twenty-four seven."

"No, not at all."

"No, then what?"

"He was under surveillance usually during business hours and on business days."

"Really? So at night, on the weekends, you had no idea what he was doing, is that correct?"

"That is correct."

My testimony continued to explain that we simply could not watch somebody twenty-four seven and that even the FBI and NYPD together did not have unlimited manpower. Then Bryant started to home in on the minutes leading up to the search of the car and the seizure of the drugs. He asked the same questions several times, changing the words only slightly.

One more time Bryant spelled out every detail.

Was meeting men at the airport illegal?

No.

Was taking suitcases from someone illegal?

No.

Were two cars driving in different directions illegal?

No.

"So then Agent Douglas, nothing my client did was illegal, yet somehow you found probable cause to believe he was a drug trafficker. That is truly amazing."

He glared at me and wanted a response. I may have responded, if he actually asked a question. No question, no answer. I stared back and let the uncomfortable silence set in.

"How do you explain that?" That was it. He broke – he blinked first and gave me the opening.

"I explain that by looking at the circumstances in toto. While nothing by itself was illegal, all the actions taken together gave me probable cause to believe that they were carrying drugs."

"Okay, then why didn't you just stop the car and get a warrant?"

"That was not practical given the entire situation."

"The entire situation? Please explain."

"Well, while we were talking to your client, we had agents and task force officers conducting surveillance at a location that we had reason to believe was stashing drugs and instrumentalities of the drug trade. The longer we waited, the greater the risk that either we would have an armed and dangerous confrontation or that drugs would find their way in to the community. Acting quickly was important."

"Then we're back to the original question. How did these facts – men engaging in completely legal conduct – lead to probable cause that drug..."

"Objection your honor. This question has been asked and answered several times already by Agent Douglas. We are going in circles."

"Your honor..." Bryant was ready to respond. Judge Sweetley held up his hand, signaling to Bryant that there was nothing more to say.

"Save it, Mr. Bryant. I have to agree with the prosecution on this one. The issue is clear and both sides have made their points. Do you have a new line of questioning for Agent Douglas?"

Bryant walked back to the defense table and stood next to the seated Sanchez. Bryant picked up his notepad and thumbed through the pages, almost too quickly and casually to appear that he was really looking for anything. He let the notepad fall down onto the table, making a small thud. He looked at Sanchez and then looked at the judge.

"No, your honor."

"Mr. Wheeler, redirect?"

"Yes, I will be brief. Thank you, your honor. Agent Douglas, in your professional opinion, is working on a task force with the NYPD a desirable assignment in the FBI?"

"Yes it is. Spots on this task force are very competitive."

"And in the NYPD, is it competitive for them to get on an FBI Task Force?"

"Well, I cannot speak for the NYPD, but from what I have

heard, yes, it is highly competitive and considered career enhancing." I was waiting for an objection from the defense, as I was testifying to something for which I did not have first-hand knowledge. I think Bryant was as curious as I was about where Wheeler was heading with this line of questioning.

"Are you a tight knit task force?"

"I would say so."

"You do a lot of dangerous things together. You have to watch each others' backs, trust each other?"

"Yes, absolutely."

Wheeler looked towards Bryant who had a bit of an inquisitive look on his face. Then Wheeler quickly scanned the courtroom, momentarily locking eyes with someone, before looking back at me, and then at Judge Sweetley.

"No further questions, your honor."

"Okay, then," Judge Sweetley said, "Agent, you are excused, please step down. Let's begin closing arguments."

I quickly stood up and subconsciously let a heavy sigh, almost getting a bit lightheaded. Though I was comfortable with my performance on the witness stand, it was a relief to get out from under intense questioning.

In their closing arguments, each attorney gave a compelling argument for his cause. As comfortable as I was with our search, Bryant's argument had me a bit concerned. There is always another opinion and perspective as valid as your own.

"Thank you. It's about lunch time. Why don't we adjourn now? I will have my decision this afternoon. Don't go too far." Court was adjourned.

Starting to walk towards the hallway, I wanted to talk to Caroleo and find out why she and Browning were at this hearing; it had nothing to do with the case against Hernandez for shooting Fremont.

Like an offensive linesman, Zucarelli placed himself in front of me and stopped me in my tracks. Placing his hands on each shoulder, he gave me a shake and told me, "That was great, Bob. You did incredible. No way we're gonna lose this thing."

"We'll see." I never liked to be too optimistic about anything. That was half superstition, half ego protection.

Just as I tried to slip around him, another hand was placed on my shoulder; this time from behind me.

"Yes, that was an excellent job, Agent Douglas. Very convincing testimony."

I turned around to see a smile of Wheeler's face as he congratulated me.

"Thanks."

Then I faked to the left and moved to the right of Zucarelli and got out to the hallway. Caroleo and Browning had their back to me as they were engaged in conversation with the man that Zucarelli so respectfully said hello to as he came in to the courtroom. As I approached, the unknown man pointed me out to Caroleo. She turned around, and noticing me approaching her, she walked directly to me. Though she wasn't quite the imposing figure that Zucarelli was, she too seemed to be blocking me from advancing on the field.

"Hello Agent Douglas."

"Caroleo, how are you?" I did not wait for, nor did I want a response. "What are you doing here?"

"I can't talk to you now. But, on behalf of the Director, you are instructed not to talk to any defense attorney for any defendant. Do you understand?"

"Yes, I understand." We never spoke to defense attorneys, unless in conference with an Assistant United States Attorney. Why she was here just to admonish me like that seemed incredibly odd.

Zucarelli came up to me. "C'mon bud, let's get a couple of those calzones you like so much. My treat."

"Your treat?

"Fuck'n A."

"Then calzones it is."

We went down the block to the pizzeria on the corner. Zucarelli went to the counter as I slipped through the crowd to grab a table in the back. I did a quick scan and moved aggressively at the first opening, almost as aggressively as nabbing a parking spot.

We kept the conversation light. We traded stories of our troubled domestic lives, talked about which girls in the office we'd like to slip it to, Zucarelli, of course offering much more detail than I. That's what made him the guy's guy and the cop's cop. I was nothing more than FBI Agent Bob Douglas – just another guy on the squad. We went on and guessed about who might be screwing who and just had a few laughs. I really needed that. Coupled with my calzone, I was having one of the most enjoyable fifty minutes I had in a while, till the call came. Judge Sweetley would have his decision in twenty minutes. We cleared the table and headed back quickly to assure time for the "check-yourself" trip to the bathroom.

This time I did not need a nudge to rise when Judge Sweetley entered. I was anxious and I was ready. As I sat down, without thinking about it, I turned around to Zucarelli. With a small smile of confidence, he nodded his head up and down. That made me smile. As I was quickly turning my head and my attention, back to the judge, I could not help but notice Caroleo and Browning sitting in the same spots, but obviously avoiding eye contact with me.

"I have carefully reviewed the arguments and am ready to render my decision. The government contends that the search of Mr. Sanchez's car and the subsequent seizure of the drugs was legal based upon probable cause and the Carroll Doctrine exception to warrantless search and seizures. The defense argues that the warrantless search was not based on probable cause; that Mr. Sanchez and his colleagues engaged in no illegal action that would give rise to probable cause and that the government relied upon a confidential source whose information and reliability has not been open to review or challenge. The defense further claims that this unconstitutional search led directly to the subsequent search warrant executed in the Bronx, and therefore all evidence seized from that search must be quashed as a result of the Fruits of the Poisonous Tree Doctrine. Both arguments are compelling."

The judge hesitated to catch his breath. Wheeler remained motionless and continued to stare ahead at Judge Sweetley. I was unsure how to interpret what the judge had just said. Was the favorable for us? Interpretation didn't matter, we were about to find out as the judge continued.

"Agent Douglas and his task force team initiated a surveillance based on confidential informant information. As I previously stated, and I hold, that the FBI did not need any further predication for this surveillance and whether or not probable cause existed for the moment in question is not predicated upon this confidential source. The defense argues that the FBI could have simply seized the car and obtained a search warrant. The defense is correct; the FBI could have done that."

My heart beat just a bit faster at that. Should we have waited for a warrant?

"Yet, being able to do that, does not mean that was a reasonable option. Had the FBI seized the vehicle and waited for a warrant, I agree that the dangers that existed while the agents and detectives waited in the Bronx created an exigent circumstance. The option of allowing the vehicle and its occupants to leave in hopes of serving a warrant after it was obtained is clearly not logical. This vehicle exemption to a warrantless search is the very basis of the landmark decision in Carroll versus the United States. However, all of this would be academic, if in fact the FBI did not have adequate probable cause. The defense argument is correct in that the defendant committed no act as described by the FBI that amounted to criminality.

Probable cause is nothing more than whether the facts and circumstances indicate, more probably than not, that criminal activity is afoot. Actual criminal activity need not be observed; observing criminal activity first-hand would clearly give rise to a higher level of assurance than probable cause. The next question to answer is whether the conclusion that probable cause existed was reasonable. Reasonable, but in whose eyes? In this matter before us, we have Agent Douglas, who is an experienced and well trained narcotics agent. And, although the argument was not made, it is fair to conclude that his partner, Detective Zucarelli and all the other agents and detectives add a significant amount of experience and training.

Based on all the facts and circumstances, considered in toto, I do not see that Agent Douglas could have drawn any other conclusion that he and his team were observing drug trafficking. I find the search of the vehicle constitutional and accordingly all evidence seized from the car is admissible. Additionally, the search warrant was properly reliant upon this seizure. The defense motion to quash is denied. We are adjourned."

Instinctively, though unprofessionally, I smiled and clenched my fist with a sense of both relief and accomplishment. There was a groan of disappointment and disapproval from the small group of spectators sitting behind Sanchez. Wheeler and I shook hands and exchanged accolades as Sanchez was led out the door leading back to the jail and the courtroom emptied. Zucarelli joined us with handshakes and back patting. I quickly excused myself and made my way out to the hallway.

Caroleo and Browning were in conversation with a man I did not know. As that man looked at me, he pointed at me and appeared to start walking in my direction. Caroleo and Browning gently placed their hands on him to stop him and I saw Caroleo mouth the word "no." The man stared at me while finishing his conversation. Eventually, he gave Caroleo and Browning a nod of agreement, but his facial expression belied any indication of accord. They watched this man until he was out of sight. Caroleo and Browning then went to speak with the mystery man Zucarelli greeted. They spoke briefly, shook hands with smiles and then Browning and the man left together. Caroleo looked at me, gave me a polite nod and left. At that moment, I was joined by Zucarelli and Wheeler.

"Well, thanks. I appreciate your good work," I told Wheeler one more time.

"You too. Let me walk you guys out." Wheeler engaged us in meaningless conversation as he and Zucarelli flanked me on each side and walked with me in that formation right up to the car door.

"So Zook," I started the conversation in the car before I started my routine of closing my eyes and hoping to catch a quick nap.

"Who was that guy in the courtroom?"

"Guy? What guy."

"Oh you know what guy. Tall, thin, very cop looking, standing by the door. You almost pissed in your pants saying hello to him."

"Oh him. Yeah, that was Chief McLoughlin. He's our Chief of Detectives."

"Chief of Detectives. That's some big shit, huh?"

"Oh yeah, he's the man."

"So, uh, why was he there? Why would this case bring out the NYPD Chief of Detectives?"

"I don't know. Maybe because of that baby getting killed. I mean, it was an NYPD-FBI operation, not just FBI, ya know. We got equity in this too."

"I know, and let's not start down that road again. But, with all the shootings and crap happening in New York, I have a hard time believing that he had such a personal interest in this particular case."

"Well, my friend. I don't know and I ain't gonna ask. Why don't you just enjoy the moment, Bob? You were great up there, really. If that little wife of yours saw you in action, she'd probably be lip-locking your dick right now, while I was driving."

"Zook, I don't get it. You make a sexual joke about my wife and I don't want to punch your face in. Actually, I'm trying hard not to laugh. How do you do that?"

"Hey, I told you. 'Cause I'm Detective Mark Zucarelli."

The rest of the ride was quiet. Word had already gotten back to the squad and we got some very nice congratulations. Reardon, D, Candelaria, Julie, Simone, even Franks and a few of the detectives I didn't talk to often complimented me. It was nice, but by the next day, it was old news.

The next few days were uneventful as we pulled all the crap together for the prosecutor, now that Sanchez was going to trial.

*****

"Hey, everybody, can I have your attention," Franks bellowed standing in his office doorway in front of the squad room. The buzz slowly quieted down.

"I have great news. I just heard that Mr. Fuckface Hernandez has agreed to plead guilty in the shooting of Fremont. He will be sentenced tomorrow."

The squad broke out in cheers. I grudgingly joined in.

"Oh, and Douglas, you need to be in court for the plea at 9 am tomorrow. They want you there just in case Hernandez pulls a fast one."

"Me, but I..."

"Yeah, Zook, make sure you drive so he doesn't get lost." Franks talked right over me and got a few laughs.

"You got it, Larry," Zucarelli yelled back and guided me back to my desk as the squad quickly went back to work – or whatever they were doing.

The next day, I showed up in court as directed, and unexpectedly was invited to sit at the prosecution table. In the first row, right behind me, were Caroleo and Browning. Caroleo sure was putting on a lot of mileage constantly traveling from Headquarters just for this one case.

Court started and I looked over at Hernandez and his attorney.

Wait a second, that attorney looked awfully familiar. Son of a bitch. That's the guy Caroleo and Browning were talking to after we won the suppression hearing. What the fuck?

He looked at me. He had no hesitation as he recognized me right away. If looks could kill…and he turned away.

Why would he be so mad at me? Why not? Now I get it. All those questions about the FBI and NYPD working so close together, being tight knit. It was all staged for Hernandez's attorney; they knew he would be there checking out the competition. My great testimony didn't just convict Sanchez, it scared Hernandez in to pleading guilty. His attorney was sure I would claim the shooting was intentional. We were all set up. Was Zook in on this?

Hernandez pled and the matter was over. We got in the car and headed back to the office.

"Hey Zook."

"Yeah."

"Ya know, I'm thinking about everything. The questions that Wheeler asked me at Sanchez's suppression hearing. Caroleo and Browning showing up. Now I find that Hernandez's lawyer was there and now Hernandez pleads guilty. I'm told to be there, ready to testify, but I never gave a statement to the Shooting Review Team. Whatta ya make of all this?"

"I think all's well that ends well. Onward and upward, buddy. We got plenty of work to do breaking up this El Gordo thing; don't you think?"

Zucarelli did it again. He made his point and redirected my attention as he planned. I tried to bring back the focus of our conversation to these unusual series of events.

"There's not something you wanna tell me, is there?" I asked Zucarelli.

"Of course not," Zucarelli answered with not a moment heistation. "We're partners; we tell each other everything, right?"

"Right, absolutely."

Once again, Zucarelli spun me.

*****

I got home exhausted that night. I hadn't done anything physical, but I was emotionally drained. I fell asleep alone; Elaine was out with the girls and got home late. My ringing cell phone woke me up.

"Douglas," was my greeting.

"Bob, it's me Zook. Where are you?"

"It's four in the morning Zook. I'm home. Where else would I be?"

"Okay then, quit chocking the chicken and meet me in the Diamond District. Right around where we're looking for El Gordo."

"Why? Wassup?"

"It's big. Very fuck'n big."

Chapter 8

As usual, there was more traffic than I would have guessed, even at zero dark thirty; which really meant I should have expected it. With a refreshing chill in the air and silence of the night, I was a bit more tranquil than usual when getting ready for my commute. Managing to get in to Manhattan quickly from our small Nassau County apartment, only six blocks from the Northern State Parkway, the Diamond District was still dark. Revolving red lights were bouncing off the buildings as police cars, traffic cones and roving police officers cordoned off the street. Though I pulled up with my red lights flashing I was stopped by a uniformed New York City police officer. Holding up my police placard, I thought that would be sufficient for him to let me through. Instead, he looked at me, clearly finding my presence annoying and walked over to the driver side.

Resting one of his fat-fingered hands on the hood, he leaned his face in to my window, very much violating my personal space. The nasal hair peeking out of his wide, thick nose was as disturbing as the alcohol on his breath and the small piece of food – or something – caught between his teeth.

"So what; we're all cops here," was his greeting for me.

Not for lack of trying, I could not think of a remark that had the biting sarcasm this deserved while accomplishing my goal of getting in to this crime scene, finding Zucarelli, and finding out what was going on. I displayed my creds to show the officer that I was not just another cop. I spoke as politely as I could to avoid the accusation of having FBI arrogance.

"Excuse me officer. I am FBI Agent Robert Douglas. I work on a task force with Detective Zucarelli. He is in there somewhere and he is expecting me."

"Alright, just hold on."

He picked up his radio from his belt and called in, "I got some Fed here, claims to work with a Detective Zucarelli. Anyone there with that name?"

"Stand by," was the response.

Though I had no idea of what was happening, this amount of police activity meant Zucarelli was not kidding when he said it was big. We stood there for a few minutes, not saying a word to each other. Normally, I would've liked to strike up a friendly conversation with a police officer. But, not with this attitude. He was just another badge carrier – one of those cops whose heart was no longer in the job, but sticking around for retirement. Ultimately, at the end of his shift and back in his locker room, he will talk about the asshole FBI Agent he met who had a big-ass ego and a "who's-better-than-me" attitude. Listening to this cop, nobody would guess that all I did was try to get to the crime scene, to which one of their own invited me. I shouldn't be so hard on the cops. We had plenty of badge carriers in the FBI. In the small offices, they sat around the office reading the newspaper, handle a minor bank fraud somewhere between breakfast and lunch followed by a long workout at the gym. In New York, you were seen as one of three kinds of agents: the gym-goers, the shoppers or the workers.

If the public only knew how much down-time and waste there was every day in the FBI.

We were glad they didn't.

Eventually, Zucarelli made his way through the crowd, flashed his detective badge to the cop and signaled for him to let me pass. The police officer stepped aside and let me in – no look, no words, and no acknowledgement whatsoever. Zucarelli pointed off to the side, signaling where I should park the car. As pissed off as I was, I steered right in to the curb. As I got out of the car, I looked back at that cop.

"What the f..."

"Forget it. We got bigger things to worry about than some asshole in uniform." Zucarelli guided me by the shoulder, knowing that this cop gave me a hard time, but also knowing its insignificance.

Zucarelli led me to a car parked on the street surrounded by cops in white coveralls, dusting for prints, photographing, and milling about – their purpose clear, but the situation unclear. Again flashing his badge, Zucarelli moved in closer for me to look through the driver-side window. It took me a second to grasp what I was seeing.

"Holy shit. What the fuck is this?"

"This was the inevitable of having an El Gordo operating in the Diamond District."

In the front seat of the old, somewhat beat-up, brown Ford, two young Hispanic males were motionless; they're eyes open, hair still combed and clothes fairly neat. All in all, their appearance wasn't bad, except that their throats had been cut open and bills were stuffed into the wide, long slashes across their necks.

"This is sick, Zook, really sick."

"Yeah, look carefully, look at the bills in their throats."

I leaned in a little closer, slightly banging my forehead against the window. Normally, Zucarelli would get a laugh out of that, but not right now.

"Those are rolls of twenties, I think. I can only make out a few; they're rolled tight." I looked a little closer at the tight little bundles of cash sat in their throats like tracheotomy tubes, only there was no wheezing sound of air coming in and out; just blood oozing from below. I held my hand over my eyes, flush against the glass to block out glare from flashbulbs, police car lights, and the rising sun. I wanted to be sure I did not miss whatever it was Zucarelli was pointing out. "Yep, that's what it looks like, they're all twenties."

"Yes, they are."

"So, we got two young guys, probably Colombian killed in the Diamond District, and money shoved in their throats. This is bad. I'm not quite sure what it all means, but it is bad."

"They weren't just shoving any money down their throats; these are twenties - currency of the drug trade. It was their own drug money."

"So, not just a robbery then, huh?"

"Nope."

"Looks more like a mob hit, doesn't it?"

"Yep. It was the mob alright. But not just a hit. This was a message."

"Message for who?" I asked.

"For El Gordo, whoever he is. I don't know how some Colombian is doing business right here in the middle of the Diamond District without us knowing about it."

"Well, obviously someone knows about it."

"You got that right. And..." Zucarelli was interrupted by a detective tapping him on the shoulder. I knew he was a detective by the badge clipped on his lapel.

"Hey John."

"Mark, how are you?"

They shook hands in a friendly exchange.

Turning and pointing to me, "John, this is my partner, FBI Agent Bob Douglas. Bob, this is Detective John Brennan; he's works Homicide."

We greeted each other shaking hands; he barely said hello before turning back to Zucarelli.

"Whatta ya think John?"

"I tell ya, we haven't seen a good hit like this in a while. Kinda like the old days, huh?"

"Sure is. Miss those days, don't we?" Zucarelli chuckled.

"Well, as I'm sure you've already seen, we got two young males, probably Colombian drug traffickers or money couriers, throats slashed and money literally shoved down their throats."

"Any clue as to what they were doing down here so early in the morning? Any witnesses or anything?"

"Well, to your first question, looks like they weren't down here."

"Huh?" We both didn't understand that; not at first.

"Which goes to your next question. We do have a witness. He saw this car being towed and then left here. We think they were towed here from Queens early this morning."

"That may make a little more sense. Can we talk to this witness?" Zucarelli asked.

Brennan held up his hands, "Sorry Mark, we can't do that."

"Whatta ya mean we can't do that? Why the fuck not?" Zucarelli was caught off balance by that response. His voice was loud, but he was not yelling. His face got red, probably some anger and some embarrassment at this rebuff from a fellow detective, especially in front of me.

"Look, Mark the guy is scared shitless and you can't blame him. We had to promise him that we would not reveal his identity to anybody, including any other cops. But, if you have any specific questions, write him down and I'll get back to you."

"Really? You'll get back to me?"

"Sorry, man. That's the best I can do."

Zucarelli looked at me with the "nothing we can do about it" look. He sighed and I could see him thinking about how to approach this, while stroking his moustache.

"Alright John. Listen, this ties in to a pretty big case we're working. So, we're gonna have to work together. Between this witness and some of the stuff we got going, we really gotta keep everything close to the vest; can we keep things just between you and I? We don't need loose lips screwing things up."

"That would be okay with me. But you know, Mark, like we just said, this got the mob written all over it. I gotta bring in OCCB."

"Organized Crime Control Bureau." Zucarelli explained to me what OCCB stood for. I already knew; I had been working with NYPD for several years. You pick up these things just from osmosis.

"I am OCCB."

"Mark, I know that, but, you're uh, you know, a narcotics detective. You know I gotta go through 1 PP. If they want to assign a homicide to you while you're on an FBI Drug Task

Force, well, that's above my pay grade."

"Alright, I get it."

"Mark," Brennan looked over one shoulder and then the other as if he was about to say something top secret, "this is obviously gonna be a big case. You know how crazy everyone is trying get their hands on a case like this that's gonna have headlines and tv and shit like that?"

Zucarelli tilted his head in my direction. "You're telling me about fighting over big cases? I'm working with the FBI." Brennan looked at me and then looked at Zucarelli. After a few seconds of silence, they simultaneously broke out in laughter.

"How true. Good point, Mark."

They really enjoyed that. I forced a smile.

"Look..." Brennan continued. "It'll take me a few days to process this crap, write the report, make the referral and blah, blah, blah. A week at most. Do what you gotta do."

"Thanks John. We'll be in touch."

They shook hands again and I too went over to shake hands and thank Brennan, though once again, he seemed to dismiss my presence as if I was nothing more than a prying bystander.

I was an experienced FBI Agent, but this was the closest I had ever gotten to a homicide. This was not just any homicide, but a likely mob hit, against Colombian drug couriers. Throats slashed, money stuffed down the wounds. *This is so fuck'n cool* was all I could think. Yet, I could not reveal to Zucarelli just how excited I really was. That would make me a punk-ass rookie. I had to be as dismissive of any excitement over tonight's events as Brennan was to my presence.

As the sun began peeking through the skyscrapers, the crime scene investigation was winding down. The bodies were transported to the morgue, the car was towed away, and the forensic processing was complete. The bright yellow crime scene tape was removed from the lampposts, cars and trash cans it had been wrapped around. The buzz of police activity subsided as they hurriedly brought the street back to normal, replaced by a new buzz of the morning rush hour crowd arriving to start the workday.

"What's up, what are you looking at?" I asked Zucarelli, who did not answer as we walked over to his car. He was looking at something or someone down the block. More than looking, he was staring, his eyebrows doing the inquisitive scrunch.

"Bob, come here." He pulled me back to the other side of the car turning our backs towards where he had been staring.

"Zook, what's going on?"

"Without being obvious, look over my right shoulder and about 3 or so doors down. You see that guy hanging out in front, just looking around?"

"Yeah, I see him. So, he's looking around after all the police activity. You said it yourself; everybody's a friggin' crook around here."

"That's um, Danny D'Albote. I went to high school with him."

"Okay, so what? He used to beat you up or something?"

"Him? Beat me up? I don't think so. He was a punk. I mean, he was kinda tough, good with his fists, but always needed a bunch of guys behind him before taking on anybody."

"Okay, so…we're go gonna over there and kick his ass right now, to make up for him being a punk in high school?"

"Shut up, you're being an asshole. What I'm trying to tell

you that he was a wannabe mobster. He was always hanging outside the social clubs; he'd join some the enforcers when they'd go put a beating on someone."

"So, he's a made guy now?"

"Nah, I doubt it. He was too fuck'n simple for that. But he's probably hanging around with a crew. Ya know, they let him hang out now and then, and once in a while, he'll help out on some minor shit, like a shakedown or something. He'll never be a made guy. But he's always hoping."

"Okay, so..."

"Remember what I told you. We don't have to know exactly what we're looking for, but when something ain't right, I 'm gonna know. Well, now I know it. Danny D'Albote in the Diamond District ain't right. There's a hit like this right by where I happen to see him. That is no coincidence my friend. This means something."

"Then wha..."

"Here's what I need you to do," Zucarelli took control, "...go in there and find out where he's going. Nothing else, we don't need to get burned. Just see what he's doing."

"I can do that." I started to walk off to follow Danny D'Albote. He had already entered through a doorway, so I picked up my pace.

"Bob, I mean it, we can't get burned."

I know how to do surveillance was how I wanted to answer, sarcastic tone and all. That would've been unnecessary. Zucarelli was not trying to sound as condescending as his warning came out. He too was pumped up over tonight's string of events. The other hard fact was that without Zucarelli, I would not have been out here tonight and I wouldn't know shit.

Walking in to a long, narrow corridor of office doors on one side only, I did not see Danny. There were a few Hassidic Jews, or "sids" as Zucarelli called them, carrying black hard-shell briefcases, with locks at each end. One had a padlocked chain around his briefcase. If that did not scream "steal me" I did not know what did. Obviously, Danny had gone in one of those offices led to shops with windows and entrances right on the street. First I thought I should casually walk down the hallway hoping to spot Danny, but realized my presence would be noticed. I walked back out on the street and started window shopping. About three stores down, I saw Danny wheeling out the glass and gold plated small showcases of jewelry. As all the other stores, the window was clearly marked with gold lettering in an old English font: Scarlotta Gold.

I tried hard not to look at Danny, although I did want to see what he looked like. Having him notice me served no purpose and only risked getting burned. I continued my efforts to appear nonchalant and looked around the windows of a few more shops before making my way back to Zucarelli.

Now who's he's talking to? I could see Zucarelli leaning against the car, talking in his animated style – his hands moving about and his body weight shifting every second.

"Mark," I said as I walked up without him noticing me.

"Hey Bob, wassup? Did you get what you needed?"

"Uh, yeah."

"Hey, this is my partner, Bob Douglas, he's an FBI Agent."

"FBI Agent? Wow, what are you guys up to?" asked the tall, very thin, olive skinned girl Zucarelli was now talking to. This was getting to be a habit for Zucarelli – picking up girls by the car while I was busy doing something. Somehow he was using my being an FBI Agent as part of his sales pitch. He was slick.

"Ahh, if we tell you, we have to kill you," Zucarelli told her.

"Oh, you are so funny," she giggled and then looked at me.

"Oh, he's a real clown, isn't he?" I didn't know what to say and then looked at Zucarelli with a clear "what the fuck?" look on my face. He got the hint. He held out his business card that suddenly appeared in his right hand.

"Well, it was great talking to you. Give me a call and let me buy you a drink or something."

"You bet," she said with a big smile and a shake of the head. She took the card and walked away just a few steps before turning back around and giving Zucarelli a quick smile and wave. Of course, he smiled and waved back. She kept walking as we watched her slim figure fade into the developing crowd on the sidewalk.

"I am gonna tap that with one…"

"Zook, I got it. I know what you're gonna do; I don't have to hear it. How come you didn't introduce her to me?"

"I did."

"No, you introduced me; you didn't introduce her."

"Oh right. Well, that's because I couldn't remember her name. So, you know…"

"Didn't know her name? Well, where do you know her from?"

"Know her from? I don't know her from nowhere? I just met her."

"You just met her?"

"Yep."

"So, if you don't know her name, how will you know it's her when she calls."

"I'll know. You're obviously a rookie at this, aren't you?"

"I guess. Let me ask you this, in the few minutes I was following Danny, how did you..."

Then I hesitated to ask the question. "Eh, just forget it."

"You might as well go ahead Bob; I know what you want to ask." Zucarelli stood there with his arms crossed and his cocked back towards his right shoulder, sporting a very smug grin.

"Yeah, and I know how you're gonna answer, 'Because I'm Detective Zucarelli, that's how.' Right?"

Zucarelli had to laugh. "Right."

*****

Busy with the task at hand, neither Zucarelli nor I saw him. Neither did any of the police officers or detectives swarming the murder scene. We were all focused on the two victims with their throats slashed. Unlike fire marshals who scan the crowd looking for the arsonist while the firemen put out the fire, we became totally absorbed in the crime scene; we had no peripheral vision and saw nothing else.

Moving slowly and cautiously, I was looking for where not to step and what not to touch. I did not want to frustrate the already delicate task of crime investigators looking for the stray bullet casing, the drop of blood, the faint footprint or the gold standard of evidence – a fully lift-able and identifiable finger-print. We were always hoping for that one little tidbit of evidence that will break the case wide open. In reality, a case was rarely solved by a sole piece of evidence. Forensic sciences rounded out the case and helped convince the jury, but invest-igations were slow and steady. For drug work- informants, surveillance, wiretaps and undercover operations made the case.

Standing back from his window, the young Colombian man dressed in a white tee shirt and blue jeans held his binoculars as he watched the activity of the murder scene. In a sparsely furnished loft apartment with the bohemian atmosphere of an artist's den, his job was to keep an eye on the comings and goings of money couriers arriving at El Gordo. A well organized drug cartel had its checks and balances and internal controls. That was one key to profitability. Violent enforcement of its rules was another key.

He looked carefully, trying to see the faces of the deceased. The darkness and police activity were obscuring his view. He wrote down a brief description of the car and took down notes like a police report – date, time, location and even photographs using a long distance lens.

Just about when he was finished and getting ready to make a call, he noticed something through the long, powerful lens. Down the street, from the window of an upscale apartment building, a round head, with thick black hair was gazing at the murder scene with its own binoculars. The young man quickly moved backwards, swinging his body 180 degrees, away from the window and rammed his back squarely against the wall. He instantly broke out in a sweat, his heart beating heavily as he tried to recapture his composure. He stood there for a second, unsure of what to do. Then he slowly moved his body so he was perpendicular to the wall. Waiting for a moment, he cautiously tilted his head forward to take a peek out the window. He did not see anything; and he did not know what he expected to see. He quickly positioned himself deeper in to the loft and in to a corner. Hands shaking, he struggled to get his cell phone and make the call.

"Hello."

"Ram.... I mean, good day. What are you drinking?" He quickly caught his mistake by almost mentioning Ramon's name on the phone. Then he went back to the script.

"Just water, and you?"

"The same."

The wording assured Ramon that the call was from his man with a message, and not with a gun at his head.

"Okay, good. What do we have?" Ramon continued.

"Can't be sure, but looks like the A and L trains are out of service."

"Running late?"

"No. Out of service."

"For good?"

"Yes, for good?"

"You know what to do?"

"Yes. But one more thing."

"What?" While Ramon did not want to talk on the phone any more, he wanted to know what else could be wrong.

"I was not alone. I saw another one."

"Did he see you?"

"No."

"Okay, move quickly."

Ramon hesitantly glanced out the window of his high rise apartment overlooking Central Park. Nothing unusual twelve stories down on the streets, no helicopters in the air; all seemed well, at least for now. Rubbing his hands together he walked in to his kitchen and opened the refrigerator. He stared. Then he closed the door, taking nothing. He walked back to the window and stood there staring and thinking. Suddenly, as sense of paranoia overtook him and he moved away from the window. Falling on to his black leather couch, he quickly stood up with a gasp as the intercom rang, the doorman announcing his guest.

"Were you followed?" was Ramon's greeting.

"No."

"Are you sure?"

"Ramon, of course I am sure. Nobody knows about me. Nobody saw me."

"Well someone knows something. How bad was it?"

"Couldn't tell; there was a lot going on. But it looked pretty bad." Looking at his watch, he continued, "I'm sure it will be on the morning news any minute now."

"Yes, yes."

They moved back to the couch, both of them wiping away the beads of sweat on their foreheads. Ramon grabbed the remote and pressed the buttons so hard and quickly, the television turned on then off. Frustrated, Ramon through the remote against the wall and walked over to turn on the television manually. He could not remember the last time he had done that. The news was coming on with the bright red Breaking News banner flashing across the bottom of the screen.

"Okay, this must be it," Ramon murmured.

"Two men found were found dead in a car in the Diamond District early this morning. The police are hunting for the killer or killers." The newscaster waited as the camera view switched to the front of One Police Plaza where the NYPD was holding a press conference.

"We can confirm that in the early morning hours of today, two men in their mid 20's were found dead in a car parked on the street in the Diamond District of Manhattan," said the uniformed officer with gold stars, gold stripes and numerous pins displayed across the chest of his well pressed uniform.

"Can you tell us anything else? What was the motive; was it a robbery?" a reporter yelled out, louder and more aggressively than the other reports, prompting a response.

"We are not sure of the motive. Robbery, however, does not appear to be the motive. At this point, it appears to be a planned and premeditated homicide. I stress, our information is only preliminary at this juncture."

"We're hearing that their throats were slashed and something was left on the bodies. Is that true?" another reported yelled out.

The high ranking police official hesitated for a moment and there was silence awaiting an answer.

"We cannot provide any more information at this time as this is an on-going investigation." He quickly turned around and headed back to Police Headquarters.

Reporters yelled out more questions. They wanted answers. They got nothing else.

"Ah, that says it all," Ramon grumbled.

"What? What did he say?" the young man asked.

"It's not what he said; it's what he didn't say," the older and more seasoned Ramon answered.

"El Tigre, you must call him now?" the young man asked, though he knew the answer.

"Yes."

The young man stood up to leave, knowing that he was not allowed to be in the room when Ramon spoke to El Tigre. Only Ramon knew who El Tigre was.

Ramon picked up his phone and within seconds important strings of numbers were being received in Medellin, Colombia.

Sitting at his large, ornate desk with a drink in his left hand, Diego Rojas picked up his digital pager that crept a few inches, pushed by the vibration of the buzzer. Rojas groaned, as he put the drink down and started at the numbers. He thought for a moment, then stood up and walked over to sliding doors on the wall to his left. Opening them up, he looked at the five different fax machines and turned his attention to one specific one. Within moments that fax started spitting out a piece of paper with another string of numbers and three words. Rojas took the paper and went back to his desk where he sat back down in his high-back black leather chair. He opened his bottom drawer and randomly picked up one of several cell phones and placed the call.

"Hello."

"Hello, this is Manuel calling for Sam."

"He is not in. May I take a message?"

"Tell him I will call back at 3:30."

"Okay."

Rojas then ended the call and walked over to a locked cabinet in a closet behind him.

There he picked one of five phones with huge antennas. He knew which one was about to ring. The codes were memorized. Procedure was clear – and was to be followed. Rojas knew that he could not stop the Americans from listening in; but they had to know which phone.

Though feeling free to speak openly, both Rojas and Ramon spoke with some ambiguity in Spanish. Rojas understood what happened.

"Who do you think it was? Mexicans?"

"Maybe, but we are thinking it could be the family."

"Hmm. This could get ugly."

"Do we move?"

"No, that won't help. They're all watching; we can't keep hidden. Just keep it quiet and slow for a little while. We can't shut down, but let's not push it."

"Do you think they have declared war on our business, senor?"

"No, not a war, but they are certainly sending a message," Rojas told him.

"How shall we retaliate?"

"We don't retaliate. At least not directly. But we will send our own message in return. A very strong message."

Chapter 9

We got back to the office, while some of the squad were just getting in. Early hours were not common in drug work and already I was exhausted. Zucarelli made a few phone calls back to some NYPD buddies who knew the working of the New York City crime families. It didn't take long for him to find out that Scarlotta was Anthony Scarlotta, known as Tony, originally from Brooklyn. When he was in high school, his parents were killed in a very suspicious car accident and he moved to Boston to live with his uncle – a capo in the New England mob. He moved back to New York about five years ago.

"C-5 has been working a case on him that apparently isn't going anywhere. I'll give them a call." C-5 was one of our Organized Crime Squads in Manhattan. They were also an FBI-NYPD Task Force and worked on the Morelli Crime Family.

This was good information. I ran upstairs to our radio room and ran Scarlotta's name through our indices – the index of names that we had moved from 3x5 index cards to computer, only in the past ten years. I couldn't believe that in my tenure as an FBI Agent, we had to sort through index cards, like a library card catalog to find if we had a file on someone. Each office had its own cards, so unless you knew where to look, a lot of information was lost.

Zucarelli sat down at the desk to plot things out.

"Did you get anything from the Morelli squad?" I asked him.

"Not much. I talked to one of the detectives assigned there. We mostly compared notes about being on an FBI Task Force."

"I'm sure you did. What about Scarlotta? Anything?"

"Nah. They were getting info that he was moving swag for the Morellis. They couldn't get anything going on him. You know their supervisor Lou Dinella, don't you?"

"Not real well. Mostly by reputation. Why?"

"Nothing really. Word is he's got a pretty good informant in one of the Morelli crews. He keeps the squad pretty busy just from the stuff he gets from that snitch."

"That's what I've heard. That informant has made his career. Management loves him - the ASAC, SAC and all the way up to Gunn."

"So, if this informant is so good, how come they couldn't dig something up on Scarlotta?"

"I don't know. He probably runs with a different crew than Scarlotta runs with. That's an Organized Crime squad for you. Unless they get some informant who spills everything 'cause he finds out he's the next to get whacked, they can't get anything going."

"Well, maybe if we get something good, Dinella could target his informant against Scarlotta."

"Perhaps. We can keep that thought in our back pocket. I wouldn't count on Dinella tying up his informant on a drug case. It won't bring his squad any stats, so, you know…"

"Okay, then, Bob. So, whatta ya think we should do to get started?"

"I think we should do what we always do, when we don't know what to do."

"Just like we've been doing?"

"Exactly. Except now, we know who we want to watch. Surveillance is always easier when you actually know what you're looking for."

"Okay, I'll check with Special Ops to see if we can get a utility van, traffic cones and shit like that, so maybe we'll only be mildly obvious."

"Well, if we look like utility workers, why would we be obvious?"

"C'mon Bob, these pukes aren't stupid. After a day or two, they'll realize that this same van keeps parking on the street right near them and they won't see any real work going on and they'll see us getting in and out doing coffee runs. That kinda gets obvious."

"I guess. But we gotta give it a try. I mean, we don't even know how your buddy D'Albote and this Scarlotta guy figure in to this El Gordo thing, if at all."

"Oh, they do, trust me. I'm not sure right now exactly how they fit in, but they do. We'll figure it out."

Then we sat there for a few minutes, lost in our thoughts and wondering if we would actually figure it out. Our pensive state was interrupted by loud yell coming in the doorway to the squad room.

"Yo, I am the man." Detective Kevin Gallagher yelled as he walked in pumping his fist in the air. Gallagher had been on our squad for only a few months. We had barely said two words to each other.

"You got it?" Simone called out to him.

"I got it, motherfucker. I am now Detective First Grade."

The squad broke out in to small round of applauds and cheers. A few of the detectives walked over to Gallagher to congratulate him with a pat on the back.

"First grade is pretty good, huh?" I asked Zucarelli who had a smile on his face that reeked of insincerity.

"Yeah, it is. Good for him."

"I see you're not over there offering your kudos with the rest of your brethren detectives."

"Well, I don't really know Gallagher all that well."

"Oh, that must be it."

Zucarelli stared at me; he knew that I knew he was full of it and was saying something without saying out. Then a small smile broke out on his face.

"Okay, you got me." Then he didn't say anything.

"So?" "Spill it Zook. What's up?"

"You know who our commissioner is, right?"

"I do."

"And, do you remember who the last detective we both knew who got bumped up to first grade?"

"Let me think for a second." I knew one of them had been promoted to first grade recently, but it was not something I gave much thought. "Yeah, that was Bill McGrath, wasn't it?"

"Yes, it was." Then Zucarelli went back to looking at me.

I stared back, tilting my head back and holding up my hands, gesturing that I did not know what he was getting at.

"Think, Bob. This ain't a tough one. I may have to reconsider what I told you about you being one of the smartest guys I know."

"Uhh, no, that's not what you said. I believe that while you were stroking me, you said that I was one of the smarter guys on the squad. Not exactly the same thing."

"Whatever. Besides, you're changing the subject on me.

Let's get back to what I was trying to tell you.

"Zook, what are you trying to say?"

"Alright, one last hint. What was the name of the homicide detective who was in the Diamond District?"

"That's a, um, good question. I don't remember. He basically ignored me and spoke to you. I can't remember his name."

"Brennan, it was Brennan, Bob. You get it now?" Zucarelli was basically yelling at me at this point. "Think Bob, think. Brennan, Gallagher, Mc…"

"Okay, okay, I got it now, I think. They're all Irish; is that it?"

"There you go."

"There I go? So what?"

"So what? That's the point. They're all Irish. You don't see any Italian names making first grade, do you?"

"Shit, Zook. The Irish control the NYPD? I thought was ancient history. I mean, most cops I meet are Italian. I thought you guys ran the PD."

"That's because most of the cops you meet are working drugs, or something like that. The first grades who get assigned to homicide are all Irish. Maybe you got a few Italians, a couple of blacks and Jews here and there to make it look good, but it's mostly Irish. Then they solve a few homicides and start getting promoted up the ranks or get all the tit jobs. That's it. This is still an Irish thing."

"Oh really. So, I kinda remember you busting my balls about how political the Bureau is. Now you're telling me the NYPD is just as bad. You're full of friggin' politics too."

"Hey, I never said we didn't have politics. I just said the FBI is obvious; they don't even try to hide it. At least we make a small effort."

"Oh please. It looks like we're all the same. I don't know if that makes me feel better that the FBI is not alone or worse that the whole world is like this."

"Forget it; it is what it is. All I know is that I've gone as far as I'm gonna go. I'll be on the streets chasing drug dealers until I retire."

Stopping to make sure I heard what I thought I heard, I did not want to talk too quickly. I was confident that I had an opening.

"Well ain't this something. The great Detective Mark Zucarelli has a petty, jealous side."

Zucarelli started giving that stare of his again, rubbing his thumb and forefinger down his moustache, with his mouth half open. Then he moved the same hand away from his face and towards me, giving me the finger. He walked away, trying to appear casual, but with a little bit of his tail between his legs. I sat there with a big, satisfied smile, trying not to laugh too heartily. Finally, I made Zucarelli blink first. That felt good.

Then I felt bad. *Did I really need to make Zucarelli face a truth about himself?* I hoped he took it as the ball-busting I meant it to be and nothing more.

"Hey Vic," I yelled out to Candelaria as he walked by.

"Hey Bob, what's up?"

"Got a quick question for you."

"Go for it."

"We're working this case on some guy named El Gordo. What does that mean?"

"El Gordo? That's an easy one. It's Spanish for the fat one, or more specifically, the fat man."

"The fat one, huh? Cool. So we're looking for a fat guy in the Diamond District. That should be easy."

"If anyone can do it, you can, Bob." At that point Candelaria patted me on the shoulder and started walking away.

"Vic, hold up, one more thing."

Reading my tone as a bit more serious than just a few seconds ago, Vic pulled up a seat next to me.

"Yeah, Bob, what's going on?"

"Nothing, I mean, after Doc's shooting, things seemed all fucked up. I kinda didn't know what to say."

"So, what do you want to say Bob. Now's as good a time as any."

"Well, I, uh, never told you directly what a good job you did. That was a tough situation and you guys really answered the call."

"I tell you, Bob, I really appreciate you saying that. Really, it means a lot to hear you say that."

"Ya know, I realize I don't thank people enough and, I uh..."

"I get it, Bob. And, if you haven't heard, Doc is coming back in the next week or two. He's doing okay."

"That is great to hear. Doc being the kind of guy he is, he's always gonna feel guilty over this thing, even though it was nothing more than a tragic accident."

"Yeah, an accident brought on by scumbag Colombian drug dealers."

"If we get felony murder charges on the table, then they can kiss their asses good-bye."

"Unfortunately, that doesn't even the score, but if that's the best we can do, we gotta live with it."

"You're right about that."

"Well, thanks Bob."

Candelaria started to walk away and then stopped and turned around.

"Hey, you wanna grab lunch some time?"

"Yeah, that'll be great. Thanks."

Candelaria smiled, nodded and walked away. Probably, we would never actually take that lunch together, but just talking about it was a gesture of friendship. It was all because I finally said the kind of things I should have been saying for a long time. I just taught myself a valuable lesson; or so I thought.

✳✳✳✳✳

"Hey boss, I wasn't sure you'd be in today. I'm sure you've heard." Danny, sitting in the back office, greeted Scarlotta as he walked in coffee and a bag of donuts or some other fattening crap.

"Of course I heard. It's been all over the fuck'n news. Not only that, my uncle heard and called me."

"What did he want?"

"I don't know, but I gotta get my ass up to New England tomorrow to see him. He's probably gonna chew my ass about something with the family not being happy with me."

"They're never happy with you. They always think you're cutting them outta something."

"Well, they can go fuck themselves. They take out my parents and then leave me out to dry. I had to move up north to some shithole town till I could get back on my feet. Where were all of my dad's goombas then, huh? Only my uncle offered to help. I owe him and nobody else. The rest of 'em can suck my dick."

"Tony, I understand all that. But you know your uncle can't protect you forever. The New York families ain't gonna take shit from their little brothers in Boston, especially not Morelli. You know what I mean?"

"Hey." Scarlotta turned to Danny, yelling and pointing his finger at him.

Danny was a bit startled. He knew that he had hit a nerve with his old buddy, but he also knew that Scarlotta stayed alive by not overreacting and trying to stay under the radar. Things were changing. Scarlotta stopped and stared at Danny.

"I know. You're right. I probably am pushing my luck a little."

"So whatta you think we should do now?"

"Well, I'm sure our pal Ramon is gonna want to talk to me."

"What are you gonna tell him?"

"I don't know. I don't wanna talk to that slimeball right now. I doubt he'll come by. He'll probably call me."

"So...?"

Scarlotta reached into his pocket and pulled out his wallet. Handing a wad of cash to Danny, "Go pick up two new pagers and cell phones. New numbers, new everything. Get one of your friends to buy them, don't put 'em in our names. I'll wait here, but I won't be answering the phone, so move quickly, okay?"

"Okay, Tony. Will do."

As Danny walked out the door, Scarlotta stared at nothing and took in a deep breath, letting it out slowly.

*****

"Bob, Larry wants you and Zook to come in and give him a

briefing." Reardon called me from the doorway of Franks' office.

"Alright."

Looking around for Zucarelli, I saw him towards the back of the office sitting on Simone's desk. This time it was Zucarelli, not Simone who seemed to be holding court. Zucarelli was smiling and animated, his arms flailing about. Julie and D were laughing like school kids.

Maybe I should be like D and use just my first initial, B. Why does that not sound as cool as D? Must be a cop thing.

"Zook," I called out, but he didn't hear me, so I called again. He was too engrossed in his talking. Julie looked over at me and I pointed to Zucarelli, and she understood. She looked at him, waving her hands to get his attention and pointed to me. Then he looked at me. I waved my hand and he held up his forefinger to show he needed another minute to finish. Three, four minutes later, he was still talking. I walked in to his field of vision as a gentle reminder. Then, he wended his way towards me, looking back and finishing his story for them.

"What's up Bob, I was on a roll."

"I see that. You really had 'em going."

"Abso-fuckn-lutely. I think a few more laughs and I could've gotten Julie in to my car and out of her pants. Mm, mmm." He finished that statement by licking his lips to highlight his fantasy.

"Oh, c'mon. Isn't she engaged?"

"Yeah, so? They all got boyfriends, fiancées or husbands. That don't stop them from screwing someone else. I can't remember the last girl I slipped it to that didn't have some guy in her life. Or some girl. Or both."

"Really?"

"Yes, really. Where the hell did you grow up anyway?
Were you raised at a nunnery or something? Look, everybody's
doing everybody. Either you're getting some of that or you
ain't. That's that."

As usual, something Zucarelli said caught me off guard and
sent a jolt through me. Now I was concerned that Zucarelli
might be right – that I had no clue as to what was happening
around me; that I was living some naive existence, and
everybody was enjoying guiltless sex and having fun, while I
sweated over every little detail of my life. I changed the topic.

"Well, whatever. Look, Franks wants a briefing on what
happened today."

"Then brief it will be. I mean, whatta we gonna tell him?
We don't know shit ourselves."

"I know. That's why I need you. I mean, who can spin
something from nothing better than the great Detective Mark
Zucarelli, huh?"

"You got that right. Let's go, man."

Zucarelli was pumped up and patted me on the back,
steering me toward Franks' office. He rarely got excited over
having a conversation with Franks. As we got in Franks' office,
he directed us to sit on the two seats facing his desk at 45 degree
angles. The window behind Franks overlooked the constant
bustle along Queens Boulevard. Reardon took a seat to the side.

"So, I've heard about the murder in the Diamond District
this morning," Franks began the conversation even before my
ass landed on the seat.

"That's correct, Larry. Zook and I were down there with the
homicide detectives. Two Colombians had their throats slashed

and wads of cash stuffed in the gashes. Pretty brutal," I told him.

"Sure sounds like a mob hit, kinda like the good old days when the mob was the mob." Franks, as many of the agents in New York, made his bones in the FBI working on the La Cosa Nostra Crime Families leading up to the famous Commission Trial. Since then, they all bemoan the lack of good mob work, like dead bodies in the trunks of burning cars.

"It does, Larry, it looks…"

'Well then, if it's an organized crime case, we should turn it over to the o.c. squads. Don't the Morellis control the Diamond District?" Franks looked over to Reardon who nodded in agreement.

"Uh, yes, they do, Larry, and uh, actually C-5 had a case on a couple of Italians we've identified, but their case is dead, and…."

"Okay, then this is theirs, we need to turn it over to Dinella?" Again Franks turned to Reardon who again nodded in concurrence.

"Larry, hold up a second here. I understand this happened in Morelli territory, but these were Colombians, most likely drug couriers. I wouldn't just assume it's a traditional mob hit. I mean these were two young Colombian males. You know that can only be the cartel."

"I don't know. From what I'm hearing this has mob written all over. Even if it is, how are you making this part of your case? How does this tie in to the seizure in the Bronx or this guy El Guido you're chasing?"

Zucarelli stopped for a moment to figure out if Franks was kidding or not. We held our laughter to a smirk. Even Reardon was trying not to react.

"Larry, do you, uh, mean El Gordo, the name we seized from the sweaty sock of the drug courier with all that dope."

"Oh yeah, El Gordo.   Gordo, Guido; they're all fuck'n crooks. What's the difference?"

"That's just it, Larry; there is a big difference. Guido would go to Dinella's squad. But El Gordo belongs here. We're not sure who he is yet, but they didn't give him a Spanish name meaning the big one if he wasn't important."

"Bob, I think you're really reaching here. Look, we got a lot going on.   Reardon's case with Miami is still ticking. He's probably going up on another wire soon. Candelaria's got a new case that may turn into an undercover op and Gordon's working on something. We can't stretch ourselves too thin. You've made a good case with that seizure. I don't think you need to keep working it. It's time to stick a fork in it; it's done."

"Oh come on…"

Sensing that my frustration had gotten the better of me, Zucarelli interrupted and took over.

"Larry, I understand what you're saying. You're right; we can't   monopolize   your   squad's   resources   on   sketchy information. This is our fault; we haven't given you a clear picture of everything."

"Okay, go ahead," Franks answered as if he was a judge looking down on an attorney about to make a losing argument.

"Alright, we got El Gordo's name and his location from Colombians we busted with about a hundred kilos of coke. What we didn't have a chance to tell you is what we saw this morning, right before we cleared the crime scene."

Franks sat up in his chair, his interest now piquing. I was concerned, because Zucarelli was about to start talking about mob wise guys.

"There was this guy, Danny D'Albote. He was a Morelli crew wannabe and..."

"There you go," Franks jumped in, "this is the mob."

"Hold on Larry, please. Danny is a wannabe, and I think he has something to do with this murder. But, like Bob said, these dearly departed were Colombian. There is no doubt that they were moving drugs, drug money or both. Now, if they were doing that right under Morelli's nose, then you know it's gonna get a little ugly."

Franks turned to Reardon. He needed Reardon's reassurance that this was worth listening to. Reardon gave his nod of approval again.

"Okay, go ahead, Zook, I'm with you."

"Great. Look, Morelli doesn't give a shit if young wall-streeters are snorting lines up their rich, coked-up noses. But, if kilo weight is moving through the District and he ain't getting his cut, then there's a problem. This could be the beginning of a mob-cartel war. This could be big shit Larry. Do you really want to give it to Dinella, or would you rather keep it here on C-13? This could be a major fuck'n case. Why give it up?"

Franks turned to Reardon, "Whatta ya think Steve?"

Oh great, he's asking Reardon if he thinks I should have a shot at a big case. Why would Reardon agree to that? He'd never let anyone else share his spotlight. Zook made a great argument, but it's gonna backfire on us. I'm always getting screwed.

"Zook makes a good point, Larry. This can be big. I mean, if we got the mob and the cartel going after each other, who knows where this may take us. We did get the lead from a drug case, so it's as much ours as it is Dinella's. You know he wouldn't give up a big to us."

"Probably not. But…"

"Larry," Reardon uncharacteristically interrupted Franks, "this kind of case can really be important to the squad. If anyone can put this together it's Bob and Zook. I think we should give it all we got. There is nothing to lose."

Did I hear that right? Did Reardon just support me give a thumbs up to me taking on a big case? Didn't Vic just say the same thing about me being able to put a case together? Maybe I need to take this chip off my shoulder?

"Okay," Franks said looking at Zucarelli and me, "run with it."

Zucarelli and I were out the door, "And one thing…"

"Yeah, Larry, what?"

"Keep Dinella's squad in the loop. He's got a great handle on all things mob. Let's keep him on our side."

"Yes sir." Franks looked a bit surprised to hear me address him as "sir." I rarely did that.

Zucarelli and I went to our desks to figure out a strategy for an investigation that we were not really sure who or what we were investigating. Reardon stayed in Franks' office.

"What's the plan, man?" I asked Zucarelli. That was a question we'd been asking each other fairly often, lately.

"Let me check with our intel guys and see if I can get some recent photos, addresses and background crap like that. Then, I think we gotta start watching Scarlotta and D'Albote just to figure out what's up and who's doing what to who. Sound good?"

"Sounds good."

"I'll assume that you'll handle coordinating with Dinella's

squad, right?' Zucarelli asked me.

"Of course we'll coordinate. When I'm ready."

"Meaning?"

"Meaning, I've played this FBI game before. We need to get this case securely under our belt before we bring in another squad, especially an organized crime squad. If they hear one Italian name, they'll go running to The Pistol asking him to give the case to them. He'll shoot somebody down, and it will probably be us. Don't forget, the mob made his career."

"Really? Going all the way to your ADIC, just over one case? What's that?"

"That's the FBI. Why do you sound so surprised? You bust my balls about stuff like this all the time, the FBI this and the FBI that, but I'm starting to see that your PD ain't much different."

Zucarelli help up both middle fingers and pushed them towards me for emphasis.

"I got work to do." He walked away.

Wow, did I get the last word with Zucarelli for a second time? I must be getting good at this stuff; whatever this stuff was.

At that moment, I saw Reardon walk back to his desk. He was picking up his phone, so I rushed over before I lost my will to say what I needed to say. Tripping on the leg of my desk chair, I called out to him, getting his attention. He appeared surprised and put the phone back on the hook. I sat on his desk.

"What's up, Bob?"

"I want to thank you for your support in there, ya know, with Franks and telling him that we should keep the case."

"Of course, Bob. Why wouldn't I support you? It looks like

a good case, you did a great job getting to where you are and we're all in this together. Right?"

"Right."

We both smiled a bit, signaling that the message was delivered and received. I said nothing more and walked away.

Things seem to be changing on the squad. I can't be sure, but I have to believe that since Doc's shooting, we are all looking at our work with a different perspective. When Fremont got shot, we were all upset. We know that is a risk we face, but a little baby getting shot? Especially from one of our guns. Well, that just makes you stop and think.

Chapter 10

Pulling up to an isolated tract of land on outside Providence, Rhode Island, about 60 miles from Boston, Tony Scarlotta heard the buzz on the intercom and then the ten foot high iron gate began to slowly open. Pulling in, Scarlotta waved to the young, husky men on the inside of the gates. He drove up to the front door, leaving his car in the circular driveway. The door was opened by another intimidating male, with two more, just like him, a few feet behind.

"Good to see you, Tony."

"Hey, good to see you guys too."

"How are things in the Big Apple?"

"Eh, you know. Scumbags, bums, crooked cops, greedy jews and too many mulignans. Other than that, everything is great."

"That sounds about right, Tony. That's why you need to move back up north," one of the bodyguards offered a lighthearted exchange.

"I don't think so, Vinny. I'm all city."

Vinny waved his hand to Scarlotta, signaling that he should walk to the table in the corner. "Sorry, Tony, but you know the drill."

As directed, Scarlotta walked across the black and white tile floor, over to the mahogany end table and unloaded his pockets – keys, change and anything else. His shoes came off and he stripped down to his underwear. His clothes were searched and a hand was run over his crotch. This was not just a search for a weapon. There was little chance that Tony would try to kill his uncle, right there in his uncle's house and surrounded by security; unless he had a suicide wish; which was not impossible. What they were really concerned about was Tony wearing a wire. Over the years the mob had learned that family loyalty had been supplanted by self preservation.

Once cleared of suspicion, Scarlotta was waved to the solid black steel door that had the look and feel of the bank vault door. He took a few steps forward and then stopped to look back at the bodyguard. Maybe his face would give some clue as to what was waiting for Scarlotta on the other side. The stoic face reflected no clues. What would it matter? Scarlotta was walking through that door, one way or another.

He tugged the heavy door open and walked in to the den where his uncle awaited him; he stopped at the doorway and made no move and made no sound in deference to both the respect and fear he felt throughout his body.

His uncle was unassuming man of average height and flabby belly, dressed in navy blue slacks and white shirt; it was hard to imagine he was ever tough and cunning enough to have worked his way up in the family. The most successful mobsters had learned that smart and silent usually beat out the loud, "look at me" wiseguys. This was a business that called for discretion.

A few seconds of silence seemed frozen in time as Scarlotta waited for some sign of where this meeting was heading. Opening his hands for a hug, his uncle welcomed him. Scarlotta hesitated; he expected that his uncle would give him a warm welcome, but he also knew what a hug could bring, especially when you have been summoned. His eyes closed and he held his breath in fearful anticipation as he felt his uncle's arms wrap around him.

"Tony, do I have to call you to get you to visit me?"

"No, Uncle Paul. You're right and I'm sorry. I should've come to see you months ago, if not years." Scarlotta opened his eyes, and began to gently push away.

"Okay, okay." Paul released his hug and motioned for Scarlotta to sit down as Paul closed the door. Letting out his breath, Scarlotta felt a chill down his spine, hearing the slam and click of steel meeting steel.

Scarlotta stood and waited for his uncle to sit first in his favorite leather chair before he took a seat across from him on the sofa. On the coffee table in front of him, Scarlotta could not miss the framed picture of his Uncle Paul and his dad, when they were in their teens. They both looked rough and ready there, in white sleeveless tee shirts, holding up their fists in a playful boxing pose. There was no small talk.

"Tony, what are you doing? Why do you look for trouble?'

"I'm not looking for trouble Uncle Paul, honestly, I'm not. I'm just trying to go about my business and not bother anyone."

"That's very nice, Tony, but that is not realistic. Actually it's more than unrealistic, it's naïve, if not just plain stupid."

"I'm not doing any family business; I swear. They have no dog in this fight. It's just a business agreement I made. Everything happens right there in my shop. It's cash for gold, that's it. I don't bother them, I ..."

'Tony, Tony, please. Now you really do sound stupid. You have Colombians carrying bags of money in to you every day. What did you think, nobody would notice? You can't snub your nose at the family like that. We have a code." Paul's voice reflected his frustration with his nephew.

"Fuck them, Uncle Paul." Tony yelled and stood up. "They kill my dad and my mom. My mom, Uncle Paul, my mother. I was a teenager. When did they start killing mothers? What happened to the code then? And they never paid for it. Nobody made them pay. Nobody."

Scarlotta had walked half way across the room, unaware of his tone and aggressive body language. Paul understood the emotion that overtook Scarlotta and allowed this outburst.

"You don't know that Tony. You don't know who paid for what." Paul kept a soft but controlling tone of voice.

Quickly moving back to his seat and leaning forward on the edge of the sofa, Scarlotta anxiously asked, "What? What are you saying Uncle Paul? You retaliated? Really? Who? Who did you take out?"

Scarlotta stared at his uncle who remained silent and looked back at him askance. Scarlotta was hoping, but he knew he would not get an answer. He was nowhere near as high in the family as he needed to get cut in on that kind of information. Information in the mob flowed like it did in the FBI – on a need to know basis.

"Tony, you know I love you like my own son."

"I do. I know that, Uncle Paul. You know I love you too. You took me in…"

"Listen to me carefully." Paul needed no platitudes. "You cannot ignore the family, no matter how hard you try to spin this. Whatever your business is with the Colombians, you are going to have pay tribute to Morelli. Midtown is his. You weren't very careful about this. You did this right under his nose. What did you expect? He is not going to back down, especially now."

"What do you mean by especially now? Cops? FBI?"

"No, nothing like that."

"Then what?"

"He's getting squeezed in all directions. The Russians, the Mexicans, the Chinese, even the Israelis are staking their claims. They're all moving drugs, money, running all sorts of rackets. The city is just not big enough for all of us. If the Colombians are going to use one of our own, the family has got to be paid. It's not just the money, Tony, you know that."

"I know. It's the respect. It's always the respect."

"Well," Paul hesitated for a second, "Respect and the money."

Scarlotta and his uncle shared a laugh over that comment. Within a moment, the seriousness of this meeting set back in. Scarlotta knew his marching orders.

"So I guess those two Colombians having their throats slashed was to send a message, huh?"

"That's Morelli's style. Make no mistake Tony, that message was more for you than it was for the Colombians."

"I understand."

Scarlotta sighed with relief as he and his uncle said their goodbyes. Just as Scarlotta was about to go out the door, Paul called out to him. Stopping in the doorway, Scarlotta closed his eyes and held his breath.

"Yes, Uncle Paul?" Scarlotta answered without turning around.

"Tony, what about that D'Albote kid you have working for you?"

"Danny? You know him, Uncle Paul. He's my closest friend." Scarlotta turned his head towards his uncle.

"I know he is Tony. But having him so close to everything is not a good idea."

"Why?"

"He's weak, Tony."

"How do…"

"Because I know, Tony. You know that I know these things."

"Yes, you do. I have it covered, uncle."

"I hope so, Tony. I really hope so."

✳✳✳✳✳

I was exhausted by sitting in the back of that van all day with Zucarelli. The air conditioner worked like crap and the two of us sweating and farting made this a completely miserable and disgusting situation. We took pictures of Colombians carrying briefcases, duffel bags or suitcases coming and going from Scarlotta Gold. We identified six couriers who came regularly. When they did, Scarlotta greeted them and took them to his back office, while Danny D'Albote minded the shop and appeared to be on the look-out; whether he was looking out for cops or criminals or both, we were not sure. He always sat at his desk, looking down towards his lap every few seconds. He had to be looking at a gun; making sure it was there if he needed it.

We kept copious notes on our surveillance log to accompany our photos. What time we saw Scarlotta on his cell phone and what time everybody came and went. Only a few times did we venture out on foot, trying to get more intelligence without burning our surveillance. Twice we followed Scarlotta to a bank with the same bag brought to him by a courier. That made analysis easy. Banks only deal in one thing – money. What happened to the money was a question we had to answer.

Three times we tried to follow one of the Colombian couriers. Once, we lost them in the crowd. The other times, they got picked up by a car parked a few blocks away. D'Albote went for coffee and miscellaneous errands; he appeared to be Scarlotta's tool.

The odor was overwhelming as Zucarelli wiped his underarms with the shirt he had removed. It was hot, but I kept my shirt on.

"You gonna put that thing back on?"

"Of course not, what am I some kind of pig?" Zucarelli answered me as he reached into his gym bag and pulled out a white sleeveless undershirt. "I got my guinea tee right here."

I moved to the front of the van as Zucarelli lifted his arms again to put on his tee shirt. He got in the passenger seat, rubbing his impressive biceps. I didn't know if he was doing that as a nervous habit or his way of reminding me that his were bigger than mine.

He grabbed the white hardhat from the floor, "Let me grab the cones and we'll blow this place." With that hat and that shirt, he looked like the quintessential utility worker. The back door to the van opened and Zucarelli threw in the orange traffic cones we used to give the van an air of legitimacy. As simple as that was, it seemed to work. Nobody gave us a second look as they went about their busy, fast paced schedule and Scarlotta went about his business slow, steady and undeterred.

"Alright, let's get back to the office and make some sense of this shit, whatta ya think?"

"I agree, Bob. I don't think sitting around and watching like this is gonna get us any more intel than we got now. I doubt we're burned yet, but it's just a matter of time. We gotta bring this to the next level. Whatta you think?"

"I agree with that. So, we agree that we agree. We have to find out his cell number and get a wire going. Then, we gotta figure out this money laundering process from start to finish."

"Before we do that, we gotta get some lunch first."

"I concur again. Anything specific in mind?"

"Absolutely. Go to the Brooklyn Bridge and I'll steer you in when we get in Brooklyn.

"Brooklyn? Ain't that a little out of the way?"

"Nah, come on. We'll get a really good pizza and then we'll just hop on the BQE. We'll be back in no time."

"The BQE? With that traffic? That friggin' thing has been under construction for ten years already. The mob must be cleaning up on that project."

"Oh, quit being such a pussy. Want me to drive, like I usually do?"

"No, I got it. Let's go."

Zucarelli navigated me to a small pizzeria in a middle class, Italian neighborhood. There were no spots in the full parking lot. That had to mean something.

"Park there," Zucarelli directed me pointing to a spot behind the restaurant.

"But it's marked reserved for owner."

"Stop worrying so much. Just park there. I got this covered."

"You always do, don't you?"

"Fuck'n A, I do. Make sure you put the police plaque in the window."

We walked in and were greeted by an old, balding Italian man, in a white apron; he was about half as tall as Zucarelli.

"Hey, hey, if it isn't Detective Mark. Come here you." Holding a menu in one hand, he reached up with the other, as Zucarelli opened his arms and walked to the man. Zucarelli bent over to accept the hug, then put both his arms around him as they both laughed. The warmth of this exchange made me wonder if this was Zucarelli's father or uncle.

"Hey, Pops, let me introduce you to my new partner." Zucarelli kept his hand on the man's back as he walked him over to me.

"Yes, yes." The man greeted me with his hand extended.

"Pops, this is Bob Douglas."

"Hello, Bob Douglas," Pops yelled grabbing my hand, shaking it wildly.

"Bob is an FBI Agent, Pops."

"An FBI Agent," Pops was just about yelling at the top of his lungs, throwing his hands up in the air. "Oh my, you really made it in to the big times, didn't you?"

"I'm doing okay, Pops. Everything is good."

"Okay. You two follow me. Hey, Connie, Salvatore, come look who's here," Pops was calling out to the waitress and chef who could not have missed our entry.

"How ya doing Detective?" Salvatore called out from behind the counter as he put a pizza in the oven."

"Doing good, Sal, how about you? How's your mom doing?"

"We're all good, thanks. You want the regular?"

"Absolutely."

"You got it, my man."

"Hello there Detective," a waitress with short, black hair greeted Zucarelli with a big hug.

Returning the hug, Zucarelli reached down and gave her ass a quick grab. Then they locked lips for a moment.

"Ya miss me, Connie?"

"I always miss you, Mark. You're my favorite. You know that."

"Well, I don't know that, but I'll take your word for it. Say hello to my partner, Bob Douglas, he's an…"

"Yes, an FBI Agent. I heard that back in the storage room. You know how loud Pops gets when he's all excited."

"Yeah, I know. That's what we love about him." Then they both turned to Pops and Zucarelli gave him a playful, fake punch to the head.

"You sit down and we'll get you started on some salads, okay?" Pops motioned to us and then to Connie.

Pops put us in a small room in the back that had only two tables with two seats each. There were no windows and just a few pictures on the white paneled walls, including the famous picture of dogs playing poker. The windowless back door had more than one deadbolt lock on it.

"Who is that, your dad? Your uncle?"

"Who, Pops? You kidding? He's just the owner of this place; he's had it like forty years or something."

"Okay, so what's with all this hugging and shit. You're not related?"

"No. This used to be my beat when I was on patrol. I came here for a meal three or four times a week for seven years."

"That's it. He's just a guy on your beat? The two of you look pretty close."

"Hey, when you patrol an area, you get close to people; that's the name of the game."

"I guess, but doesn't being that close, get, I dunno, a little dangerous maybe?"

"Dangerous? How?"

"I don't know. Some kinda conflict of interest; ya know, something like that."

Zucarelli leaned back in his chair and started to laugh.

"Oh man, you feds are so anal. You can't be so afraid of everything. Listen, staying close to as many people as you can is what keeps us alive. You can never have enough friends out there."

"I get it. It's just that getting too personal may…"

"Getting personal means getting them to trust you. When you get their trust, you get their information. We probably get more information from people on our beat than the FBI gets from paying all your supposed informants who are usually playing you for fools anyway."

"Okay, I give up. I got it." I threw my hands up in the air to surrender in this ongoing "NYPD is better than the FBI" battle.

Once again, Zucarelli was able to outplay me with that cop card. I couldn't act like I knew what it was like to be on patrol and getting to know the people in your area. That was another one of those big differences between being a cop and being an FBI Agent. He also knew some of the stories of how the FBI got screwed by their informants - and well paid informants to add insult to injury.

About halfway through the meal, which was extraordinarily

good pizza, with extra cheese and pepperoni, Zucarelli stared out the doorway from our little, secluded room in the back and appeared to be nodding his head.

"Hey, lemme have the keys to the van." Zucarelli downed one last bite and held out his hand.

"Huh?" That caught me off guard.

"The keys, give me the keys, c'mon." He seemed to be in quite a rush.

'What's wrong?"

"Nothing is wrong. I left something in there. Just give me the damn keys already."

"Alright, here you go." I leaned back in my chair to dig the keys out of my front pocket of my jeans which had been sticking to my sweaty legs.

Zucarelli grabbed the keys out of my hand and left. I could not imagine what he had left in the van that could be so important at the moment. We were enjoying a good meal and I did not plan to interrupt mine. Several minutes after Zucarelli left, Pops poked his head in the doorway.

"How is everything FBI Agent Bob?" Pops yelled at me.

"This is great, Pops. Thank you very much." I was hoping that I was not being too familiar with him by calling him Pops, but it seemed like the right thing to do, and I didn't know any other name to call him. "I appreciate your hospitality." I tried sounding a bit more formal, just in case.

"Ahh. Stop it. Just eat and enjoy." Pops waved his hands at me, then turned around and left.

After sitting there several more minutes by myself, I started feeling a bit uncomfortable. I had stuffed my face with about as much pizza as I could take. Though I had no real need, I took a bathroom break, also wondering what Zucarelli was doing. The path to the bathroom went by the kitchen, and the back door to the alley was open; our van was in plain sight. I didn't give it a second thought until I saw the van move a bit, just as I passed the doorway. I stepped backwards to take a second look. Where was Zucarelli?

I knew it. Zook got too comfortable with these people and he got set up. I don't know what, but we were in trouble. I don't even know where we are, except somewhere in Brooklyn. I'm on my own.

I took off out the front door and around the bend to the van. The doors were closed; the engine was running. I pulled my weapon and moved slowly and quietly, approaching from the rear of the van.

The windows to the back of the van were blacked out; you could see out, but not in. That was a tactical disadvantage for me at the moment. Hunching over, I ducked below the windows and made it to the driver area, where the windows were not blacked out. I peeked in the driver window, but could not see anything. I heard whispers. The make-shift door we had installed to block off the rear of the van was ajar, but I had to get to the other side to see in. Moving across the hood of the van, the sun reflected off the windshield. I didn't want to, but I had to hold my one hand against the passenger window to block out the sun and peek in and hold my weapon in the other. That was a vulnerable position. I could not discern the image I was able to see. Then I could.

I quickly holstered my weapon, unsure of how to respond. I had to lean over and held my hands on my knees. Seeing Zucarelli's gyrating ass almost caused me to heave every morsel of pizza I had just eaten. I walked around in a daze for a few minutes, when the rear doors of the van opened up. Zucarelli jumped out, turned around and seeing me said, "Man, it's hot in there." Then he walked back over and helped Connie get out. She straightened out her clothing and patted down her hair. I think she even adjusted her boobs. Without even acknowledging me, she walked right back in to the restaurant. Zucarelli watched her with a smile on his face.

"Really, Zook? What are we, back in high school?"

"What? So I grabbed a little muff. Big deal."

"While we're working and in a Bureau vehicle? That is a big deal."

"Oh shit, here we go again. Look, I'm on lunch break. Don't worry about the van. I left no evidence, no DNA, if you know what I mean."

"That's great, Zook. So, I guess it's time to head back, huh?"

"Not quite. I'm starving now. Lemme finish my meal, then we'll go. Chill, my friend."

Zucarelli walked back in, like nothing happened. I leaned against the van, almost out of breath, as if I had run full speed in to a brick wall. After a few minutes, I rejoined Zucarelli who was finishing up his meal and guzzling down the last drop of soda from the red plastic cup.

"Okay, let's go." He stood up, wiped his moustache a few times and threw the napkin on to his plate.

Walking out, Pops came over.

"I hope to see you soon, don't be a stranger," he said to Zucarelli.

Then they hugged again. Zucarelli appeared to be hunching over just a bit more than before and holding Pops a little closer. The hug lasted a few more seconds. Then we walked out."

"Uh, Zook, aren't we forgetting something?"

"I don't think so."

"Like paying for this?"

"Oh c'mon already. Pops is like family to me."

"Maybe, but you know we..."

"No, no." Zucarelli stopped in his tracks and held up his right hand to me. "I see where you're heading with this and let me stop you right now. This was not a pay-off; you're not going to get arrested for corruption. You don't have to report me to Internal Affairs or your office of whatever-the-fuck you call it. It was lunch; that's all. This is how cops work. Really, Bob, I like working with you and I consider you a friend. But, you've got to chill the fuck out. I mean it."

He did mean it. There was no sarcastic smile. No wink of the eye.

Was he right? Was I that anal? Or was I just being a cautious FBI Agent? We knew there were differences between us. I had to strike the right balance. If Zook dropped me as a partner, no cop would ever work with me. I'd probably find my ass on FCI, working Mongolian espionage. That would be a killer.

Back in the van, and driving back to the office, I thought there would be no conversation.

"I suggest we go home, clean up and get some rest." I was relieved that Zucarelli's tone was now more friendly.

"Whatta ya mean?"

"We're working tonight."

"Huh?"

"Yeah, our timing was good. Did you notice Pops whispering to me on our way out?"

"I thought something was happening with that hug. I

wasn't sure. Wassup?"

"Well, that room we ate in is for some special guests."

"Okay, educate me."

"Think, it had no windows, and a back door. That should be a hint."

I looked at him with a blank stare. I had an idea, yet thought it was better to remain silent than say something really stupid.

It's one of many meeting spots around the city the family uses now and then. They've been using it for years, showing up on short notice. The Morelli's are having a meeting there tonight. Don't know exactly who and what about, but that's okay."

"You're kidding. How the f..."

"That's what I was trying to tell you. It's all about having friends and getting information. Pops is so open about giving cops free meals and treating them like gold, that the mob would never suspect he tips us off. They can't imagine that anybody from the neighborhood would double cross them. They don't know Pops. He's got big balls."

"Holy shit. I tell you Zook, you really amaze me sometimes. You get this great meal, you get great info..." At that point I hesitated.

"Go ahead; say it. And I got to bake this big Italian sausage in one hot oven," as he grabbed his crotch, now laughing like the devil.

"Ya know, Zook, as fucked up as I think you are, I don't know how you do it."

"What do I always tell you? "Cause I'm Detective Zucarelli, that's how.

*****

After dropping Zucarelli off at his car, I checked with Franks to let him know what we planned. He concurred without hesitation, and without checking with Reardon. Reardon must've really gotten to Franks, and convinced him that Zucarelli and I had a good case.

"Hey, what are you doing?"

"Just at work, like always, what's up?"

"Nothing. Do I need a reason to call my beautiful wife?"

"No, but you don't call too often during the day. You're always out on one of your missions."

"Well, I'm on my way home now, so I thought it was a good time to give you buzz. I know you're busy." Working as a paralegal at a Midtown law firm, Elaine usually had a hectic day; every lawyer was in a rush and everything a lawyer was a priority.

"Yeah, I am, but why are you going home? Is everything alright?"

"Everything is fine. We gotta work tonight. Zook and I stumbled in to something and we gotta do a surveillance. I was hoping to see you before I left."

"What time you leaving?"

"Around 7 or so."

"Oh, I'm sorry. I have to work late on a project; then a few of the girls were going out for some drinks."

"Out with the girls again, huh?"

"Yeah. There's always someone's birthday or a new baby or something. You know how it is."

"Yep, I think I do. I guess I'll see you later."

"Okay, bye."

She hung up the phone before I said goodbye in return. I couldn't really decipher that conversation. We hadn't been arguing recently; we weren't mad about anything. Things haven't been terrific either. We've just been muddling along. I was trying. I didn't know if I was attracted to marriage or avoiding divorce. I'm sure she was feeling the same way. Clearly, that was the problem.

I sat in bed hoping that she would surprise me and come home right before I left; maybe a little fooling around. Plain-old married sex would do; I couldn't aspire to have the fun Zucarelli had. My heart pounded when my cell phone rang, until I saw who was calling.

"What's up, Zook?"

"Just checking. Making sure you're on your way."

"What else would I be doing?"

"I dunno. Maybe you and momma doing the nasty or something. Knowing you, you'd probably get so excited you'd pass out and forget where you were, you..."

"Zook, enough please. Besides, I thought wives were off limits for those kind of jokes."

"No, they're off limits for me saying things about her doing the nasty with me, not you."

"And you say the FBI got fucked up rules. I'll meet you at the O."

Off to the office I went.

Did Zook know he hit a raw nerve with me? Was that his intent?

✱✱✱✱✱

"Look, we gotta keep this really loose. We can't burn Pops.

They'll tear his old body apart if they knew he was snitching for us."

"I know, I know. The FBI has been pretty good at handling informants. We keep 'em safe."

"I'm just nervous, Bob. You never wanna be responsible for getting someone killed when all they did was try to help you. Ya know?"

"Yes, I know. That's not a hard concept to grasp."

We picked a surveillance point across from the back door where Morelli's crew and whomever they were meeting would come in. We had our binoculars ready. With no idea of what to expect, we had absolutely no plan.

"Shouldn't you have turned this over to OCCB?" I asked Zucarelli.

"Fuck 'em. My snitch, my case. We'll see what happens and we'll take it from there."

I didn't respond. Zucarelli knew his way around NYPD politics. He didn't need me worrying about him. I was plenty busy worrying about myself.

As with all surveillance, it was hurry up and wait. Wait we did. Zucarelli asked me questions about my home life. I deflected those and asked about his.

"Eh, what's not to like. We live together and the kids are happy to see mommy and daddy together. We tolerate each other and..." He couldn't find an ending and left the sentence dangling.

"Zook, are you really sure the kids are happy?"

"We do things together. We go to all their ball games and shit like that. Why wouldn't they be happy?"

"I don't know. With dad out all the time either working or

screwing some bim somewhere, may…"

"Hey, who I screw is none of your business."

"Whoa, a little touchy there, aren't we? Look, you make it my business every time you put it in my face; and unfortunately that is literal. I'm still having nightmares."

"Let's drop this conversation. Obviously neither of us wants to discuss our home lives."

That sounded as if I struck a raw nerve back. I don't like getting to Zucarelli; he is a good partner and a great cop; but, I do feel like I need to even the score every now and then.

Silence set in and remained until we saw some action.

"Okay look, a car is pulling up now," Zucarelli's voice reflected some excitement.

We grabbed our binoculars and homed in on the back door.

"Ahh, ya see that. Good ole Pops left that upstairs light on. He knew we'd need that to see anything."

"He's good Zook, you developed a good snitch."

The driver stepped out of the black sedan and opened the passenger door. Another man, in a business suit then stepped out and looked around.

"Mother fucker," Zucarelli whispered.

"What?"

"Mother fucker. I don't believe it."

"What Zook, what?"

"You know who that is?"

"No, I don't. Who is it?"

Zucarelli continued to look through the binoculars, his lips mouthing out indiscernible words.

"Zook, Zook, c'mon already. Who the fuck is it?"

"That's The Ragman."

"The Ragman?"

"Yeah, Johnnie The Ragman Ragusa. He is a top level capo for Morelli. He's big. If he's showing up, this is no small meeting, whatever they're meeting about."

"Too bad the place ain't bugged," I said just to add something.

"Get me the camera; quick, the camera."

Though fumbling, I was able to get it from the floor of the back seat, although we were not expecting to take any pictures. From that distance, at night, we couldn't expect any great photos.

Zucarelli started clicking away. "I doubt these will be any good, but if I have to swear that I saw The Ragman here, a fuzzy picture is better than nothing."

The Ragman walked in to Pops' restaurant; the driver stayed close behind, his back turned to Ragusa, keeping an eye on the rear as he stepped in backwards.

"The Ragman is one nasty dude, Bob, he'll bash your head in...Wait, look another car."

Again, Zucarelli started taking photos as I kept notes in the log. This was great stuff, but it didn't tie into our case; so, despite Zucarelli's enthusiasm, this was getting turned over to his OCCB, or one of our Organized Crime squads.

The driver door opened and someone stepped out, still in the dark. This time, there was no passenger, just the driver who made his way to the door and under the light. He assumed the position and was frisked by The Ragman's bodyguards.

"You ain't gonna believe this, Bob." Zucarelli's voice was quivering and his hand shaking with excitement.

"What?" I grabbed at Zucarelli's binoculars. He pulled away.

"Grab your own. I'm not missing this."

I managed to get my binoculars focused on the right spot just in time to see Scarlotta walk in.

"Holy fuck, Zook. What the, I mean, how, uhh, what.."

'Alright, alright. We gotta calm down here."

"Yeah, yeah, okay, we're calm, we're good. But really, what were the odds of that? What the hell is going on?"

"I don't know, Bob. We gotta do something, I just don't know what."

"Zook, we gotta get a closer look at those cars. We need the plates. If we don't get at least that, we haven't got shit."

"I know, but I can't burn Pops. They got those two gorillas watching the cars. If they make us, who knows, that could fuck up everything and everybody."

"If we can just get a little closer, I could probably make out the plates. That's all we need."

"Whew, I don't know. It's risky."

"Zook, we can't sit here with our thumbs up our asses. We gotta walk away with a little intel. This is gonna break open something."

"Alright. I got an idea. You're not going to like this."

Zucarelli drove the car up the BQE and pulled over on the shoulder opposite of where Pops was. Camera in hand, I crossed the highway, hoping there was no asshole driving with his lights off. I wouldn't see him and I'd be dead. Horns honked as I made my dash. We were far enough away to avoid getting unwanted attention; even they heard the horns, that would hardly sound out of the ordinary. Carefully stepping over the shoulder barricade, I crawled down the hill and through the brush, while Zucarelli watched from the highway.

Speaking to me through our radio, he kept me alert to the movements of the bodyguards watching the cars. I could not get noticed. No matter how fast Zucarelli could respond, I would be dead before he got there. Of course, with that thought in mind, I tripped over my feet and tumbled down the hill for a few feet.

When I made it down the hill, still tucked behind some bushes, I did the paranoia check – wallet, gun, badge – all where they belonged. Pulling a few thorns out of my sleeves, I brushed myself off, wiped my lips with the back of my hand, spit out some dirt and tried to regain my composure. Readjusting my earpiece, I told Zucarelli that I was in position and to let me know as soon as he saw any movement. Fortunately, he did not see my roll down the hill; he would still be laughing and I would never hear the end of it.

Once settled, physically and emotionally, I took pictures of the cars, the license plates and the bodyguards. Then I got out of there, quickly, but carefully, running up the hill. We got back in to position from a safe distance. While sitting there, Zucarelli reached over and grabbed a small twig dangling in my hair.

"You got an ear full of dirt, my man. Have a little problem staying on our feet, did we?" Zucarelli chuckled.

No response was the best response, other than flipping him the bird. Then we sat still and quiet and waited, as we so often did.

"Okay, the door is opening. Here they come."

Scarlotta, followed by The Ragman came out the door. They spoke for a few minutes and shook hands. As Scarlotta walked to his car, he took out his cell phone and made a call.

"His phone," I blurted out.

"Huh?"

"His phone, Zook, we gotta get Scarlotta's phone number. I think we can put together enough p.c. for a wire. We gotta get it."

"How? We can't just go over there and ask."

"We can't let him just drive away, we gotta get that number."

"Bob, we can't pull him over. That'll be so fuck'n obvious; Pops will be burnt and he's dead. No can do."

"Well then, get a patrol car to pull him over. Make something up. I don't know, but we can't let this opportunity slip by."

After hesitating for a few seconds while rubbing his moustache and staring at me, Zucarelli called in to the police dispatcher as an anonymous private citizen.

"I think he just robbed a restaurant. Someone was yelling for help." Zucarelli described Scarlotta's car, location and direction of travel.

His description was so specific that an experienced dispatcher should have realized that it was no regular citizen making the call; dispatchers were so busy, they probably took no notice of things like that. We kept a loose tail on Scarlotta. Within about five minutes, and a decent distance from Pops, a marked patrol car pulled Scarlotta over. One cop talked to him and had him step out of the car and empty his pockets while the other cop stood back keeping an eye on things. We pulled over a few feet behind. The second cop quickly took notice and reached for his gun. Zucarelli expected that and quickly displayed his detective badge.

"Just wait here," he directed me. He went to have a quick

conversation with the uniformed cop who then went to talk to his partner. Zucarelli walked back over to me.

"Okay, they're on board."

"What's the plan?"

"They're gonna move Scarlotta over to the patrol car leaving his crap on his hood. As soon as they get him spread eagle and looking away, grab the phone. Let's try to make sure he doesn't see what's going on. Got it?"

"Got it."

The cops did as Zucarelli said they would, escorting Scarlotta by the elbows away from his car. We heard Scarlotta demanding to know what was happening, asking who we were and throwing out threats. That only pissed off the cops.

I grabbed the cell phone off the hood of Scarlotta's car and brought it back to Zucarelli. He dialed a number and when answered, he gave his name, badge number and some code words I didn't understand.

"Got it. Ready to copy?" I heard the party speaking to Zucarelli.

"Go," he answered. He wrote down the numbers told to him and ended the call.

"Okay, now just let me delete this call off his phone and we're set."

Wiping off the phone with his shirt, Zucarelli quickly returned the phone to the car hood as the cops kept screwing with Scarlotta. Scarlotta knew something unusual was going on, every time he tried to look back, the cops pushed him back in to the position. Hopefully they had him convinced that they were responding to a call of a possible robbery. We got out of there quickly.

"What was that call you made?"

"It's one of our hello phones. It's always answered with nothing but hello. It's not listed to the department, does not trace back to a location, or anything like that. We use it for shit like this, undercover ops or whatever."

"Cool. I assume it had caller id, and captured his number."

"Oh yeah."

Chapter 11

The next day in the office, Zucarelli and I knew that our job now was to build probable cause for a wire tap on Scarlotta's phone, if he didn't dump it after getting stopped last night. The Colombians coming to his office with duffel bags and suitcases and leaving empty handed was suspicious but not enough to get a warrant. Scarlotta's trips to the bank right after those meeting was a good tidbit for us to allege he was taking drug money. If we could have tied those murdered Colombians to him in any way, we would have had probable cause coming out of our asses. Though we suspected he was involved at least indirectly, we had nothing. Everything changed when he was seen meeting with a known mobster. One little fact was sometimes all you needed to cross the probable cause threshold. We had arrived. The next step was to subpoena Scarlotta's cell phone and bank account records. Then, we would have to figure out what all that data meant.

Coming in a little late, having gone to 1 PP first, Zucarelli saw us getting ready to leave the office, "Hey, what's going on?"

"Reardon's new wire has been active. They picked up something. Let's go. I'll drive since you just took that trip in to Manhattan."

"What a guy."

We hustled to the garage; Mel the garage attendant recognized our fast pace and knew we'd be pulling out in a hurry. He opened the gate and waved to each one of us as we pulled out.

"Be safe, guys," he yelled out as the last car left the garage.

"What did we get on the wire that's so hot?" Zucarelli asked me.

"Well, they got a load being picked up in Queens and then it's supposed to head to the Fat One."

"The Fat One? As in El Gordo? Our El Gordo?" Zucarelli asked.

"Sounds like it. Can be one of the same."

"Then let's not be surprised if we wind up at Scarlotta's. He's gotten big enough to qualify for that nickname. I saw some old mug shots of him when he was young; man, he was cut. Now he's just a slob."

"That would help. If we get anything hinting that he is this El Gordo, we're good. Though, I think we got enough p.c. for a wire anyway."

"Then does favorite son Reardon get to steal our case? All he has to do is tell Franks that his wire found him, we're not sure if he is El Gordo from our wire and all that bullshit."

"Eh, I don't think so."

"No? Why not? You're the one always bitching how he hogs the spotlight."

"I know. I think maybe I've seen another to him, and ..."

"And what?" Zucarelli knew I was reconsidering what I was about to say are started giving me that stare of his.

"I don't know. I mean, he did back us up there in Franks' office."

"Yes, he did. So, you completely changed your mind about him because one time he doesn't screw you?"

"It's not that simple. It's just, well, I could've been wrong. You know I'm man enough to admit when I'm wrong."

"Sure I do, but…"

Hey, what happened down at 1 PP by the way," I quickly changed the conversation. That seemed to work.

"Oh yeah, very interesting. Some lawyer, presumably working for Scarlotta, called in to check if there was a robbery called in last night in Brooklyn."

"No shit. So what happened?"

"Exactly what we hoped would happen. Dispatchers checked the log and confirmed that they got an anonymous call that described Scarlotta's car. It should sound legit and hopefully convince Scarlotta that it was nothing but a mistake and that should be the end of it."

"He is one suspicious motherfucker, isn't he?"

"He should be. After all, we should be tapping his calls pretty soon, right?"

"Hopefully. Let's just get this done first. If it doesn't take all day, we'll start a draft affidavit and then go see an AUSA."

"10-4." Zucarelli closed his eyes for a quick catnap as I usually do. Getting up early to fight your way in to Manhattan was exhausting.

"Oh and by the way," he continued, still with his eyes closed, "Nice way to change the conversation."

I started to respond, but realized that no response was the better option.

We set up as we always did on surveillance, looking for that strategic spot. Having a wire up made it easier. Hopefully, we would hear when things began to move so we didn't have to get that close and risk getting burned.

The wire room called out on the radio every time a little more intel was learned. Then Reardon called out his directions to our squad. Usually that was nothing more than to stand by until we were ready to move.

As with almost all surveillance, we sat and waited. Though I was in the mood to talk, I kept quiet and let Zucarelli catch a few zees. If it was me trying to sleep, he'd probably keep interrupting with a story of some babe he was banging. Unfortunately, I had no such stories. Or maybe that was fortunate; at least for today, I was still married. We sat there for about another ten minutes, Zucarelli napping and me staring in to space, when the call came from the wire room that our subjects were on the move.

"Okay, everybody, we got two Colombian males leaving now carrying two black suitcases and one gym bag." Reardon described them and the car.

"You know the drill," he continued. "Larry and I will start out with the eyeball. Try to parallel or stay a few cars behind. We'll call for a switch every few blocks."

We knew the drill very well; well enough to know to not get on the radio and try to coordinate our positions which would change every few minutes. We did it by instinct. About twenty minutes in to the moving surveillance, Reardon got back on the radio.

"I don't know what they're doing. They don't seem to be destination oriented. Let's keep it loose and see if what happens."

After a few more minutes, Reardon got back on the radio.

"Okay we're well out of familiar territory for these dope deals. No idea what they're up to. We're heading over the

Williamsburg Bridge."

"Well, I guess they're not heading to the Diamond District, unless they are taking a really circuitous route, which is possible," I suggested as an idea.

"Maybe, but if they're carrying around a load of cash, the more time they spend on the road, the more the risk. Who knows?"

We kept driving; over the bridge, a few turns on Delancey, then Mott Street and Mulberry Street.

"Shit, Bob, what the hell are they doing in Little Italy. This ain't Colombian territory in case you haven't noticed."

"Ah, it's a little hard not to notice. Every Vinny Goombatz is staring at them, and then at us. We gotta be burned by now."

"This ain't right, Bob."

Reardon got back on the radio for an update and reminded us to keep it loose. He then mentioned the street the car turned down. Zucarelli immediately picked up the radio and asked him to repeat the location. Then Zucarelli thought for a moment.

"Fuck." Zucarelli yelled out to me then grabbed the radio.

"Steve, this is Zook. Listen, they're gonna be driving right by the Ravensworth Social Club, you with me?"

"10-4, Zook. Thanks. All units stand by," Reardon replied on the radio.

"Ravensworth? *The* Ravensworth Social Club?"

"Fuck'n A. That's where one of Morelli's crews hangs out. I think you FBI guys got that placed bugged, don't you?"

"Huh? Yeah, I think so. I don't know."

We generally didn't discuss wiretaps on mob places all that casually outside the office.

"Why would they drive right past a mob place?"

"Coincidence? Maybe they don't know what it is?"

"No way. Everybody knows."

"Then what?   You think they're working with Morelli? Maybe making a delivery to them?"

"I can't imagine that, Bob. This is fucked up."

"We got the eye. They are moving very slowly" Simone called on the radio.

A few minutes later the car pulled over. The passenger walked out with the gym bag and went in to a local corner store – the Italian version of a bodega. Several minutes later he left, without the gym bag. On they went, slowly driving away. Moving up 6th Avenue, past Canal and Houston and making our way to Midtown.

"Maybe we are heading for Scarlotta's place."   Zucarelli suggested.

"Then what was that whole Little Italy thing about?"

"No clue."

We moved as slowly as traffic did. When we got stuck in the crosswalk, pedestrians walked behind us, in front of us with some banging their fists on the car; and one smartass walked right over the car.

"Motherfucker. I'll make him eat this car. What…"

"Is that gonna help anything? Just forget it. It's a Bureau car anyway." I said in the most calm voice I could muster up as Zucarelli opened the car door and started getting out. I was tugging on his arm as I spoke, and he stopped.

"But they don't know that. It's just the point."

"Forget the point. Let it go, Zook. We got more important things to worry about, like catching up to the surveillance."

"I know. You're right." Zucarelli backed his way in to car seat.

"Hey, is everything alright? Seems like you're ready to fly off the handle at any moment. What's up?" I asked, as he seemed to be increasingly on edge.

"Ahh, nothing. I don't know. Just the same shit at home. My ex drives me friggin' crazy."

"Well, buddy, you're the only guy I know who divorces a woman and then moves back in with her with no intention of saving the marriage."

"I told you, you can't…"

"I know, I know, I can't judge you. I'm not in your shoes, I get it. I'm just pointing out that the situation seems to have you all stressed out. That's all."

"Okay, fair enough. Sorry, I'll bring it down a bit. Let's go and catch up with everybody."

Nothing more needed to be said and I maneuvered in the traffic the best I could to catch up, with moderate success. The guys back in the wire room got on the radio to broadcast the new intel that was overheard.

"You're burnt, repeat, the surveillance is burnt, they know they're being tailed."

"Great, that should help."

"Well, Bob, maybe getting caught back here was a good thing; they can't blame getting burned on us."

"Yep, let's see what they're gonna do now."

"13-2, if they know we're on them, we should probably just pull 'em over and see what's up. Whatta we got to lose?" Simone asked Reardon over the radio.

"Stand by. All units stand by, please," was Reardon's response, meaning he was discussing it with Franks. After a few moments, Reardon was back on the radio.

"They're pulling over, they're pulling over."   Reardon screamed in to the radio, revealing his surprise.

"Okay then, let's catch up," I said to Zucarelli as I picked up the pace, only to be cut off by a cab, then swerving lanes and getting stuck behind a bus.

"They are out of the car. They are out of the car. We're coming in from behind, can someone grab them, quickly," Reardon screamed in to the radio.

"We got it. We'll get 'em." Simone called out.

We heard the sirens go off as we were just a few blocks away and I flipped the sirens switch as Zucarelli put the red light on the roof. The traffic was unimpressed and nobody yielded. I didn't want to miss the action and I knew Zucarelli felt the same way, though we would never actually say that.

Simone called in that he and Julie stopped the two subjects walking up 6th Avenue, just a few blocks south of the Diamond District. Reardon and Franks pulled in behind the car, quickly joined by Gallagher and his partner, rookie FBI Agent Garcia.

As we pulled up we found ourselves on the west side of the street, while everything was happening on the east side. Trying to move laterally across 6th Avenue seemed impossible.

"Fuck it, just park here," Zucarelli directed me, jumped out of the car and started running.

I left the car in the middle of the bus stop. Running in between cars and across the street, we could see Simone and Julie talking to the two subjects about a block north of the car. Grabbing them by the elbows, they started escorting them back. As Reardon walked across the front of the car, we saw Franks by the opened driver door and reach down.   Gallagher, shadowed by Garcia, then reached for the trunk. At that moment, the two men pulled away from Simone and Julie. They turned around, knelt to the ground and covered their ears. Simone looked at them and then quickly turned around holding his hand up and began yelling something.

Silence. Darkness. Numbness. Nothingness. I was dead. I had to be. What else could it be?

I could not remember who I was or where I was. I felt as if I was lying down, but was not sure; was I afloat, ascending to my final destination? I remained motionless, waiting for something, anything to explain my state of being. Time was moving neither slowly nor quickly. Was time moving at all?

Eventually, I heard a slight ringing and a buzzing. I blinked my eyes a few times as the darkness began to dissipate; there was no light, just less darkness. Sensing the hardness of the ground, I could feel that I was lying down. I waited, as my darkness evaporated and my sight slowly returned, though nothing looked real. I heard noise and static.

My head was partially resting on the wheel of a taxi cab. Just to get moving, I had to push my own head forward; I felt the blood in my hair and held my hand there, circling and rubbing, thought I felt no pain. Rolling over on to my knees, my first attempt to hoist myself up was unsuccessful, falling back on to the ground. I tried again, a bit slower, and aware that my sense of balance was off. I looked around, not fully capable of comprehending what I was seeing. The ringing in my ears remained, but now I heard alarms, screaming and noise. I remembered seeing a flash. Now I saw smoke, debris and stuff floating around. I saw people lying on the street. Where was everybody? Where was Zook?

"Zook, Zook. Where are you?" I called out, almost crying.

No response. Trying to get my bearings, I walked in no particular direction with no purpose other than to walk. Almost subconsciously, I walked towards the car, which was nothing but a frame on fire. I saw bodies, and partial bodies, and parts of bodies. Then I saw Julie leaning against a wall.

"Julie, Julie." I yelled to her as I ran over.

She didn't hear me, or just did not respond. Leaning over, she was resting her hands on her knees, spitting out blood. I stood next to her and put my hand on her shoulder. She held her hand up, acknowledging me.

"You guys alright?" Simone came over, putting his hand on my shoulder. His face spotted with bloody cuts, his speech was a bit slurred from the shard of glass I could see sticking in his lip.

"I'm okay, but don't move" I answered him; slowly I reached up and pulled out the shard. His eyes opened wide from the surprise of not knowing that was sticking out of his face. Then we both looked at Julie. She held up her hand again to show that she heard us and was with us, but needed a moment.

"Julie, stay here. Ray, let's go."

Ray and I ran to back to the car to see…whatever there was to see; and to help whoever needed help. Amongst the dust and smoke, hundreds, if not thousands of tiny pieces of greenish paper whirled around and snowed down upon us as we sadly scanned the area. The scene was ugly. We looked around. With each look, the scene only got uglier.

How did this happen? Where was Zook?

Chapter 12

ADIC Gunn took his familiar stance at the window of his office overlooking downtown Manhattan. Not looking at anything in particular, he absorbed the serenity that comes from being 28 floors above the reality of a busy city street. Gunn knew the conversation he was about to have. High profile positions in the FBI brought crises and headaches. Any crisis and any headache was a fair exchange for holding one of the most prestigious and powerful positions in the FBI. Gunn welcomed any opportunity that would put him front and center of attention from the media or Congress; any publicity was good publicity. Gunn expected that publicity would pay off, sooner or later.

"The Director is on the phone, Mr. Gunn," came over the intercom.

"Thank you."

Gunn walked over to his desk and slowly sat down. He took a deep breath and gathered his thought before hitting that button that would connect him with the FBI Director.

"Good morning, Bill."

"Pete, this is bad, very bad."

"I know. But all I can say that this is another example of the dangers these drug cartels pose to…"

"Pete, I know what you're gonna say. As true as that may be, we can't keep playing that same sound bite every time we get our ass kicked."

"We have to turn this around, Bill. We need to get the public and Congress angry at the drug cartels. Maybe then we can get the money we need and take over this drug war once and for all."

"I think you're getting a little ahead of yourself. This hardly puts us in a strong position. Forget Congress, I got the police commissioner up my ass. Two innocent citizens killed and a cop's brains were literally splattered on the streets."

"Well, it's not like we had a picnic out there; we had an agent killed as well, and one seriously injured. It's a war; there are casualties, we ..."

"Pete, Pete, stop, please. That's why the commissioner called me. He didn't think you were listening to him. He knows what happened. But this is the second police casualty recently on the same squad, not too long after they killed an innocent little baby. Pete, he's ready to pull off the task force and work only with DEA. The city can't take any more black eyes like this. This is not some small town police chief we're talking about here. This is the New York City Police Commissioner. If he starts making a lot of noise, this will go right to the Attorney General, maybe the President. That can't happen, Pete."

"I understand; I do. I'll fix this."

"How? How do you plan on fixing this and calming him down?"

"I, uh, I'm gonna hold some people's feet to the fire. Accountability, Bill, it's all about holding people accountable. We'll clean house and show that we..."

"You know what Pete, don't tell me. I don't want to know. Just take care of it. I want the commissioner off my ass and his cops on our task forces. If we don't handle this correctly, we'll be lucky if Congress doesn't kick us out of drugs altogether and gives the whole thing to DEA. Once that starts, who knows what else. You know we got Customs and ATF licking their chops, hoping to steal away half our programs. Losing anything won't help either one of us, Pete. You know what I mean?"

"Absolutely. Don't worry. I got this. I promise. Please, Bill, relax. We'll be fine."

"Okay. I'll talk to you later."

Whew, that wound up being a lot easier than I thought it would be. Ahh, Muffins, you speak loud, and carry no stick. You're so easy.

Smiling at that thought, Gunn picked up the phone again for his next call.

"Section Chief Borton. How can I help you?"

"Hi Rand. Pete Gunn here."

"Whoa, a call from The Pistol."

"How are you, Rand? It's been a while."

"Yes, it has. And not to that I don't enjoy small talk, but something tells me you didn't call me out of nowhere just to catch up."

"No I didn't. So I guess I'll get right to it."

"Okay, Pistol, shoot."

"Well, you are looking to get out of HQ, aren't you?"

"You know I am. Who isn't? But its gotta be the right SAC slot. Getting close to retirement, ya know. I want be somewhere that will lead to the big bucks in the private sector."

"Alright then; how does SAC, Criminal Division in New York sound? Ca-ching, ca-ching?"

"Criminal SAC, New York? Are you kidding? Kinda my

fantasy job. I'm there. Except for one thing, what about…"

"That's just it. He's not planning on going anywhere, which is the problem. His time has come. We've had a few problems in the criminal division here lately."

"No shit. That rogue drug squad of yours out in Queens has been the topic of conversation fairly often around here."

"I'm sure it has. You're probably thinking that it's due for an inspection, aren't you?"

"I, umm, am starting to think that, yes. But, we're looking at one…"

"We are looking at one chain of command that is broken. From case agent to supervisor to ASAC to SAC. Each one is out of control. Inadequate supervision that has resulted in these tragic events. It's time to hold people accountable, shake things up, make some transfers. You with me?"

"I think I am. Now, you know we can't guarantee how…"

"Cut the crap, Rand. You know that an inspection finds whatever the inspector wants to find. We're not talking anything new here; it's the FBI way. You do this right and there is a spot waiting for you."

"Okay, Pete. What about the Director? Is he gonna buy off on this?"

"You just leave Muffins to me. If he even hesitates, I'll simply remind him that if we don't handle this, the Inspector General will."

"Oh, good point. He quivers at the thought of the IG poking around."

"That's right. So, you just get the right team out here and everything will work out just fine. When can you start?"

"Wheels up tomorrow? Sound good?"

"Nah, not so soon. That would be a bit brutal. More than that, it would be kind of obvious. Give it a couple of weeks. We got everyone going to Employee Assistance, their shrinks, their priests, their mothers and crap like that. So, you know."

"Yes, I know. See you soon."

ADIC Gunn hung up the phone and leaned back in his chair to stare at the ceiling for a moment. A smile broke out on his face. Then he stood up and walked back to his favorite spot at the window. The smile expanded and morphed into laughter.

Hah, like we used to say in high school: what a tool. He'd sell his mother to be SAC. They shouldn't call me The Pistol; they should call me The Magician. There is no trick in the FBI that I cannot pull off; no illusion I cannot create. This is almost too easy. That thought sent Gunn into full blown laughter as he stood there by himself, leaning against the window frame, staring down upon New York City.

✳✳✳✳✳

"So whatta ya think?" I asked as we both stared at our coffee, mindlessly stirring slowly and steadily, almost like synchronized swimming, sitting in the diner across from the office.

"I don't know what to think. Everything sucks."

"Sure does."

"Listen, I don't wanna get queer or anything here, but I gotta tell you, Bob, I really appreciate how you were at my bedside in the hospital that night. I mean, when I woke up and didn't know what was happening, I saw you with that stupid smile of yours and everything kinda fell back in to place." Instead of rubbing his moustache as he would normally do, Zucarelli was now rubbing his fingertips over the wound extending from his forehead to behind his ear, not too far from the grazing he took at the shooting in the Bronx.

"You kidding? Where else would I be? You're my partner; you would've been there for me."

"Well, thanks, man." Zucarelli did not look up; he was very uncomfortable with this verbal exchange of friendship and support. I let it end there.

"It never should've gotten this far, Zook."

"Of course not."

"We should've seen this coming. I mean we walked right into this friggin' death trap."

"Huh, what..." Zucarelli was having trouble staying focused.

"Look, we had these cocksuckers driving through Little Italy, right by the Ravensworth," I continued.

"And?"

"And you said it yourself. That made no sense. We shoulda realized something was wrong. The money wasn't even real; if was just fuck'n paper. This was all for nothing. The whole thing was a set up."

"Why would they set us up? Going to war with us is never a good idea. They know better than that."

"They weren't setting us up, Zook"

"But, you just said..."

"I said it was a set up, not that they weren't setting *us* up. This was a setup against Morelli's crew. That's why they drove right past his club. By getting in their face, they were trying to goad his goons into ripping them off. It worked."

"What for?"

"Revenge. What else."

"Revenge? You mean for the…"

"Absolutely; for the throat slaying of two of their couriers. This wasn't meant for us, Zook." This was the first time I was out-talking Zucarelli. He wasn't himself. He's been through a lot of crap in his career, but this seems to have knocked the wind out of him.

"You think the Cartel is willing to go up against the mob? Can they win that war?"

"I don't know. But they can't be bullied around either. You slash two of theirs, they're coming back at you."

"I guess; that sounds right. I hadn't really thought about it."

"Zook, you almost had half your fuck'n head blown off. You were totally out of it for almost twenty-four hours; it's okay that you haven't given this much thought."

"Well I'm thinking about it now." Zucarelli moved to the end of the booth, leaning against the wood panel wall and stretching his legs out.

"So am I. You wanna tell me how a drug task force of NYPD detectives and FBI agents walked right in to that. How the fuck did we not figure out that this was some kind of trap?"

"We really took some beating out there, didn't we?" Zucarelli leaned back and reached in to his pocket, pulling out a bottle of aspirin. As he dumped a few into his hand and quickly downed them down with his coffee, I put my hand out and waved my fingers, before he put the aspirins back. He poured two in to my hand. I looked at him and kept my hand out. He poured one more in. My hand did not move; nor did my stare. He gave me one more and I chugged those down with my coffee.

We did take a beating. Detective Gallagher, two days away from his transfer was killed; his head literally blown apart from the blast that came from the trunk that he opened. His partner, Agent Garcia, got hit in his face with so much glass and shrapnel, he would be lucky to get any of his sight back. Only two months on the job and a new dad, his future was not bright. Franks, only a few months from retirement age was dead. Julie had a collapsed lung. The rest of us had varying degrees of cuts, gashes and bruises.   We were living on aspirin, prescription pain killers and alcohol. Most of us had loud ringing in our ears. Maybe it would dissipate over time – some of it, perhaps none of it. Either way, our hearing would never be the same.

Our respective agencies mandated psychological counseling. We all acted as if we didn't need it. We all knew that we did. Two innocent citizens who just happened to be in the wrong place at the wrong time had died. A few others had serious injuries. We didn't protect ourselves and we didn't protect the public. This was a complete failure. We deserved every bit of the guilt we were carrying around.

There was a very painful truth that was rubbing salt in to our deep wounds. The two drug couriers who set this whole thing up and were ready for the blast made their getaway, probably without injury. We knew we would never see them again.

"Life is funny, huh Zook?"

"Given everything that just happened, how do you figure?"

"Well, I didn't mean funny like in humorous. I meant funny like strange. Think about it. If we didn't get stuck in traffic, if we didn't wind up on the other side of the street, we would've been right on top of that car too. That would've been us, Zook.

That might've been our brains blown all over the street. We really got lucky."

"I don't know Bob. How much luck is any one person entitled to in a lifetime? It was close at Doc's shooting, and I got lucky there. Maybe this time I got more than my fair share. Maybe I'm..."

"Zook, you can't do that. It's like you're having survivor's guilt. You can't blame yourself for getting lucky enough to not get killed. It's just how things go. Look, I'm no shrink. I'm sure we're all getting enough shrink time, but we got work to do and somehow we've got to keep going. If we don't then we really suffered through all of this for nothing. We're gonna have to get past this and move on.

"Alright. Let's go."

Without waiting on the tab, Zucarelli took out a ten dollar bill and laid it on the table for two cups of coffee.

"Zook, get your change."

"Fuck it. C'mon."

We crossed Queens Boulevard at the crosswalk, with the green light. We never did that. We didn't have the energy to dodge traffic. Going back to the office was the only thing we could do, though was probably not helpful. The office was a like a ghost town. Those who came in, hardly spoke. They came, they went. No questions were asked. If nothing else, the quiet gave us a chance to focus on the mundane tasks of looking through records, taking notes and drawing out flow charts to help us understand the flow of people, phone calls and money. Now we were posting these charts and drawings on the wall. A few weeks ago we were hanging up pictures of half naked women.

"Hey guys, how's it going?" Reardon sat down with us.

"Hey Steve, how you doing, buddy?" I responded to his social overture.

"You know, it ain't easy. Franks and Gallagher gone. Both of them so close to moving on to another stage of life. Garcia, his career over before it starts. Innocent people dead. I don't know guys, what is this all about?" Reardon wanted to have the same cathartic conversation with me that Zucarelli and I just had. Couldn't blame him.

"It's all about fighting crime and doing our job."

"I know, but we really screwed this one up. I mean..."

"Yeah, this was a screw up. But let's not forget something – we didn't slash anybody's throat, we didn't line a car with explosives and drive it through the city. It was the mob and the cartel going after each other and taking it out anybody who happened to be in their way. They're all scumbags and we should get more fired up about going after them. We can't get discouraged. Even with all this crap happening to us."

"That's my partner." Zucarelli stood up, grabbed my shoulder and walked away. I wasn't sure why he left.

"So, you're covering the desk now Steve; tough time to be in charge here. You think they'll give it to you when it goes to the Career Board." I was trying to change the subject.

"Are you kidding. Bob? I guess you haven't heard."

"Heard what?"

"There's an inspection coming our way. They'll be here next week."

"Okay, so?"

"C'mon, Bob. You know what these special inspections are all about. They're never for good reasons. There's a contract out, and my name is on it. I got two, maybe three weeks before something really bad happens."

"You don't know that."

"Yes, I do."

"How can I help? What should I tell them when they come around asking those stupid questions?"

"Thanks, Bob. I appreciate it, but you know where this is heading. Look, we haven't been the best of friends, but I know you've always been a stand-up guy. Just do what you always do – tell the truth no matter what."

"Well, telling the truth hasn't done much for my popularity around here."

"No, it hasn't." Reardon chuckled. "But, we all knew where you stood. You always had everyone's respect. That means something."

"Thanks, Steve."

"You and Zook got some good leads to follow up on. We'll do what we can. I'll try to get help from some of the other squads. I'll get whatever I can for you until they take me out. Okay?"

"Sounds good."

Reardon stood up to walk back to the office. I stood up with him and extended my hand.

"Hey, Steve."

Reardon stopped and turned around.

"We'll do what we gotta do, just like always. We'll get through this."

We shook hands and smiled. We both knew that what I said were empty words. The FBI die was cast.

"So, you and Reardon are asshole buddies now?" Zucarelli

said as he came back and sat down next to me.

"Let's get working, Zook."

"Okay, let's do it."

$$*****$$

The next two weeks were quiet and sad. We visited with Garcia, both his eyes still patched with heavy gauze pads. Fortunately his hearing, like most of ours, was coming back and we were able to talk to him. His wife sat at his side, holding his hand, every moment while we visited. Wooden crosses and pictures of Jesus adorned his living room with baby toys strewn across the floor of their studio apartment on the 16th floor of a Long Island City apartment building.

We promised to be there every step of the way and to do whatever they needed us to do. Yet, we all knew that promise had a short life span. In a few weeks, Garcia would be retired from service and given whatever a permanently injured FBI Agent was entitled to. Of course, we would pass the hat and chip in ten, maybe twenty bucks each. It would never amount to much, certainly not enough for a young man looking forward to life as an FBI Agent. Eventually he and his wife would settle into a new life, his short lived career as an FBI Agent would fade in their memories amidst their struggle to overcome very difficult obstacles. We would go back to work, where Garcia would become a sad memory for us and a story to be told for a year or two, and then forgotten. That was a harsh reality.

"Poor kid. This sucks," was all Zucarelli said, lighting a cigarette as we left Garcia's apartment building. I was about to respond, but he picked up his pace as we walked to the car. He leaned against the passenger door, inhaling with long, deep puffs that quickly burned the cigarette out. He flicked the butt onto the street, hitting a passing car.

"He's obviously a man of faith. You think that will help get him through this?" I asked, not sure I wanted Zucarelli's answer as I leaned against the car, next to him.

"I sure hope so, Bob. I don't think I have any faith left in anything anymore."

"Zook, listen, I'm not much on the whole religion thing, but whatever you believe, you got to hold onto. On this job, buddy, we can never lose sight of what we have to do, and how we have to do it. We've taken oaths, remember? We gotta live up to them, no matter what."

"Yeah. No matter what; you got that right." Zucarelli got back in the car.

We spent the next few days at our desks working slowly and sluggishly, often taking breaks to eat, drink coffee or just bullshit about nothing. Laying documents and records out side by side, taking notes, drawing diagrams and re-writing the flow charts we posted on the wall, we were looking for that elusive probable cause. The time-lines showed a fairly consistent pattern of activity. Scarlotta's phone records showed him getting a call within minutes of some Colombian currier showing up at his store. Then surveillance logs showed he would go to the bank with the money. A few minutes later, phone calls, wire transfers and the process repeated itself a day or two later. When we discussed it, the probable cause sounded good; when we tried to reduce it to writing, it was not as convincing.

"You think we're getting enough p.c. for a wire, Bob?"

"We're getting close. If we stay focused and I can get this

flow of activity in to one cogent document, we can get with an AUSA and start drafting an affidavit."

"Right, staying focused. I guess going to funerals can be a bit distracting, huh?"

I did not answer him. There was no answer. I just kept staring down at the work on my desk.

The next day was Franks' funeral. Afterwards, we were in no mood to work. Nobody was. Everyone just went home. No personal leave requested; no explanations of where we were going. We all got in our cars and left. No questions were asked.

Getting back early, I sat in the living room watching television, waiting for Elaine to come home. I was hoping just to have her listen to me. I had nothing in particular to say, but a lot to get off my mind about Garcia, Franks, Gallagher and the whole drug war business. We went out for dinner and surprisingly, she listened patiently and seemed to care. It was kind of like our dating days - talking about stuff, not our fledgling relationship. I guess discussing something other than our marriage was refreshing. Back home, we washed up, spoke a little bit more, watched television in bed and fell asleep. No sex, not even a kiss or warm embrace.

The very next day brought the expected solemnity of a funeral for a police officer killed in the line of duty. Hundreds of police officers from the surrounding area were there to show their support and pay their respects. The funeral procession of sirens and flashing lights went for miles as it snaked from the chapel to the graveside through congested city streets. Dress uniforms, bagpipes and military precision complimented the sense of honor and duty that permeated a police funeral.

The temperature quickly changed from cool to warm and

back again as the cloud-pocked sky vacillated between sunny and shady. I stood next to Zucarelli, who looked pretty sharp in his dress blues. I had never seen him in a uniform. Doc showed up, bravely facing the sadness of the day, despite his own inner turmoil that he was trying to quell, as he readied to return to work and resume the good fight. The flag was folded and handed to Gallagher's widow, flanked by their young son and daughter. She held her hand in front of her face as she broke down, as all widows do at that moment. The casket was lowered in to the ground, and Zucarelli whispered to me.

"Someone has to pay for this." He was tugging at his tight fitting collar. The sun peeked through, raising the temperature a bit and Zucarelli's forehead was spotted with beads of sweat.

"They will, Zook, they will." I did not believe that was true. Maybe if we caught the scumbags driving the car, a good case would be put together. They were gone and there was very little chance we would find out who they were and get our hands on them.

Zucarelli knew that too. Yet, he did not seem to be accepting that. With every passing day Zucarelli was getting closer and closer to that thin line separating an aggressive cop from a cop on the edge.

At the end of this funeral, we did not go home. Zucarelli changed into his civilian clothes and we went to one of his cop bars in Brooklyn where we met up with many of his police department buddies. Loud and raucous, nutshells crunched under our feet with each step. Zucarelli shook hands or hugged almost every guy and gal in the place as they passed each other. He did not introduce me to anyone, nor did anyone seem to want to be introduced. We grabbed the last of two empty stools at the bar. We drank beer and listened to cops tell stories, each one trying to outdo the other. Most of the stories sounded like pure bullshit, yet they were entertaining and brought laughter from the crowd. I hadn't seen Zucarelli laugh like that in a while. I hadn't laughed like that in even a longer while. This was a much better way of dealing with loss than sitting home mindlessly watching television. We were having fun while respectfully honoring the dead and burying our sadness. What a concept. Cops and FBI Agents were very different.

Chapter 13

Wwe circled around the block two or three times before finding a tight parking spot. Zucarelli had to bump the cars in front of and behind us before fitting our car in. Most of us would look around, concerned that the car owners would've seen that. Zucarelli could not care less. He threw the police plaque in the windshield.

"Let's go, Bob."

"Okay, Zook, let's do it."

There was a cool breeze and a mist in the air; the streets were slick on this dank and dreary day. Ignoring the traffic lights and crossing the street in the middle of traffic, a black Mercedes came to a screeching halt right in front of Zucarelli, stopping only inches in front of him. Looking down at the inches that separated his legs from the car's front grill, Zucarelli banged on the hood and then gave the driver the finger as he continued crossing the street. We weren't expecting anything to happen, but the driver got out of the car. About ten years younger and almost the same size as Zucarelli, dressed in a business suit that probably cost more than my weekly salary, he pointed his finger at Zucarelli,

"Hey motherfucker, how about I bang your face like that?" He was ready; dark, steely eyes covered by thick brows, stared straight at Zucarelli. Zucarelli stopped, turned around and returned the stare with the same resolve; he was not about to blink.

"Bang my face, really? You're gonna eat this fuck'n car before you make it down to Wall Street, you coked up little puke." Zucarelli picked his hands up to his chest and started shaking them, loosening them up for a fight. The driver stepped away from the door and started rubbing his hands together; he was not backing down either.

This was not a high school bluff, where Zucarelli was actually hoping for someone to stop him. He was going to fight this guy. I ran fast, getting in front of Zucarelli and blocked him. I grabbed his arms.

"Zook, you can't do this. You're a cop. He's a dick. You have too much to lose. Please, let's go." Facing Zucarelli, I spoke softly and was trying to block any view of his badge and gun. If this hotheaded motorist found out that Zucarelli was a cop, things would only get worse. It was difficult pushing Zucarelli, trying to get him to back up. It took a few tense seconds, but he gave in, knowing it wasn't worth it and started walking away. As we did, the driver just couldn't let it go.

"Yeah, you'd better run, you pussy."

That did not help. We both stopped and I closed my eyes in frustration, knowing what was about to happen. Zucarelli turned around and pushed aside my hands as I again tried to stop him. He was walking quickly and deliberately. I got in front of Zucarelli and again ran, this time right to the driver. I held up my badge to him.

"Listen asshole, I'm trying to get my witness here in to court to testify against some people a lot tougher than you, if you know what I mean. Now, we have a couple of choices. I can lock your ass up for obstruction, or I can have my friend rip your face off, or you can just drive away. Your choice." He took a moment to think. I help up my hand to Zucarelli signaling for him to stop, which he did.

"Fuck you." He needed to get in the last word as he got back in to his car and drive off, waving his middle finger out the driver window.

We started back across the street, still in the middle of oncoming traffic. That was one of my better bluffs.

"I would've killed that cocksucker."

"You know what Zook? I believe that. I really do. You gotta get hold of yourself, man. I don't wanna sound too trite here, but, you are really on the edge, and I'm worried about you."

"Bob, I'm okay. I just got a lot of shit going on now, and it gets to me sometimes. I mean, watching our own get their heads blown off and all…"

"Zook, my life is not so great either. My wife is like a friggin' stranger to me. I was there with you, you know. I saw what happened. It haunts me too. But we can't go around ready to take it out on anyone who happens to push our buttons. We got guns and we got badges. We've got to be more careful than everybody else. You with me?

Zucarelli didn't answer me. We walked in silence crossing the streets, up the steps and he stopped.

"You know, Bob, I'm just sick and tired of watching good people pay the price for all the bad ones. Haven't you noticed that lately? Every damn thing we do seems end up with the wrong people getting hurt. The punks and drug traffickers walk away. Cops, agents, innocent people and even babies are getting caught in the middle. I mean…what the fuck?"

"You're right Zook. The world certainly seems upside down

right now. We can't let it get to us. We've got a job to do. Even when things get bad, and they really suck right now, we have to keep our heads in the game. It ain't easy, but that's why we get paid the big bucks, right?"

"Yeah, right." Zucarelli gave me a small smile and a pat on the back. "C'mon, partner, let's get a wiretap and put some of the fuckers in jail."

Making our way to the United States Attorney's Office, we checked in with the receptionist and found our way to the office of Assistant United States Attorney Jay Fromberg.

"Agents Douglas and Zucarelli, nice to meet you." Fromberg politely stood up and walked out from behind his desk, stepping over stacks of files to shake our hands.

"Bob Douglas. Nice to meet you, Jay." I introduced myself and let him move to Zucarelli, and I knew what was coming.

"Mark Zucarelli, Jay. But, that's Detective Zucarelli, NYPD. I'm not an FBI Agent, I'm a detective." Zucarelli was giving him a strong and animated hand shake. Fromberg's hand, arm and most of his skinny body seemed to be vibrating.

"Of course, I apologize, Detective. I should have known that." Fromberg seemed a bit unnerved by that exchange, waving his hand over his thinning black hair and then readjusting his round wire rimmed eyeglasses.

"No prob. I was just busting your hump a bit." Zucarelli added some light hearted relief.

"Well, I read the file about the search warrant. Congratulations, that was a great job. I understand that now you want to get a telephone wiretap. Is that correct?"

"That is correct," I answered. "We were gonna reconnect with Brevard, but couldn't get an appointment with her. Not that we don't want to work with you, but wouldn't it be easier since she already knows about the case?"

"Well, she, uh, she's, umm, she's been transferred to the Eastern District," Fromberg told us.

"Eastern District? She got banished to Brooklyn? Holy shit. Who did she piss off?" I asked, honestly surprised; though I suspected something was up when she did not show up in court, replaced by Wheeler.

"No such thing, Agent. The Eastern District had an opening that she was very qualified for. She asked for the transfer. This is nothing like what you're suggesting." Fromberg sounded a bit defensive.

"Oh, come on. Nobody voluntarily transfers out of the revered Southern District. What other U.S. Attorney's Office produced a mayor and an FBI Director?"

Fromberg moved quickly to change the direction of the conversation away from U.S. Attorney office politics to the task at hand, which was the wiretap affidavit. Zucarelli and I looked at each other with a smile. We knew we were making Fromberg uncomfortable, which we sort of enjoyed, but he was right to refocus the conversation. I wouldn't want an AUSA wasting my time prying in to FBI office politics instead of getting the job done. We showed him our logs and flow charts. We explained the timelines of activity, from phone calls, to deliveries to bank deposits to wire transfers. Fromberg asked many pointed questions and listened carefully to our answers, which sounded as if we were complicating things.

"Let's get this down to its simplest form. In a nutshell, Scarlotta gets bags of suspected money delivered to him by unknown Colombian males."

"Correct," Zucarelli and I answered in unison.

"Then he deposits this alleged money in to his own bank account. Then he either sends a wire transfer to this gold dealer in Los Angeles or to other accounts in South America or some of these Middle East countries like Saudi Arabia or the United Arab Emirates. Is that right?"

"United Arab Emirates? Oh yeah, that's right." I looked over at Zucarelli and we hid our laughter. We had seen the wire transfer to the bank, but didn't know what UAE was. Now we knew.

"This Castle Gold in Los Angeles; what did you find out about them?" Fromberg asked.

"Oh, they're legitimate gold wholesalers. We think they sell to Scarlotta who uses the gold to wash the drug money, somehow. We're not exactly sure what they're doing. But, with a wire, we can figure it out."

"Well, if Scarlotta is a gold dealer and he's buying gold from a gold wholesaler, I 'm not seeing a lot of criminality in that."

"Yeah, but what about all this drug money he gets from the Colombians? That's criminal," I offered.

"First of all, that's alleged money. We're not sure its money he's getting."

"What?" Zucarelli chimed in. "Right after he gets those suitcases and duffel bags, he runs to the bank to make a cash deposit. What's that?"

"That's us concluding that the money was in the bags. We don't know that, we're just assuming. Since we do not know what, if anything was in the bags, what he brings to the bank could be cash receipts from legitimate store sales. Your surveillance logs show customers coming and going," Fromberg responded.

"Okay then, we have Colombians bringing in these suitcases and bags. If we don't assume it's money, let's assume it's drugs. How about that?" Zucarelli was starting to get a little angry now.

"Why should we assume that, detective? Because they're Colombians? Is that what you want to do Detective, racially profile these individuals without knowing anything about them? "

"Hey, we've been..."

"Hold on," I interrupted Zucarelli. "Jay, we can't swear that this is cash coming in or that it is from drug trafficking. We are not proving this beyond a reasonable doubt; we're only saying we have probable cause for a wiretap, that's all. Nothing more, nothing less."

"I appreciate that, I really do. I just don't think we've crossed that threshold. We need more. Can you intercept one of those deliveries - the suitcases or duffel bags, before they get to Scarlotta and see if it is full of cash? That would give us something."

"Of course we can. We've always had that option. If we do that, we risk blowing everything; they'll know we're watching them. Scarlotta will move or change his operation and the Colombians will scatter like cockroaches."

'Well, then, can you source these deliveries to Scarlotta? You know, track them back to some drug operation."

"That's kinda what we were counting on the wiretap to do. There is no way for us to know where the money originates from."

"Can you..."

"We tried following the couriers back." I interrupted Fromberg, knowing exactly what he was going to ask. "Never worked. They drove around enough to lose any tails they may have, or they went out to eat, or went into some huge apartment complex or just hung around all day. Following them was a complete dead end. We need the wire to connect all the dots here."

Zucarelli and I persisted in trying to counter Fromberg's perception that we did not have enough probable cause for a wiretap. He always countered back.

"We saw Scarlotta meeting with a known mob member."

"We already know he is associated with mob figures. So, are a lot of people. How does that give us p.c. for his cell phone?"

"The drug couriers we busted had the name El Gordo on a piece of paper."

"Great, what proof do you have the Scarlotta is El Gordo?"

Nothing was sticking. Naturally, we saw him as an over-cautious AUSA who could not distinguish between probable cause and absolute certainty. Fromberg undoubtedly, viewed Zucarelli and me as over-anxious cops thinking only about the short-term and not concerned about getting all the evidence from any wiretap quashed at a suppression hearing. What Zucarelli and I thought had no significance. The AUSA had the final word on whether we were going to a judge or not. Obviously, we were not. What Fromberg wanted us to do to get the probable cause had a high chance of burning the investigation. We were stuck in a quagmire at this point.

"That little twerp. He's pulling the old 'I am prosecutor, you give me what I ask for, or no warrant' line. This is the stuff I hate about our job. If we could only do things our way…"

"Zook, I think that if right now, we were doing things our way, we'd probably be in jail. Let's figure out how to get him what he needs without screwing up this already screwed up case. Okay?"

"Okay, but I tell ya, I didn't like this Fromberg guy. He's was a little too...I don't know, just too."

"Go ahead, Zook, say it; too what? Too Jewish? Is that what you want to say?'

"No, and don't be putting words in my mouth. You keep acting like I'm some kind of bigot and I don't appreciate it, 'cause I'm not."

"I know that. But you do like categorizing people in ethnic terms, don't you?"

"Maybe. That's just how cops talk though. I'm no bigot. I don't got one prejudiced bone in my body."

"Okay, buddy. I'm sorry. I didn't mean anything by it. Just busting your balls a bit."

"I know. Besides, saying he's too Jewish is racial profiling. We don't want to be doing that, do we agent?"

We laughed a little and let it go at that. Zucarelli was being honest; he was not a bigot. He was a New York City cop being a New York City cop when he described people with words that were generally understood as derogatory. To him, it was police jargon; nothing else.

Chapter 14

The interrogation room seemed different now that I was the one answering questions. While not under arrest, I was certainly not free to leave. I had nothing to hide, yet I did not like the questions I was being asked. No windows and no fresh air. Bland white walls marred by black scuff marks. Handcuffs hanging off the gray restraining bars for holding our prisoners, bolted into the wall below the two way mirror. I knew there was nobody on the other side of that mirror. There never was. We rarely had reason for someone to observe our questioning. I didn't like the FBI Agent facing me; I didn't like where this was obviously heading. There was nothing about this I liked.

"Agent Douglas, let's talk about the minutes just preceding the entry and subsequent shooting." Agent Brian Cherrybrook, from our Office of Professional Responsibility was discussing the shooting from the Bronx that we were all trying to forget.

"Didn't all these questions get asked by the Inspection Shooting Review Team? Why are we going over this again now?"

"This is different. The Shooting Team was only reviewing whether it was a good shooting. What we're looking at now is the planning and execution of arrests on this squad, and how we wound up with a dead baby at one place and dead cops and agents at another. You know that already, Douglas, don't you? You're a senior agent. Word has it that you've been pretty critical of the way things run around here. Now's your chance to get it on the record."

"Listen, Cherrybrook, this is bullshit and you know it. You come in now while we're still grieving our dead friends. All of a sudden, you're interested in getting my thoughts on the record. Fuck the record."

"Hey, hey," Cherrybrook yelled and stood up from his chair. "I am a Unit Chief with OPR and I expect you to address me accordingly. Let's bring the animus down and show some respect. We represent the Director, ok?"

"Okay, okay, animus brought down. But, I think we should be honest here. There isn't one guy on our squad - cop or agent - that thinks you guys aren't here with an agenda. This is nothing but a charade."

"Well, that's just not true, Douglas. As a matter of fact, as soon as we got here, Section Chief Borton called a meeting and told us to make sure we did this fairly."

"Oh he did? Why would he do that? Aren't all your inspections done fairly?

Why would you need special instructions about being fair now?"

"Obviously, you're going to find fault with whatever I say, so there is no point in my trying to convince you otherwise. As you know, it really doesn't matter what you think; I am going to ask you questions, and you will answer them honestly. Those are Bureau rules and if you do not comply, you will be charged with insubordination. Are we clear?"

He was clear and unfortunately for me, he was correct. Insubordination had a pretty broad definition in the FBI. Any wise-mouthing to a superior could be considered as insubordination. I had probably already crossed that line. We went back and forth with his questions and my evasive answers.

"Did the SAC and ASAC provide adequate oversight over drug enforcement activities?"

"I don't know, I never have occasion to speak with the ASAC or SAC."

"Really, so you would say that they don't engage in hands-on management."

Those kind of questions reinforced what we already knew. The outcome of this inspection was pre-determined. Anything and everything that we would say would get spun. Then Cherrybrook went in for the kill.

"Isn't it true that right before you raided that apartment in the Bronx, several squad members suggested that you use the NYPD Emergency Services, is that correct?"

"Yes, that was discussed."

"Didn't Agent Reardon disagree and convinced Franks to move forward with only the SWAT member on the squad, and not wait for a full SWAT call-out?"

"Uhh, no. Actually, I think it was The Pistol who called for that."

"The Pistol? Are you talking about ADIC Gunn?"

"Yes, I am, he..."

"Then address him accordingly. ADIC Gunn is a high level FBI executive who deserves your respect. Nicknames are not appropriate."

"Yeah, okay, then ADIC Gunn made that decision."

"How do you know that, Douglas? Did he speak with you? Did you hear him say that?"

"No, I didn't speak with him. I, uhh, no...I heard, that's all. I just heard that."

"You heard? Well, as you know, unless you actually heard it directly from ADIC Gunn, then I have to dismiss that as rumor."

"Of course you do."

This was getting brutally obvious. Gunn put the blame on Franks. Without Franks around to defend himself, that was an easy one. Reardon probably told OPR that Gunn gave the order; it was the word of an Agent who was being targeted against the word of the Assistant Director in Charge of the New York Office. That was not much of a contest.

Now I got a question for you if you don't mind," I asked, not sure of what his response would be.

"Can't promise I will answer, but go ahead."

"Are you an attorney?"

"What? Why is that..."

"Just to satisfy my curiosity, are you an attorney?"

"Yes, I was prosecutor before I got in the FBI. Does that help answer whatever it is you are wondering about."

"Yes, it does. Thank you."

We exchanged a few more questions followed by my answers, which weren't answers as I carefully teetered along the thin line separating bad attitude from insubordination. When I was finally released from my obligatory questioning, I met up with Zucarelli at my desk.

"Did you get interviewed too?" I asked Zucarelli.

"Fuck'n A. What bullshit that was."

"Yes it was. I'm surprised you agreed to be interviewed. This is FBI stuff, and I know you cops don't like getting involved in our internal crap."

"We don't. But we got a memo from Division Command. While they knew our union rules didn't allow us to be forced to talk to your goons, they requested our cooperation in furtherance of our close working relationship with the FBI, to use their words."

"Since when did you what was requested of you."

"Eh, you never know when I may need a favor from somebody at 1PP. May as well be as cooperative as I can."

"How'd it go?"

"I gotta tell ya, Bob, I don't get it. This young FBI Agent was putting words in my mouth; he wasn't even listening to my answers. How the fuck do you guys tolerate this shit without representation? If this was a PD inquiry, forget about it, we'd all have our union reps with us. How do you let the FBI walk all over you like this? Don't you have any protection?"

"No, we don't. The FBI can really steamroll over someone if they want. They often do, when it suits them. There's no way to stop that machine once it starts."

"Oh man, I don't know what to say, Bob. I find it very strange. How about you? How did it go?"

"Not good. I had some douche bag unit chief asking loaded questions."

"What's a unit chief?" Zucarelli asked.

"Oh, it's probably the worst position in the FBI. They're only at headquarters and it's for supervisors who can't get promoted to ASAC. They take that spot hoping some face time with the decision makers will help their careers."

*****

The next weeks continued to be slow and dull. We worked

with some other squads, sat on wiretaps, followed suspects around, and in between meals, breaks, and wasting time doing nothing, Zucarelli and I tried to brainstorm ways to get enough probable cause to get a wiretap on Scarlotta.

"This really sucks, Zook. We've accomplished nothing since, umm, I don't know when. It's been a while. I'm really hating, my job these days."

"I know. I agree. I can't remember the last time I found work so fuck'n depressing. I'm thinking about putting in for a transfer. Maybe go back to anti-crime or something. Whatever I do, I gotta start seeing some action soon. I'm losing my edge, not to mention my mind."

"No Zook, don't do that. Don't leave me here all alone." I faked crying, but in reality I did not want to lose my partner and was concerned that he would leave. Everyone on the squad was feeling down and sticking to the one or two people they felt close to. There was no anger or hostility amongst us; we just were not in social moods.

"Well, I'll give it a few more weeks. I'd rather be here than back at a precinct, but this is killing me."

"Okay, let's really beat the bushes with Scarlotta. Maybe try a little more surveillance and try to track these Colombian pricks back to some drugs or…"

"Or maybe, we do something bold and rip off one of those loads of cash; excuse me, alleged cash."

*****

The drive to work this morning seemed to go fast, mostly because my clouded mind was far from the frustration of slow moving traffic. Walking in to the office, I heard some laughter and conversation. In the back of the office Simone, Julie, D, and a few others were sitting at their desks sporting smiles and having an animated conversation; Julie's smile was coupled with curling her hair with her forefinger. Candelaria was at his desk reading the paper and Doc, who was easing back in, was getting up from his chair and making his way to Simone and the others, though he appeared hesitant. That was how things used to be in our office; maybe things were starting to return to normal. Reardon was sitting at the desk in the supervisor's office, talking on the phone while holding up a piece of paper in front of his face. Walking over to get my office mail out of the rickety, tan filing cabinet, I looked out on our panoramic view of the Long Island Expressway and the apartment buildings on the other side, staring right at us.

Did the cartels ever think of getting an apartment there and just watch us, looking at all the flow charts and intelligence we post on the walls? Would they put a sniper there? It's amazing what we accomplish while we are so lax on operational security.

"Hey Babs, wassup?" I greeted our squad secretary, Barbara sitting right outside the supervisor's office.

"Oh there's plenty going on this morning."

"Really? What?"

"Read your mail. It's all there in black and white."

Grabbing my mail out of my folder, I quickly got back to my desk and started sorting through mail of mostly meaningless papers, documents and notices to find what Barbara was talking about.

"Good morning," Zucarelli greeted me as he came with two cups of coffee in his hands, handing me one of them and interrupting my frantic search.

"Hey, thanks, Zook, wassup?"

"Oh nothing really. My life is as fucked up today as it was yesterday. And you?"

"Ditto, brother. I'm not sure if my wife hates me, likes me as a friend or just finds me physically repulsive."

"You two been fighting a lot?"

"No, we're not fighting at all. That's the problem. She's polite and cordial, doesn't complain, but she's totally disengaged. Like a couple of college roommates just getting along."

"I don't know, Bob. I think that sounds pretty good. I'd take that over all the arguing and sniping I'm living through."

"I don't like it, Zook. I really want to stay married. I'm not the single and carefree type."

"Being afraid of being single is no reason to stay married, my friend."

"As opposed to what you're doing, living with your ex-wife."

"I told you, I've got kids. That changes everything. One day, you'll see."

"I know, you're right. It's so frustrating. I can't get to the bottom of what's wrong. I'm horny as shit, we don't have sex; we don't even kiss, nothing."

"Well, that's an easy problem to solve. I can introduce you to some babes."

"Thanks, but, uh, I'm not like that. Things may suck, but I don't want to cheat on my wife."

"Okay, but it sure sounds like..." then he stopped.

"Sounds like what, Zook?"

"Oh, nothing. I was just gonna say that it sounds like you're umm, really, uh, unhappy. That's all."

Pretty confident that Zucarelli was not saying what was on his mind, I didn't pursue it any further. He was not going to say what he did not want to say, and I was not sure I wanted to hear what he really wanted to say. I returned to my hunt for the news of day in my mail and found it. I read it. I was not surprised, but at the same time, I was surprised.

"Did you see this?" I asked Zucarelli as I passed the papers across the desk.

"What's this?" he asked as he put down his coffee and grabbed the papers from me.

"Oh, just an intra-office memorandum from ADIC Gunn to all NYO employees. You'll notice it's entitled 'personnel changes' which understates the matter at hand."

While the information was couched in euphemistic terminology, the message was clear: people were getting screwed and careers were getting ruined.

The SAC was removed from his position, but he handed in his retirement papers. The ASAC was also removed and transferred to headquarters as a unit chief. The FBI would claim it was a lateral transfer. It was the same pay, but it was, without question, a huge demotion. Zucarelli read through the memo.

"Ouch; that's an all out scorched earth assault. Gunn left no man standing."

"No, he didn't. I don't know how far you've gotten. You see who's out; did you see who's in?"

"Let's see." Zucarelli scanned down the memo and started reading again.

"Hmm. Rand Borton and Brian Cherrybrook? Weren't those the two douche bags from your internal affairs?"

"Yep, my words exactly. Only, we call it OPR, not internal affairs; but that's not the point."

Section Chief Borton was named the new SAC and Unit Chief Cherrybrook was named the new ASAC.

"How the hell does the FBI get away with this shit?"

"Which shit we talking about?"

"You kidding? Two guys who want a job, screw the guys who have those jobs, and then steal those jobs. What is that? If the NYPD was doing that, our union would be all over this like stink on shit. As a matter of fact, I don't think the brass would even try something as obvious as this."

"I'm surprised you're so surprised. You always talk about FBI politics."

"This is beyond politics, Bob. This is, uh, I don't know, this is fucked up."

"Yes it is. I hate to admit it, but I'm gonna do what every other FBI agent does when shit hits the fan."

"What's that?'

"I'm gonna consider myself lucky for not getting swept up in this, keep my head down, my mouth shut and keep doing what I'm doing."

Zucarelli did not respond immediately and just looked at me. "Whatever," he then answered me.

"Zook, I don't have a dog in this fight. It's none of my business."

"Yeah, whatever." He picked up his cup of coffee and walked away.

I wanted to stop him with a snappy retort. The word "whatever" with his dismissive attitude called for a response. Yet, as I often did in verbal sparring matches with Zucarelli, I decided not to take this any further. I knew Zucarelli was right - FBI Agents ran for cover whenever internal trouble started to boil up; it was every man for himself. This was not the end of this personnel shakeup.

Reardon was taken off the desk as the acting supervisor and was transferred to an FCI Squad. Without Franks around, they had to hold somebody on the squad accountable. Reardon was the second in command who participated in the assault that resulted in the death of a baby; he was the case agent when the car exploded. He was an easy target and he knew he was going down. Lou Dinella from the Organized Crime Branch was coming over as our new supervisor.

Like the last time I wanted to speak with Reardon, he was on the phone. This time I was not going to rudely interrupt him and I waited for him to hang up the phone. When he did, he turned his chair around to stare out the window. I gently knocked on the door frame. Reardon turned around and invited me in.

"Hey Bob, what's up?"

"Nothing, Steve. Listen, I, uh, I'm really sorry about what's happening here. You don't deserve this. Putting a guy with your experience on an FCI squad is just plain fuck'n stupid. How is that helping us accomplish our mission?"

"That's not even the worst of it, Bob."

"What? What else?"

"They busted me back to a GS-10. I'll be making the same as a rookie agent. This is really gonna hurt and not just me. My wife, my kids are all gonna suffer from this. All these years..."

"Steve, that sucks. I can't believe they'd come after you like this. Nothing that happened should fall on you."

"Well, it is what it is Bob."

"This probably is not the best time for this, but I want to apologize, Steve."

"Apologize? What for?"

"Nothing specific. It's just that I've always been a little jealous of you. I wanted to be in your position on the squad, you know, second in command and getting all those good cases; shit like that. I should've been a better team player instead of bitching all the time."

"I appreciate that Bob. But, you weren't completely wrong."

"What?"

"Yeah, I kinda took advantage of my relationship with Franks and worked it to my advantage. I should've shared the wealth a little more. I was greedy, so I owe you and the rest of the squad an apology. Maybe I'm getting what I deserve."

"No, you do not deserve this, Steve, not this." We both hesitated for a moment, collecting our thoughts. Then I continued, "Look what it takes for you and me to have a conversation like this. It was long overdue."

"Sure was, Bob."

Reardon stood up and held out his hand. I stood and walked around his desk. He was surprised when I added the man-hug to our handshake. I was a bit surprised myself. I gave him one more pat on the shoulder and walked out of the office.

Chapter 15

"Okay, Bob, here comes that skinny courier again with a bag of money. Wanna jump him?"

"I don't know Zook. We should; how many times are we gonna watch the money go in to Scarlotta and do nothing, just hoping something will change and we'll get a lucky break. How many more weeks are we gonna sit out here taking notes and pictures of the same old shit? I know it's time to jump 'em but then I keep thinking we'll blow it. What do you think?"

"The only thing I think is that we are definitely doing the insanity dance."

"The insanity dance?"

"Yeah, you know, we're doing the same thing, the same way, expecting different results. That ain't gonna happen."

"I know," I said with resignation, unable to make a firm decision.

"We got about five seconds to get out of this car, run down the block and jump him before he gets in to Scarlotta's office. Cast your vote."

"Fuck, I don't know."

"Well, I guess if we sit here for a few more seconds and make no decision, we've made a decision."

"I guess so. We spend the entire summer screwing around with Scarlotta and got nothing to show for it. I gotta believe there's a better way than ripping off one load of cash and risking the whole investigation, if you can even call this cluster-fuck an investigation. I mean, if by some miracle there's not money in there, or we can't get any information from the courier, once again, where does that leave us?"

"As usual, it will leave us holding nothing but our dicks."

"Just make sure we're holding our own dicks." I thought that was funny. Zucarelli didn't respond; he stared straight ahead rubbing his fingers across his moustache.

"Before you know it, the Christmas season will be here and it'll be impossible to work surveillance out here, with all the shoppers and tourists and whatever else the wind blows in."

We drove back to the office feeling demoralized. We had a lot of information and we knew we had a good investigation staring us in the face but we couldn't get it off the ground. We needed that wiretap to put it all together. The information we needed would only come from a wiretap. What a Catch-22.

Zucarelli and I decided that this would be a good time to break off and handle the bullshit administrative tasks that tended to get backed up and then get you in trouble. I had to drive upstate one day for firearms qualification. I had to go in to Manhattan another day for mandatory legal training. I was randomly selected for drug testing, which meant another trip in to Manhattan. I helped Doc on a few surveillances for one of his cases. One night, we made three arrests and executed two search warrants from an undercover operation that Candelaria and Simone had put together. Dinella was keeping a low profile, trying to get an understanding of how the drug squads worked. Like drug cases, mob investigations were mostly informants and wiretaps but didn't have as much of the street activity and excitement of drug work. Dinella seemed to be enjoying himself. He kept asking me for a briefing of the Scarlotta case, since he knew all about Scarlotta and his mob connections. I put him off, asking for him to wait till Zucarelli got back, so I wouldn't miss any important details. Actually, I didn't really need Zucarelli to help me give a briefing; I was just dodging Dinella because I had a strange feeling about him – one of those "I can put my finger on it" type of feelings.

Zucarelli had a few NYPD tasks at 1 PP that he needed to take care of and wanted a few days off to go hunting. He was the only person I knew from the city who went hunting. Before becoming an agent, I never touched a gun. I did not know anything about hunting or the outdoors – unless we were talking about outdoor basketball courts, schoolyards or street corners where we hung out as kids.

Like a dating couple who decided to take a break from each other, it seemed Zucarelli and I were both ready for a little "me" time. We'd spent a lot of time in the car together for the past few months. We were getting frustrated from our case going nowhere and were starting to get on each other's nerves. Nothing serious, nothing that threatened our partnership, but enough to welcome a break.

*****

Getting back from a cup of coffee and a few laughs with some of the squad, I found a message on my desk. I immediately returned the call.

"DEA, may I help you?" the phone was answered.

"Yes, Agent Dave Marcus please." The phone went silent for a moment.

"This is Agent Marcus."

"Dave, this is Bob Douglas with the FBI returning your call."

"Hey Bob. Listen, I think I may have some good news for you. We may be able to help you with your case on Scarlotta."

"My case on Scarlotta? How…"

"We checked DECS. We had an informant that is into Scarlotta and we saw that you indexed his name and address, so we're calling you like we're supposed to."

"Wow, thanks. I didn't think anybody really checked that system, never mind actually respecting it. I appreciate it."

"Yeah well, DEA is not all bad, huh?"

"Of course not. What's up?"

DEA Agent Marcus called me with what proved to be a lucky break. DEA arrested a drug dealer turned informant who was delivering money to Scarlotta. DECS was the acronym for the Drug Enforcement Coordination System. DECS was an interagency database for entering names and places that were under drug investigations. It was designed just for this purpose – so the multitude of different agencies working drugs didn't start targeting the same subjects. I had never heard of a time when the system actually worked; this may be a first. Marcus had one lighthearted demand – I attend the DEA undercover training they were offering, that I had so far avoided. If I went, he would share his informant. That sounded fair and Marcus seemed like a descent guy. I called Zucarelli. When he heard the good news, he said he would come back a day early. In reality, I knew he was looking for any reason to get out of the house and away from the ex and kids.

*****

"In other words, white guys in plaid shirts does not make

for a good drug surveillance," Marcus told the audience of cops and federal agents from many agencies fighting in the drug war.

"Do we ever wear plaid shirts?" Zucarelli whispered under his breath to me.

"I don't think so."

"Too bad."

"Too bad? Why?" I asked, also in a whisper.

"That might've explained why our surveillances of Scarlotta never worked out. Now, where back to square one. Oh well."

We got a chuckle out of that, but kept it silent; we didn't want to be disruptive or disrespectful. DEA was trying to provide a valuable service that they thought they were uniquely qualified to offer their law enforcement peers. I am not so sure the audience appreciated the offer; probably everyone there was forced to attend by their agency in the name of "inter-agency cooperation."

Cops from NYPD, Nassau and Suffolk County PDs and the State Police were there. So were federal agents from IRS, Customs and the Postal Inspectors.

"Shit, is there any federal agency not trying to claim a stake in the drug wars? Zucarelli asked, again under his breath.

"They're just following the money. It's all about the money, right?"

"Fuck'n A."

We listened to the rest of Marcus' presentation, not really paying attention while trying to appear attentive. When it was over, Zucarelli and I hung around as everyone mingled for a bit, waiting to speak with Marcus. Eventually, Marcus made his way over; we made small talk, thanked him for the presentation and then got down to business.

During a drug bust, one of the arrested drug dealers decided to cooperate and dropped the name El Gordo as the one who they delivered their drug money to. He didn't know what El Gordo did with the money, but it made its way back to the cartel in Colombia. The drug dealer took Marcus to the man they knew as El Gordo and that wound up being Scarlotta. To avoid prosecution, the drug dealer was now an informant.

"We see you got this case on Scarlotta that you put in DECS quite a while ago, so it's all yours," Marcus told us.

"Really? You're gonna hand over your informant to us just like that? No strings?" I was appreciative yet very skeptical.

"No strings, except you gotta babysit him. He's looking at a lot of years, so if you take your eyes off of him for a moment, he's in the wind. The AUSA agreed to hold off any plea agreements until you're done doing whatever you gotta do. Sound good?"

"Yeah, it sounds real good. I appreciate it. I gotta tell ya, Dave, I, uh, I've never seen this kinda cooperation between our agencies. I can't honestly say we'd do it for you."

"Well, to be honest in return, normally we wouldn't turn over an informant to you just like that. We've had a few heated discussions about it. But, everyone knows what you guys have been through lately and we want to show our support for the loss you've had. We compete a lot, and even screw each other over now and then, but, when it comes down to it, we are brother law enforcement officers. So, you got it. Just don't lose him, okay?"

"Okay. Thanks."

I guess being the object of pity wasn't all bad. If that's what it took for DEA to make such an unusual but generous offer, who am I to argue? Zucarelli and I kicked around a few ideas and planned out our approach to Dinella. Keeping an informant out of jail for a few days while working him on the street was manpower intensive. We'd have get a hotel room and stay with him 24/7. We would debrief him about everything he knew and then keep close tabs on him while he carried out some illegal activities under our watch. As Marcus warned us, we could not lose him.

Dinella, having been anxious for a briefing, made time for Zucarelli and me to meet with him. He listened carefully, asked some good questions and gave us some useful suggestions. That shouldn't have surprised us; Dinella was an experienced organized crime agent. He was used to protecting witnesses and operating informants.

I briefly reflected on my arrival in the New York Office as a young agent assigned to protect a mob witness to and from court. He was testifying against some of his own after working as a paid FBI informant with a contract. He was running a gambling racket for a small mob crew in Brooklyn. During cross examination he was asked how much he was getting paid. The other young agent and I were shocked to find out the informant was getting paid more than we were, though his benefits were questionable. I think the jury was just as shocked. The two defendants were found "not guilty." Sometimes, working with informants rubs juries the wrong way and they express their dissatisfaction via the verdict.

We had Luis Jiminez in our care and custody. He spoke excellent English, but sometimes acted as though he couldn't understand us. That was when we knew we were on to something. After a few hours of debriefing him and understanding how things worked, we became more comfortable with him, talking about his family and his hometown. We bought him lunch, shared some laughs and started calling him LJ. That was another risk of working with informants; usually they came off as regular, friendly people and despite their criminality, we developed relationships with them. That was not professional and spelled danger. When a male agent operated a female informant, there was a good chance a career was about to get ruined.

LJ, a short man with short black hair and a baby face, wore faded jeans and a plain dark blue, button down shirt; he was fairly non-descript and would never attract anyone's attention. I guess that was the best way to look when transporting hundreds of thousands of drug dollars at any given moment. LJ's job with the cartel was simple. He would get paged and call the number. He was told where to pick up the money and take it to a man named El Gordo. LJ knew El Gordo's real name was Tony Scarlotta but never called him by his real name. They were cordial with each other but visits were short and to the point; they never discussed business or much else.

LJ knew the money came from drugs, but he never saw the drug deals. Each step in the process was segregated from the other. He did not know the drug couriers by name, did not know where they lived or how to reach them. That was by design for events just as these. If he got arrested and decided to cooperate, he could not give up any information that would hurt cartel operations. He could still cooperate, but it would be difficult and dangerous.

Using undercover identity, we rented a room at one of the

hotels surrounding LaGuardia Airport.   We sat in the hotel room with two queen-size beds, watching television as we waited for LJ to get the next call to pick up the money.   That would be a critical opportunity for us to identify the drugs dealers and lay out a drug and money laundering enterprise on an affidavit for a wiretap.   We would have to run a very discreet but successful surveillance of LJ and everyone he met.   Lots of coffee and pizza consumed, as were cigarettes smoked by Zucarelli as we waited.   Night time came and Zucarelli and I had to switch off staying awake.   I called Elaine to tell her that I would be out all night.   She didn't seem to care.   The next morning, waking up in the same clothes, with no toothbrush, I felt disgusting.   It was early and I thought we could get someone to cover for us so we could get home to clean up, but the call finally came.   LJ had a pick-up to do.

*****

Fortunately, our squad was used to responding quickly and everyone moved with lightning speed to get in place.   Despite our years of experience, we still got excited over these street operations.   I got LJ wired up.   That was never fun - taping wires and equipment to someone else's sweaty body.   Candelaria was in the car with us, monitoring the radio on the transmitter's frequency, since all of the conversation was going to be in Spanish.   Zucarelli drove while I kept the squad advised of what was going on.   We had to stay out of the immediate area.   I was too white.   Zucarelli looked too much like a cop – yet he was successful in undercover work during his career.

  With all the talking in to the radios we were doing, we would get burned in a minute.   Yet, we had to stay close enough to pick up LJ's wire; it did not transmit very long distances. We also had to keep LJ under our surveillance every moment so he didn't try to run. We had to keep our undercover cop safe. Face to face transactions with drug dealers are never safe, especially if they are worried about being ripped off, arrested or both.

LJ had to remain cool and not let on that he was wired or cooperating. Any hint that there were cops around would mean a bullet in LJ's head. There was only one way this could work well; there were many ways this could turn to shit.

Detective Pena was the undercover, which on the radio, we referred to as the "uncle." Pena drove LJ in the undercover car.

"Okay, we're turning on 38th Avenue. We'll be pulling up in front of target location in a few seconds." Pena transmitted over the radio that was secreted in the undercover car.

"We got eyes on uncle." Simone called out. Simone was ethnic looking enough to fit into the neighborhood. Having Julie next to him made them look more like a couple than two cops.

"10-4, all units stand-by," I broadcast in response.

Simone told us when Pena pulled up and he described the location as a small, one story house of white wooden shingles. He could see in the windows, because there were no window shades, which sounded strange for a drug house. LJ got out of the car. Pena stayed in the car; I imagined he did nothing more than remain silent and stare ahead. Any indication he was talking on a radio, looking for back-up or showing any signs of being nervous, it was over – in more ways than one. LJ made it to the door. Simone must have found a good vantage point as he described the scene in detail.

"Source at door. Two Hispanic males at the door talking to him. I can see through the window; another male has a weapon pointing towards the door," Simone reported.

"That's not good," I turned to Zucarelli.

"Sit tight," he answered. His stroking of his moustache told me that he was as concerned as I was with that scenario.

Candelaria held up his hand and admonished us to "shh" as he listened to LJ on the wire. Candelaria started explaining what he was hearing.

"They want to know who is in the car. LJ told them it's his friend; he's just waiting for him. They want him to get out of the car."

I was thinking of what, if anything we should do, when the radio crackled again.

"Something's happening, they just pushed source out of way and came out. They're yelling at uncle," Simone's voice was loud and high pitched; he was nervous from what he saw.

Candelaria kept listening. "They're yelling for the uncle to come to the house."

Biting my lip, I wasn't sure what to do. If we charged in there trying to stop this whole thing, we may trigger a gun fight. If we didn't, our undercover may get killed. There was no good answer. I was waiting for Zucarelli or Candelaria to say something; they didn't.

"Uncle getting out of car. Repeat, uncle getting out of car," Simone was back on radio. "All units stand-by."

I knew Pena was an experienced undercover cop; he must've had a plan. I hoped he did.

"Alright, they are yelling at each other." Candelaria was trying hard to keep up on the translation while keeping us advised. "They want uncle to come over to the house. Pena's saying fuck you, I'm not coming out in the open. I can see those guns in the house."

Candelaria continued listening. "Come here, they keep telling uncle. Uncle keeps saying fuck you and now he yelled at LJ to come back to the car. Uncle told them to keep the money; someone else will come for it."

"Zook, this is fucked, whatta ya think?"

He did not answer immediately. He thought for a moment. He rubbed his moustache.

"I think we should let it play out. Pena's good; he knows what he's doing." Zucarelli stated what I was hoping, which was mildly reassuring.

I was expecting to hear a gunshot at any moment. Zucarelli had to be thinking what I was thinking: *this squad cannot take another shooting.*

"Okay, uncle yelled back that he is not coming over, they should keep their money." Candelaria gave us the update. We listened, waiting for the next shoe to drop.

"Uncle back in the car. I repeat, uncle back in the car." Simone brought his voice down to a whisper.

"10-4," I responded. "All units hold your position, we are monitoring the situation."

Everyone knew we were listening in, but I said that just to reassure them that were in control, though I wasn't really confident that we were.

"Okay, LJ is talking to them. He says that if they don't give the money, El Tigre will think he is getting ripped off. They may not like who he sends next."

"El Tigre?" I looked at Zucarelli.

He gave the "I don't know either" look.

"Okay, okay, it looks like they're giving him the money. They're giving him something." We could hear the relief in Simone's voice.

"Source in car with uncle. Source in car with uncle. They are driving off."

"Okay, Simone, hold your position and make sure they leave the house and try to follow the uncle." I told Simone and then let out one big sigh.

"That's 10-4."

"All units, keep surveillance on the uncle. Be alert for a rip-off." The squad knew that, but we still send out those broadcasts to remind everyone. We do not want to leave the safety of our operations to chance, any more than we have to.

Everyone acknowledged on the radio and we began a mobile surveillance. As usual, we knew how to switch off keeping the tail; we operated intuitively. We were good. We were better than good. We had no doubt we were the best in the FBI.

The first stage of this operation was a success. We got the money and identified a drug house. That will be a starting point for tracing the money back to a drug trafficking organization. Making it back to the office safely, we had to move fast to get everything done, before the next step of delivering the money to Scarlotta. If too much time went by, he and the cartel would get suspicious. We counted and copied the money, making sure each serial number could be read and recorded. This was evidence. We took stacks of cash and put them in plastic bags, shaking them vigorously. From each stack of cash, a small amount of white powder would accumulate on the bottom. Once we accumulated a good sample, we ran a preliminary test that showed positive for cocaine. No surprise. Most cash in the United States, especially twenties, would test positive for cocaine. But, a baggie of cocaine coming off money headed to a money launderer added to the probable cause. Every little bit helped.

"Okay, LJ, who is El Tigre?" I asked him as Zucarelli and I got him alone in the Interrogation Room.

"El Tigre. Everyone knows El Tigre. He is the boss. Everything is his. The drugs, the money, everything."

"What's his real name?"

"Ha, are you kidding me? I don't know that."

"Well, you're the one who brought up his name. How do you know him?"

"He's El Tigre. We all know EL Tigre. We don't know who he is, but we all know his name."

"Where is he? Where does he live?"

"He's in Colombia. I don't know where. You must be joking. I am nobody. I would not know El Tigre if he was standing right in front of me."

"Then who does know him? Who knows how to find him?"

"I don't know. Don't you know how this works?" He was trying not to break out in full laughter and really piss off Zucarelli and me. I didn't like that.

"Alright funny man, just wait here." I handcuffed LJ to the restraining bar and Zucarelli and I walked outside. Zucarelli slammed the door. That may have startled LJ, but I doubt it scared him.

"Whatta ya think, Zook. You believe him? Is it possible he doesn't know anything about this El Tigre?"

"I don't know if I believe him, but it's possible. That's how these cartel cells work. They keep each other in the dark. The mob could probably take a few lessons from them. Look, we can't be dicking around here much longer. We gotta get this scumbag back on the street and get that money into Scarlotta's hands."

We re-wired LJ as we got the cash back in the suitcase. The squad went back on the street with cameras in hand and the same basic plan. We needed LJ to hand the money to Scarlotta. While we wanted the conversation taped, we didn't want LJ engaging Scarlotta in any conversation different than usual. Drug dealers, mobsters and any criminal worth his salt knew when he was getting set-up. As soon as everybody took up a position around the Diamond District, we sent LJ in, although this time with no undercover agent. LJ always came alone, so that would have been too risky. We had five of us on the streets, in case LJ decided to run for it. We dropped LJ off at the corner and we watched him at every step. About one hundred feet before getting to Scarlotta Gold he was met by Danny D'Albote.

This conversation was easy to follow, it was all in English. D'Albote turned LJ around and started walking him back to the corner. Zucarelli called that out on the radio. We didn't expect that; we needed a hand to hand with Scarlotta as LJ said he always did. The plan remained the same. All we needed to was watch, take notes, take pictures and be ready for anything.

D'Albote asked LJ what he wanted, why was he there?

"I have a delivery for El Gordo. You know that. What's going on?"

"I don't know what you're talking about. Nobody here is

expecting anything. You need to leave. Don't come back here, ever."

LJ knew something was wrong, though he did not know what. He looked at D'Albote and then looked side to side, wondering if he was about to get killed. He looked back at D'Albote, then took a step backwards. He turned around and started running north on 5th Avenue.

"What the fu…" I couldn't believe what was developing.

Zucarelli got on the radio and gave out orders. "Source is running north on 5th Avenue. Get him, get him. Let the other male go."

"Doc and I got him. We'll cut him off," D got on the radio.

"I'm out on foot backing them up," Julie called in.

"I'm there too," Candelaria yelled into the radio as he was running.

Zucarelli and I were frozen in our seats; we knew we had enough out there to catch LJ; trying to run with his short legs and carrying a suitcase full of cash, he would not get far.

"What just happened, Zook?"

"I don't know Bob. No Scarlotta. No hand-off. We get D'Albote shooing off our informant."

"You think D'Albote sensed something was wrong?"

"Nah, he ain't that smart. He was tipped off, he was ready for this. The way he met LJ in the middle of the street and walked back to the corner. How many months did we sit out here watching these Colombians walk right into the store and hand the money directly to Scarlotta? This never happened."

"We got the source. Repeat source in custody." Julie got on the radio, a little out of breath.

"Let's get back to the office. Let's just go." Zucarelli was yelling, making no attempt to hide his anger and frustration.

Within an a couple of hours of setting out to what was to be the big break in the case, we found ourselves back in the Interrogation Room talking to LJ, handcuffed to the restraining bar. We didn't know how he could've tipped off Scarlotta. There seemed to be a lot we did not know.

"What happened out there?" Zucarelli sat on the desk, hovering over LJ.

"I don't know. You tell me. I didn't know what was going on?"

"Really? Why did you run?"

"Because I was scared. I thought I was about to get killed. I thought you set me up."

"You thought we set you up?"

"Yeah, why not? I did everything you told me and look what happened."

"So you conveniently ran off with the money, huh?" Zucarelli was now on his feet. Normally, I would think he was just playing bad cop. Now, I was afraid that he was becoming unhinged.

"No, I ran for my life. I wasn't gonna just dump the money right there on the street. Can you blame me? I didn't know what was happening."

"How did Scarlotta get tipped off LJ?" I asked, trying to bring down the hostile tone.

"I have no idea. You know I didn't do it."

"What about the guys at the house? Could they have called him?"

"What? They don't know who Scarlotta is. They wouldn't even know his name."

"Why not?"

"I told you. Don't you know how this works? Nobody knows anybody else."

I looked over at Zucarelli who nodded at me; what LJ was saying sounded right.

"Wait a second." I had an insightful thought. "What about those guys at the house? Now you know them. You know where drugs are being held. Aren't they worried you can target them for a rip off? Maybe things aren't as isolated as you're saying."

LJ looked at me and then looked at Zucarelli, expecting a response from him. None came. Zucarelli wanted an answer.

"Oh man. You just don't get it, do you? That's no drug house."

"Whatta ya mean?" I asked.

"C'mon, this is what I am trying to tell you. They brought the money there, that's all. They're gone. That's not their house. They somehow got in just for to this. There is nothing going on there."

Zucarelli and I looked at each other, trying not to show our surprise, or lack of understanding.

"Wait here," I told LJ, not that he could go anywhere. I looked at Zucarelli and nodded my head to the door. He understood.

"Are you thinking what I'm thinking?" I asked him.

"I think so."

We asked Simone and Julie to go back to that house and see what was going on. They did and what they found was exactly what we thought they would find. That was a vacant home, up for rent. The For Rent sign was taken down and the back door was forced open. Simone checked with the rental agent and did a quick background on the owner. It all checked out. The house was broken into only for this money transaction. We should've seen that. One again, nobody saw what should've been very obvious. Were we not as good as we thought we were?

"How did we get burned, Bob? Who could've let Scarlotta know?"

"I have no idea, Zook. I can't believe how bad this sucks."

LJ was returned to the DEA with our thanks. We had to let them know that LJ did what we asked him to do, but to no avail. We couldn't blame it on LJ, but we couldn't admit to our own screw-up, though we were sure LJ would let them know how naive we were.

Scarlotta changed all his phones and closed his bank accounts. Any wiretap we were hoping for, seemed more elusive than ever. We drove by Scarlotta Gold a few times and did a periodic surveillance. Scarlotta was keeping a low profile; at least for the time being. We didn't see any activity other than jewelry shopping; the weeks were passing and holidays were approaching quickly. Zucarelli and I had to re-group. Our investigation had a major set-back.

Chapter 16

December came and it was time for our squad's Christmas Party at McCormick's Pub across the street from the office. We rented out the second floor party room at fairly reasonable rates. McCormick's liked that we hung around their bar after work or when we had those endless waits for the undercover drug deals that never went on time, if they went at all. Everything in life is a little give and take. Much to my surprise, I talked Elaine into coming with me. I thought a nice night out, a little squad camaraderie with some alcohol and laughs would give our marriage a much needed boost. As usual, our squad secretary Barbara took control of the decorations. Red and green streamers, a wreath, a miniature Santa and a menorah sat on a table that had bottles of alcohol, soda, ice and blue plastic cups with cigarette butts floating in the remainder of the drink at the cup bottoms.

"Hey Zook, how's it going brother?" We gave each other a firm handshake and man hug as I came in to the party with Elaine.

"You know my wife Elaine."

"Hey, beautiful." Towering over her thin, 5'2" frame, he reached down and gave her a hug. For a moment, it looked like he was reaching down to grab her ass. Surely he wouldn't do that to his partner's wife. I watched anyway – just to be sure."

"Where's the Mrs. Or the ex-Mrs?" I asked him.

"That's the point, she's still the ex. I'm here alone."

At that point, Simone and his wife came in, arm in arm. Simone smiled at Zucarelli and started walking over. When he noticed me, he turned and kept walking.

"What the fuck was that, Zook? Some reason Simone didn't want us meeting his wife?"

"Eh, that's just it, Bob. That's not his wife. That's his girlfriend. Don't you recognize her? She works at the bank on the first floor of our building."

"No, I don't know her. Isn't Simone still married?"

"Yeah, but you know…"

"Holy fuck, you're kidding," I reacted as Elaine let go of my hand and stepped back, a look of shock on her face.

"Ya see; he knew you'd react like that. That's why he avoided you."

This was not a conversation for Elaine's ears; I turned to her, "Hey, you know Julie and our secretary Barbara. She brought some friends with her. You want to mingle with the girls?" I asked Elaine.

"Yes I do." She walked away.

"Zook, Zook."

"Huh? What?" He was obviously distracted.

"Stop checking out my wife's ass, please."

"I wasn't doing that."

"No?"

"No. I was checking out the babes Barbara brought with her. You know why they come to our parties, don't ya?"

"Open bar?"

"Well, that too. But more importantly, they're all cop groupies and I'm gonna be sticking my cop cock into one of them tonight. You can count on that."

I moved on to socialize with the rest of the squad. Doc was with his wife and he seemed to be in good spirits. Dinella also came with his wife; he had been the supervisor long enough to be one of the squad. Reardon also showed up and we all gave him a warm welcome. We re-lived a few of the cases – the good and the bad – and had some good belly laughs. As far as office parties went, this one seemed to be going pretty well. Within about ten minutes of that thought, things changed when I felt a tug on my arm.

"Let's go," Elaine ordered me in a firm commanding voice.

"What? We're having a good…"

"No. Let's go right now. I'm serious."

I looked around to say good-bye to Zucarelli, but did not see him within the few seconds I thought I had before Elaine went into a complete meltdown. We grabbed our coats and I tried to act like I didn't see everybody eyeing our unexpected, hasty departure. She was mostly mumbling to herself as we walked across the street towards the garage. We got to the car and as she was about to open the door I heard her screech. She was looking at the car next to her as she stepped back, yelling and cursing. Reaching for my weapon, I ran around the car to where she was just standing. Moving Elaine aside, I looked in the car. It took me a second to understand what I was looking at; and when I did, I did not know how to respond. There was Zucarelli, sitting in the back seat, with a smile on his face, while some girl was sucking his dick. Our presence had no effect on him or his companion. Nothing stopped. He nodded his head, casually acknowledging me, as if we were simply passing each other in the office hallway.

"What kind of disgusting animal is he? That's your friend

that you look up to so much?" Elaine was yelling at me as I drove home.

"He was just…"

"Just what? Getting a blow job in a car in a parking lot. That's gross enough, but he's married."

I was going to point out that he was not married, but that did not seem like the right thing to do.

"Okay, but why were we rushing out of there to begin with?" I was trying to get off the topic of Zucarelli.

"Because I couldn't believe what I was seeing and hearing. I guess I shouldn't have been surprised by your partner. You are all sick. Those girls were a bunch of tramps. I think they all came to your party just to screw some cops."

"Well, that's them, I…"

"Oh and that female agent you think is so nice…"

"Who, Julie?"

"Yes, Julie. She's screwing around with that other guy on your squad, what's his name, D or Z or something like that?"

"Yeah, D. They're not…"

"Their like everyone else there, all screwing each other."

"What? They were both there with their spouse or with somebody. I don't…"

"You don't see anything, Bob."

"I don't see anything? What does that…"

"You can't see what's staring you in the face, Bob. But I do. I saw them both leave for the bathroom at the same time. Then they came back at the same time. They kept looking at each other like little children who just played doctor. You are all a bunch of disgusting pigs." She was yelling at me.

"Hey, hey. Why you mad at me? I don't do that. That's

them. Why are you taking this out on me?"

"Because you seem so happy there these days. And you love this Zook guy. Maybe you are just like them. What should I think?"

"You should think that I just like my job. And yeah, things have been better. We've been through a lot there. You shouldn't..."

"I shouldn't what, Bob? I shouldn't trust my husband, is that it?"

Where did that come from? Why would she accuse me of that just because of everyone else?

I would not find out where that came from. The conversation simply ended.

✳✳✳✳✳

"Hey, you've been pretty quiet the last few weeks. What's up?" Zucarelli asked me as we found ourselves once again out on surveillance. Doc had put a good case together and we were sitting in the car as usual, outside of a restaurant.

Pena was back at it, trying to lure some drug dealers to launder their money through our undercover operation, all while having an expensive meal, courtesy of our undercover bank account. If that worked, it would be a lot easier than trying to do track the money back to the drugs as we attempted with Scarlotta, unsuccessfully. Zucarelli and I had not given up on Scarlotta. With no hot leads at the moment, it was best to let things cool down. Unless DEA or some other agency started hounding him, Scarlotta's suspicion would subside and sooner or later, he would go back to doing business they way he used to. We were sure of it. We were hopeful. We wanted his ass in jail.

"Not much. I'm just got a lot of things on my mind," I answered him with little emotion.

"I bet. How about telling your ole partner here what happened at the party. Why did the two of you go storming out of there? That's kinda been the subject of office scuttlebutt, ya know?"

"Scuttlebutt?"

"Yeah scuttlebutt, that means, like gossip…"

"I know, Zook. I know what scuttlebutt means. It's just not the kind of word I expect to hear from you."

"Well, you know me. I like to surprise you now and then."

"No shit. Like having my wife walk up on you getting a bj in the car. That was quite a surprise."

"Ahh, now we're getting somewhere. I take it that upset her."

"Yes, it upset her. She thought it was pretty nasty, especially since you're living with your ex-wife."

"Hey Bob, I don't mean to disrespect your wife or nothin', but in all honesty, if I feel like getting a bj by some bim in the back of the car, that's none of her fuck'n business."

"No, I guess it's not."

"Besides, from what I hear, she was pretty steamed before you saw me; that's why you went running out of there. Yes? No?"

"Yes, she was pretty steamed."

"Let's hear it partner."

I explained to Zucarelli how disgusted Elaine was with what she thought was a lot of loose sex going on in the squad. Simone showing up with a girlfriend and then thinking D and Julie left the party to get it on somewhere, really upset her.

"Well, she's right about that," Zook said.

"Right about what?"

"About D and Julie. You didn't know that? I thought everyone knew that. It's one of the worst kept secrets I've ever heard."

"I heard the rumors; I didn't believe it. I guess I don't see what's going on around me."

"Maybe you don't."

"Even so, why did she lash out on me, though? Why accuse me of cheating like that?"

"Guilty conscience, why else?" Zucarelli responded immediately with no hesitation.

"Hey." Instinctively, I swung my arm at him, with the edge of my hand heading for his face. He leaned back as far as he could in the car, turned his head and blocked my swing enough for this to be nothing more than a few of my fingers slapping his temple.

"What the fuck was that?" Zucarelli turned, his eyes opened wide and a bit of spit making out of his mouth as he yelled at me.

"Well fuck you. You just said that my wife is cheating on me. How the fuck…" Zucarelli did not interrupt me, but his stare spoke volumes and I stopped.

"You know what, Zook?"

"What Bob?"

"Whew. You're probably right. No, actually I'm pretty confident you're right. She's doing somebody. I'm sure of it. I've been kidding myself, but I guess hearing it like that was like getting hit by a train. It was too much to absorb at one time."

"I kinda suspected it, and wanted you to at least consider it.

I'm sorry to bring it up Bob, but I don't like watching you get played. Cheating on a good guy like you. That's bullshit Bob. Who is he? Who is he, Bob?"

"I think it's some friend of hers from work. She was always saying he was good to talk to; he was like a girlfriend, all that bullshit, like we were still in high school. I shoulda known."

"Yeah, but who is it? What's his name?"

"What's the difference? We can't do anything about it."

"Oh no? Some cocksucker decides he can sleep with your wife while you're out here on the streets keeping his fat ass safe. I don't think so. We'll take a fuck'n baseball bat right to..."

"Zook, c'mon; I appreciate your support, but unfortunately you know we can't do shit like that."

"No, *you* can't do shit like that. I tell you what, one time, when I was in uniform in the Bronx, we found out someone was screwing our sergeant's wife; we found that prick and beat the..."

"Zook, Zook, stop. Stop right there. Do not say another fucking word. Please."

"What, you don't believe me?"

"No. I do believe you. I really do. That's why I don't want you saying one more thing. Remember, my creds say FBI, not NYPD. Things are different for us. We got different rules."

"No, we got the same rules. But FBI Agents aren't NYPD cops; that's all."

*****

The holiday season and even the days following New Years were very slow, even for a usually busy FBI-NYPD Drug Task Force. Vacations and the general malaise of returning to work after a week or two off, kept things quiet. The good news was that things were returning to normal after all our setbacks. The bad news was that things were returning to normal. We all loved working drugs, but there was no escaping the squad dynamics. Personality differences were re-emerging. We were more willing to argue, insult each other and talk behind each other's backs. We had a few new FBI Agents and NYPD Detectives on the squad who didn't go through all those crises with us. They were choosing their sides and the divide could be seen by who sat with whom when we were just hanging around.

"Agent Douglas, may I help you," I answered the phone.

"You sick bastard. You are a bunch of crazy goons. I can't believe you carry guns and badges. What is wrong with you?" The screaming hurt my ears. Elaine sounded maniacal.

"What? What's wrong?"

"Don't do that, Bob. You know exactly what I am talking about. How dare you do that to him?"

"Do what to who? What the fuck are you talking about?" I was trying not to yell, but it was impossible to keep my voice from getting loud.

"To Bruce, that's who. What did you care, Bob? This marriage was over and you had all those girls hanging around you just giving it away. What did you care if I found somebody?"

That pierced my heart. I had to hear it again, this time right from her lips. That shut me down. Sweat and chills overcame me. I could barely speak; I could barely breathe.

"What Elaine, what are you talking about?" I was trying not to cry.

"You almost killed him. He had to go to the hospital. He's pretty hurt. Who was behind this, you're crazy friend Zook? Huh?"

"Elaine, why would you think he would do something like that?"

"Because they said they were cops and threatened him, that's why. He never saw them coming. He can't describe anybody or anything. That sounds like your cop buddies to me."

"Elaine, this is…"

"This is it, Bob. I will be gone by the time you get home. Don't ever call me or speak to me again. You'll hear from my lawyer." Then I heard that click. I held the phone for several seconds before hanging up.

Sitting there silently, I lowered my head and stared at the floor; I had to gain some level of composure. Too many thoughts were going through my head for any one of them to be coherent. Then, as I grabbed the sides of my head and looked up at the ceiling, something told me to turn around. As I did, I was met by Zucarelli's stare. He smiled at me and gave me a wink. Sitting next to him was Simone, who held up his cup of coffee as if proposing "cheers."

I never did speak to or see Elaine again. With no kids, no house and hardly any assets, the divorce was handled through our attorneys. I could not decide if I was sad that my marriage failed or happy that I was free from a failed marriage to a cheating bitch. It seemed like the answer was easy; but it was not. Some nights, lying in bed by myself, I would break down and cry. At work, I put on a face of bravado. Zucarelli saw right through me, but always pretended he didn't.

*****

The weeks and months went on and we worked as usual. As the winter subsided, the workload seemed to pick up. Ironically, the busiest day for drug dealers was Christmas, because they knew so many federal agents had a holiday day off. Zucarelli and I picked up a few new cases and worked them as we always did. Surveillances, undercover deals, search warrants raiding homes and arresting people. We lived for that. We helped out with the other cases on the squad. Zucarelli would entertain me with his stories getting laid here, getting a blow job there, and doing a threesome somewhere else. I no longer judged him; I envied him – not just for the action he was getting, but for his carefree attitude to life and everything in it. Why was being good and loyal and following all the rules the right thing to do? Look where that got me. I was one miserable bastard.

"Hey, Zucarelli, can I see you for a minute." Dinella came out of his office signaling for Zucarelli to come to his office.

Zucarelli and I looked at each other, both of us a little surprised at that. Dinella rarely spoke to us. We had no problem with him, but had no reason to talk with him. Zucarelli and I got up and started walking to Dinella's office. Dinella gave us a strange look as we approached the door.

"Uh, Bob, I only asked to talk to Mark."

"Oh, I'm sorry, I thought..."

"Forget it; no problem, you are partners. Have a seat guys."

That was a little embarrassing, though I realized that Dinella did ask to speak only to Zucarelli and not me. Here we were, back in the same seats where we used to listen to the stupid ideas from Franks. Now that he was gone, I felt guilty for having had such little respect for him.

"Mark, my old squad has put together a RICO case on one of the Morelli strongmen. Looks like he got tipped off, now he's on the lam. I know have you have some good sources into the Morellis and thought maybe you could help us out."

"Sure, I'd be happy to, Lou. But, you're known to have some pretty good informants yourself. I'm surprised you need my help with that."

"Well, Mark. You know how informants work. Sometimes they can help, sometimes they can't and sometimes they screw you."

"Amen to that. So whatta ya need."

"We have a good case against an enforcer who answers directly to Morelli himself. He's known as The Ragman; his real..."

"Johnnie The Ragman Ragusa."

"You know him?"

"Oh yeah." Zucarelli and I looked at each other and Dinella saw the smiles.

"What? What's up? What's so funny?" Dinella asked.

"Nothing's funny, Lou. It's just that we saw Ragman meet with Scarlotta sometime last year. We thought that was pretty important for probable cause, though the AUSA didn't seem to agree."

"Scarlotta met with The Ragman?" Dinella asked, even though that was what we just told him. He seemed alarmed.

"He sure did. This is good. If we grab his ass, maybe he'll flip and give up something on Scarlotta," Zucarelli suggested.

"I bet he will. Just about every wiseguy who's been up against a RICO has cooperated. Whatta you think Lou?" I felt the need to add something to the conversation.

"Hold up a second," was Dinella's response. "How come I didn't know about this?"

"Uhh, well, Lou, this happened before you got here." I wasn't sure how to answer that.

"I understand, but you know I come from the Morelli Squad; wouldn't you think I would want to know this; that a Morelli enforcer showed up in your case?"

"I, uh, I, guess so, Lou. It never crossed our minds. I mean, nothing came of it and I kinda forgot it." I wasn't sure why Dinella was getting irritated.

"I didn't think of it either, Lou. In all fairness, we didn't keep anything from you. It was some intel we had in a case that didn't seem to be going anywhere, that's all." Zucarelli was running interference between me and my supervisor.

"Alright, anyway, like I said, we got a RICO warrant against him. We had a source give him up on an old homicide. Then DEA got him on some drug counts and they want to get hold of him too. We need to get him first and somehow cut DEA out of this thing."

"Cut out DEA? If they have evidence and a good case, why would you cut them out?" Zucarelli asked, though I was sure I knew the answer.

"Because this is an organized crime case that happens to involve drugs. We, the FBI have jurisdiction over the mob, not DEA. It's bad enough you drug squads have to fight with them, but we can't have Congress or anyone else thinking that DEA has a dog in the fight against the mob. It's our thing. That cannot change." Dinella was slamming his middle finger against the desk as he pontificated the FBI's steadfast position on its investigative primacy.

"Wow, he is tightly wound, isn't he?" Zucarelli asked when we got back to our desks.

"Sure is. So, whatta ya think? You gone be able to get any info on The Ragman? You got anybody to call?"

"Ah, I don't have to call anybody. I'll be getting a call in a day or two. I'm positive about that."

"Agent Douglas, may I help you?" I answered my phone a few hours after our meeting with Dinella. Every time the phone rang, I hoped it was Elaine calling, though I could not imagine what that would lead to.

"Bob, Dave Marcus from DEA here. Remember me?"

"Of course I remember you, Dave. How you doing?"

"Doing good. How were your holidays?"

"All good and you?" I was not about to share my woe with him.

"Good. I'm sorry things didn't work out with that informant we handed over to you."

"That was unfortunate. We really appreciated your helping us out like that."

"No problem, but I could use a favor in return."

It wasn't as if I didn't see that coming. I knew he wasn't calling just to chew the fat with me.

"Sure what's up?"

"Listen, we put a case together on a mob guy named Johnnie Ragusa; did you ever hear of him?"

"Yes, I have." I had to keep myself from laughing; for some reason I was not surprised by the timing of Dinella's request and Marcus' call. Something stunk and somebody wasn't telling me something.

"Well, we know that one of your organized crime squads put a RICO case together on him and we think they're trying to go around us."

"What makes you think that?"

"We got him doing a hand to hand drug deal with an undercover agent. We were ready to lock him up, but it seems he took off 'cause your guys were going to charge him with RICO. We'd like to work together to find him, but we're kinda getting the FBI could shoulder."

"Oh, okay. So what can I do for you?"

"We were hoping that maybe you could talk to your fellow FBI Agents and let 'em know how we helped you. We know you have good informants in the mob and we have some good intel that may help finding him. It would probably be better for all of us if we worked together."

"Sounds good. I'll see what I can do."

Zucarelli knew something was up with that phone call and waited patiently to hear what it was about. When I told him he broke out in a big laugh, and I followed.

"It doesn't take long for this shit to make full circle, huh?" he said.

"I guess not. It's a small law enforcement world out there. What should we do? Go to talk to Dinella?"

"You can't do that. He's made it pretty clear how he feels about involving DEA. He's already upset that you didn't tell him about Ragusa meeting Scarlotta. You go in there now, after what he just said, suggesting that we work with DEA and it'll probably get worse for you than when Franks was around. You don't want that."

"No I don't. But you know, we kinda do owe DEA a favor."

"Bob, there is no such thing as owing a favor. If it was really a favor, there is no chip to cash in, kapish?"

"I kapish."

Zucarelli was right. Didn't I learn my lesson about trying to do the right thing? I keep screwing myself over.

*****

As Zucarelli said would happen, within a day he got the call he expected. We knew when and where we would be able to find The Ragman. That night we had a briefing for our squad and the Morelli Crime Family Squad, who was working with us, at Dinella's invitation. The operation had one goal - arrest The Ragman.

"Okay everybody, you have your assignments. Remember, we cannot make the arrest at the primary location. Our information is that Ragman will be dropped off at the location and according to our intel, he will be there for only about twenty minutes. When he leaves, we will conduct a very loose surveillance. If we get burned, lives can be lost. Any questions?" I asked.

"Umm, I have a question. So, if it starts getting hot, we let him go rather than get burned? Is that the call?" an agent from the Morelli Squad asked.

"Yes, at least for the first two or three miles. We cannot have them suspect that we were on them at the first location. Keep it loose."

We broke up and spent the next few minutes talking, getting our gear, running to the bathroom and then out on the street. Positions were taken surrounding Pops' restaurant at all intersections ready to begin the surveillance when Ragman arrived.

"I'm nervous, Bob. We can't mess this up. If we get burned and there's even a hint that Pops gave Ragman up, you know what will happen."

"I know Zook. We got a lot of experience out there. It'll be okay."

I was not that sure. Surveillances get burned all the time. One car gets too close or stays on the tail one too many blocks and it's over. Zucarelli was right. If this got burned, Pops was dead. Within thirty minutes, we took positions up around Pops' restaurant. Zucarelli and I set up on the highway from where I had fallen down the hill last time we were there.

Standing there in the dark on the side of the BQE, Zucarelli watched with binoculars, not expecting anything to happen for another fifteen minutes or so, according to our information. We were taking it easy and talking about nothing until we saw some bright flashes down the hill. Watching the car arrive, we saw Ragusa walk in to Pops' place. Our information was good. We called on the radio that Ragusa was there, and for everyone to sit tight, waiting for Ragusa to leave. Only minutes later, we heard the blasts of what we knew were gunshots. More flashes, more blasts.

"What the fuck is happening?" Zucarelli called out in a panic.

"Holy shit, what the…"

As quickly as it started, it stopped. We called it in on the radio and everybody rushed to the scene. We were waiting to hear tires screech and see a car fleeing. We did not, which should not have surprised us; we never saw any cars approach.

"Take the car, I'll meet you there." Zucarelli jumped the barrier on the shoulder and ran down the hill. I got in the car and headed to the restaurant. With reds lights on and siren blaring I was screaming in to the radio, asking if anybody saw a get-away car. Nobody did.

I went to the back entrance that led to that little meeting room in the back. Moving cautiously, careful not to step on any shell casings, bloody footprints or any evidence, I knew I was heading to a blood bath.

The Ragman's body, riddled with bullets, sprawled on the floor, lying in his blood. Another male that I had never seen looked the same. I walked out the door into the restaurant and back towards the kitchen. There was Pops. Two bullet holes in his head. As I turned to walk back to the front of the restaurant to clear my head, Doc signaled for me to come to where he was standing behind the food counter. Connie was also dead.

Other than knowing this was a mob hit, I could not figure out what this was all about. Who had to kill The Ragman right now? Pops and Connie were collateral damage, unless they someone knew that Pops made the call to Zucarelli.

Zucarelli. This is going to destroy him. Where is he?

I wanted to be with him when he actually saw the bodies; everything he feared would happen, did happen, and it was even worse than he imagined. Where the hell was he? He was not in the restaurant. Nobody had seen him. I went into a panic. All this gunfire and my partner was missing, again.

Flashing back to the day the car exploded and couldn't find him, I remembered how sure I was that he was dead, but it all worked out. He and I talked about luck. Tonight, I feared our luck had run out. Grabbing our flashlights, some of us ran back to the hill behind the restaurant where Zucarelli had been running down. Everybody wanted help, but we needed cops and agents to secure the crime scene and wait for the crime scene investigators and medics to do their thing. Yelling at the top of our lungs, we spread out. Moving quickly, yet carefully and methodically like a crime scene search, beating aside the brush hoping to find something, anything.

"Shh, shh, I hear something," Candelaria yelled out.

"Zook, Zook is that you? Where are you?" I yelled as soon as there was silence.

Nothing. We waited. Looking at each other with fear written all over our faces, we readied to resume the search.

"No wait, I heard something," Simone said.

"Yes, yes I did too." My voice crackled and I got choked up.

"There, there." Julie pointed to some movement in the brush.

Yelling his name, we ran in that direction. I got there first and there was Zucarelli, holding the back of his head, trying to stand up. I could see the blood on the back of his head, dripping down his hand and arm. He was talking, but was incoherent and fell back down.

"Easy buddy." I held him by his elbow. Then I yelled, "Get an ambulance, right fuck'n now."

✳✳✳✳✳

"You know, this sitting by your hospital bed is getting a little old." I told a now awake and alert Zucarelli.

"And you being by my hospital bedside tells me something."

"Like I said last time, nothing you wouldn't do…"

"No, that's not it. It tells me that working with you is bad for my health. "

"Hey, I never promised you a rose garden, asshole."

"Bob, what happened?"

"It was bad, Zook. Real bad."

"Pops?" Zucarelli leaned forward, trying to prop himself up on his elbows.

"I'm sorry, buddy."

"Motherfuckers." He fell back onto his pillows with his hand on his forehead.

"That's not all."

"What?"

"Your girl, Connie. They got her too."

"Holy fuck." Now both hands were covering his face.

Zucarelli had been hit from behind, most likely with the butt of a gun. The wound and the circumstances made that clear. The killers were hiding in the brush that Zucarelli was coming through, and made their escape the same way, to cars not too far away, waiting for them. They must've known he was a cop; that's why they didn't kill him. That also explained why we didn't see or hear a getaway car. They knew what they were doing and they were well prepared. Someone high up in one of the crime families thought Ragusa was so much of a threat that he had to be taken out right away.

The doctor came in and after looking at charts, x-rays, gave Zucarelli the once-over. He assured Zucarelli that while the hit was not serious, it was going to get more painful, especially as the painkillers that were pumped into his veins wore off. The doctor wrote him a prescription and he was released.

"You know, that head of yours can't take too many more blows, I mean, it's not screwed on that tight to begin with." We got settled in the car.

"No shit. This is fucked up. First the shooting in the Bronx, then the car bomb, and now this. My luck has got to be running out."

"Let's not talk like that, Zook. Though, I was kinda thinking the same thing."

"It's alright, Bob. In my will, I left my ex-wife and kids to you. If I check out, at least I get the last laugh."

"Now we're getting stupid. We gotta figure out what happened tonight. It doesn't make sense. The mob takes out a hit on The Ragman, and from the look of things, they knew we were there. Why would they do it right under our noses?"

"Obviously they were in a rush. Besides, they seemed to know exactly how we'd be set up. I guess they didn't expect me to come down that hill on foot, though."

"Yeah, but…"

"Hey, Bob, not for nothing, but can we leave this brainstorming session for tomorrow. I gotta give my brain a rest." Then he settled back in to the car seat and dozed off.

Pulling up in front of his house, I had to nudge him to wake up.

"So, when do you think you'll be coming back to work?"

"When am I coming back? Whatta ya mean when?" I wasn't sure if Zucarelli was confused by my question or still in a daze.

"I'm talking about when you're coming back. You need a few days off."

"I don't think so. Sitting around my house is gonna suck. We got some work to do. If I just sit around thinking about this, I'll drive myself friggin' crazy."

"Okay buddy. Hey listen, I'm really sorry. I know what you lost tonight. This is…"

"Pick me up at 7. See you in the morning."

Zucarelli walked slowly along the cracked pavement to the doorway of his modest Long Island single family house, still a little unsteady on his feet. He will be with his children and ex-wife, a situation I consider strange. I will go home alone to my empty apartment.

Chapter 17

"Look, this is a little bizarre, sitting here in the car in a dark alley. What's going on?"

"Sit tight. You'll see."

"Okay, but what are we doing in Valley Stream? Aren't we a little out of your jurisdiction?"

I wasn't sure why Zucarelli was acting so mysteriously, having a meeting in Nassau County, just over the border of New York City. If we were meeting an informant of his, I didn't think all this drama was necessary.

"That's the idea. We didn't want to risk getting spotted. Nobody out here should recognize us."

"Okay." It was obvious that asking any more questions was pointless.

We sat there in silence, awaiting something or somebody. In a few minutes, headlights appeared and the car stopped. Zucarelli turned off his headlights and then flashed his brights twice. The other car hit its brights three times. Zucarelli then hit his brights one more time and kept the headlights off. The other car then approached with its headlights still on, turning them off before pulling up next to us. Sitting in the passenger seat, I could not see who was driving that car, and Zucarelli seemed to be deliberately blocking my view.

"What the fuck, Zucarelli, who's that?" The voice in the other car was low and raspy.

"FBI Agent Bob Douglas." Zucarelli answered.

"Oh fuck." The driver put the car in gear and started to pull away."

"Hey, hey it's okay. He's a blue. He's my partner," Zucarelli yelled at him.

The car stopped and pulled back slowly.

"You know you don't spring people on me like that. I've worked too hard to stay deep."

"I know, I'm sorry. What did you find out?"

"It's not good. The Ragman had an agreement to cooperate with the DEA; that's why he was still out on the street. DEA wants to get him back and have him spill his guts."

"No shit. The Ragman flipped. Well, fuck my grandma," Zucarelli answered. I hadn't heard that one, and was about to laugh, but knew this was not the time.

"He was going to cooperate, then he found out the FBI was coming after him with some new charges, so he knew his plea deal would fall apart," our mystery man told us.

"I think I see where this is going," Zucarelli said, then looked at me, getting only a blank stare in return.

"You got it. Somehow, Morelli found out that Ragman was cooperating and knew where to find him. They took him out while they had the chance."

"Son of a bitch, how the hell did they know…"

"That's just it, Mark. They knew exactly where to find him. You guys got a fuck'n leak somewhere. That's the word."

"Leak? Who…"

"That's all I got. I gotta go. This is not a good idea, meeting like this. If I get any more I'll let you know through the channel. Don't call me and I'm not gonna be meeting you. Make sure your partner here is cool. Okay?"

"Okay," Zucarelli answered him.

The mystery man drove off, quickly. Zucarelli was motionless and stared out the windshield in to the darkness. The rubbing of his moustache began. I knew what the meant. Then he looked at me. This was his ballgame. I waited for him to speak.

"Well, you heard it. You've got a leak in the FBI."

"That's not what I heard, Zook. I heard that *we* had a leak. Maybe it's NYPD."

"Bullshit. No NYPD on our squad is leaking."

"Well fuck you; it's not an FBI Agent either." My voice was getting loud to match his as we became defensive.

"Alright, alright. Let's just hold it right here. All we know is that there is a leak and we gotta figure this out or we're dead."

"We don't know shit. Who is this guy anyway? Maybe he don't know what he's talking about."

"Oh, he knows. He's one of our intel detectives. He is in deep cover. He took a big risk meeting with us. Believe me, he knows."

The silence overtook us again. Sitting in the dark seemed so symbolic at the moment.

"DEA didn't know about this, did they? Did you tell that Agent Marcus anything?"

"Hell no. Besides, they conveniently forgot to mention that they had a deal with Ragusa. Is anybody around here telling the truth?"

"Doesn't seem that way. What do we do now, Bob?"

"I don't know, Zook. We gotta move carefully. Let's regroup and think this out. I think we need to keep this between me and you. You know what I mean?"

"Well, we can agree on that."

*****

"Move, move, make the arrest." With that order over the radio, Zucarelli came running in to the parking lot to arrest the poor schmuck who just sold 5 kilos of cocaine to our undercover agent. Zucarelli and I had spent the last several weeks trying to help out anybody and everybody on the squad, with whatever they needed. We took midnight shifts on the wiretaps, surveillance on the weekends, processing evidence, fingerprinting and transporting prisoners to jail and getting our firearms qualifications and annual physicals out of the way. We did anything we could to stay busy, but not move on our case until we had a better idea of what to do and who to trust. Now, we were just sitting at our desks, shuffling paper.

"Zook."

"Yes, Mr. Douglas."

"Time for you to take a smoke break, ain't it?"

"I think it is." Zucarelli gave me an inquisitive, yet understanding look. We got up and left the office to take our walk down Queens Boulevard.

"You got an undercover drug squad in NYPD that isn't in bed with DEA or FBI or anybody else, just NYPD?" I asked him.

"Of course we do. Everything we do on a federal task force, we also do on our own, just to make sure it gets done right, if you know what I mean."

"After all this time, I think I know exactly what you mean. I got an idea."

"We can use some ideas. Let me hear it."

*****

We went back on surveillance, only Zucarelli and I, with nobody on the squad knowing. We weren't going to do anything; we just wanted to see what the action looked like. It was back to normal. Young Colombian men would occasionally come to Scarlotta Gold with suitcases, knapsacks or gym bags stuffed with what had to be money. Apparently, no law enforcement agencies had been watching Scarlotta; he and the Colombians must've thought it was safe to get back in business. It took a few days for the opportunity to present itself and I was relieved; I was concerned that a squad of busy, action-oriented undercover detectives was getting impatient.

"Okay, Scarlotta is out. Wait for confirmation and bring the undercover in," an unknown voice called in on the police radio Zucarelli was holding.

"Look, if shit hits the fan, just slip out the back door, and I'll pick you up later."

"You got that right," I answered Zucarelli. We agreed – I was never there.

Scarlotta was seen getting in a cab and he was followed across town where he was at least thirty minutes away, in case he decided to return. The signal was given, an undercover detective, who at least could pass for Colombian walked in to Scarlotta Gold, holding a gym bag, clearly stuffed with cash. From outside, we could see the undercover detective engage in conversation with D'Albote.

After a few minutes, they went in to the office and shut the door. After a few more minutes, the detective came out without the gym bag. Part I was a success.

Barely five minutes later, Part II began. D'Albote locked up the store and carrying a small bag, ran to his car, where he carefully put something in the trunk, tucked under a bunch of crap, while constantly looking over his shoulder. He hit the car alarm five or six times before running back to Scarlotta Gold.

The rest of the day dragged on. Scarlotta came back and nothing noteworthy happened. The day ended, Scarlotta and D'Albote said good-by and Part III was about to begin.

Once D'Albote got several miles away and we were sure we weren't being watched, D'Albote was pulled over by two unmarked cars. I couldn't get close enough to hear what was going on, but I knew the plan. It was my plan and it appeared to be working. D'Albote was caught skimming about ten thousand off the delivery of $200,000 to Scarlotta. D'Albote's choice was clear. He could cooperate, or the detectives would go straight to Scarlotta and play the tapes – the whole transaction was recorded and Scarlotta would not be happy about being ripped off. The NYPD had to let $190,000 walk, so this case was now theirs; D'Albote was their informant. That was just what I wanted. I couldn't believe it, but this was coming together.

"What's the call, Bob? This is your brainchild," Zucarelli said.

"You and I get our asses back to the office and look busy. Then you get a call from one of your detective buddies inviting us to debrief D'Albote. Strictly as a courtesy, of course."

"I like it. I like it a lot. I knew you had it in you."

That is what we did, and we did it well. We were just screwing around in the office, when Zucarelli got a call. Then he yelled for me and we left in a hurry. No overacting and no dramatic exit; just responding to a lucky break.

D'Albote was easy. He gave up everything. He told us about Scarlotta's money laundering organization. D'Albote didn't know enough details to give us names and numbers, but he gave us enough to know where to look. All in all, it wasn't a very complex money laundering scheme. Couriers brought Scarlotta cash. He recorded it in his books as a sale of gold; he even wrote a receipt, destroying the original and keeping the carbon copy. It looked like a legitimate transaction. Later, he would record a purchase of gold at the lower price and wire the money to a foreign account. He would get a receipt for that transaction from a gold wholesaler in Los Angeles who got a cut for their cooperation. On paper, it looked legitimate. It was so simple, the IRS never asked questions and an FBI-NYPD Task Force couldn't break it up; it worked.

More importantly, D'Albote gave up how Scarlotta was getting close to Morelli ever since he agreed to pay tribute to Morelli, giving up a small percentage of his profits from laundering all that cash. When D'Albote was asked if he was willing to go back wired and help us put the case together, his answer hit us hard.

"How can I do that? I'm probably already burned."

'Whatta ya mean burned? How would Scarlotta know you're talking to us?" I asked him.

"Are you kidding? You're FBI, ain't ya."

"Yeah, so?"

"Oh, c'mon. Everybody knows Scarlotta got an FBI Agent in his pocket."

"What are you talking about, you lying fuck." I stood up and moved towards D'Albote when Zucarelli stopped me and directed my back to my chair."

"Really? You don't know that Scarlotta's an informant for you guys." D'Albote sounded genuinely surprised.

"An informant? What? How can he be an informant and you all know that. He'd be dead."

"No, 'cause he only gives up bullshit information. His handling agent gives him more information about what's going on with FBI investigations than he finds out about the family. It's a big joke. We all know he's playing some FBI Agent for a fuck' n fool."

This was like Elaine telling me that she was screwing someone all over again; that shooting pain in my heart, shortness of breath and the cold sweats. How many ways can my trust get betrayed?

"Who? Who's his handling agent?" I demanded to know.

"I don't know. He doesn't say. But, everyone knows about it. Even Morelli knows. That's how he found out..." and he stopped.

"Found out what, Danny? What did he find out?"

Danny hesitated and looked around, biting on his upper lip. Whatever it was, he knew once he said it, his life would never be the same.

"Ragusa," he said.

"The Ragman? What about him, Danny? Let's fuck'n hear it."

"Whew." Danny let out a deep breath. "Tony knew where he was; his agent gave it up. Then he told Morelli and Morelli called the hit."

"Are you sure, are you absolutely sure?" Now Zucarelli was yelling and getting in D'Albote's face. I didn't stop him.

"Yes, I'm sure."

*****

"It's kinda hard to believe, huh?"

"Sure is, Zook. I gotta stop being so blind and not seeing what is right in front of me. That's why Scarlotta always stays under the radar. He's been playing Dinella."

"Are we sure it's Dinella?"

"Gotta be. It all makes sense. You saw how Dinella reacted when he heard about Scarlotta meeting Ragusa. Then, Ragusa gets whacked right under our noses. Scarlotta plays Dinella, then Dinella plays us to find Ragusa. What a circle jerk."

"Well, then Dinella got Pops' and Connie's blood on his hands. He has to pay."

"I get nervous when you talk like that Zook. You can't take out Dinella. He's still an FBI Agent. Whatever you're thinking about is probably a federal crime."

"I'll turn it over to NYPD homicide. They won't care that he's an FBI agent. If anything, that will make them more determined. A case like that makes careers."

"I don't think that will do any good. Dinella will never admit to giving up Ragusa to Scarlotta. Then it's the word of a smalltime scumbag against an FBI mob guru. Who would you believe? "

"Actually, now that I think about it, we're better off if Dinella never gets implicated."

"How do you figure that?"

"Think, Bob. He's been working the families for a long time and he has a good track record for getting wiseguys locked up. If it gets out that he helped Scarlotta set up a hit, then every mobster who Dinella has put away would probably get sprung on some appeal. Ain't worth it. We're better off forgetting it."

"I would have never thought of that.   Shit, everyone's getting away with everything.

"Not everybody. I think Scarlotta may have pushed his luck a little too far this time."

"I'm listening."

"There's something I didn't tell you, Bob. Connie wasn't your ordinary waitress. Her uncle was Carmine Genova."

"*The* Carmine Genova?"

"Yep, that one. Mob boss of the Tavella Family."

"Zook, you were screwing a mob boss' niece?"

"Well, it's not like she was a made member or nothing. She was just a niece. It wasn't like…wait a second, that's not the point. The point is when her daddy goes crying to his brother Carmine for revenge, there will be revenge."

"Do they know it was Scarlotta and Morelli in on this?"

"Trust me, if we know, they've already known for a while. They won't go after Morelli himself, but a punk like Scarlotta – they'll take him out in a heartbeat. He'll get his."

"This is too much. What a clusterfuck this has been."

"I should've seen it, Bob. I really let Pops down."

"Zook, you can't feel that way. We did the best we could. We couldn't see this coming; no way."

"I guess I'll let that rationalization carry me through, at least for now."

✶✶✶✶✶

"Sit, Tony. Would you like some wine?"

"No thank you, Mr. Morelli." Scarlotta sat at the opposite end of Morelli's white marble dining room table, surrounded by dark maroon walls adorned with expensive still life paintings.

The mood was serene.

"I am glad we've been able to keep things under control for as long as we could."

"Yes, Mr. Morelli, I am too."

"I appreciate your help with that little matter. That could've been problematic for us."

"My pleasure, Mr. Morelli."

Morelli looked over his shoulder to the man standing behind him, who leaned over to hear what Morelli had to whisper in his ear. The man left and returned with a sealed, large manila envelope, which he brought to Scarlotta.

"You can deliver this and then call your friend?"

"Yes, I will do that."

"Very good. Then we will take care of everything. It's going to get a bit nasty around here for a while as you can imagine. Do what you have to do, go wherever they put you and keep quiet for a few years. Things will eventually calm down and we can talk then."

"Understood. Thank you, Mr. Morelli."

*****

Zucarelli and I had a new case assigned to us. It was a spin-off from one of Reardon's old cases, all of which had been reassigned. It was nothing new – a drug distribution cell operating in Jackson Heights was getting large loads of cocaine shipped in. The next weeks were spent the usual way – surveillance, record checks and trying to find informants.

We were also waiting for word on Scarlotta. With D'Albote's cooperation, the NYPD was putting together a case to charge Morelli and Scarlotta with murder. That was the great thing about charging mobsters with killing mobsters – it was win-win. It wasn't just Ragusa; they would also get charged with killing Pops and Connie. Dinella would not be able to protect Scarlotta from the NYPD.

Zucarelli's phone rang. He was listening intently, walking in small circles. Restricted by the length of the telephone cord, he moved the phone from ear to ear. Zucarelli did little talking during the conversation. When Zucarelli finally hung up the phone and sat down, he gave me the Zucarelli stare.

"Zook, what?"

"He got away with it, Bob. The motherfucker got away with it."

NYPD detectives arrested D'Albote for the murder of the two Colombians we found with cash stuffed in their slit throats, sitting in their car in the Diamond District. Based on a tip, they got a search warrant and found the knife that was used hidden behind D'Albote's refrigerator. Forensic analysis found that the blade matched the cut pattern on the throats, the blood matched and a hair belonging to D'Albote. D'Albote went from witness to suspect. His cooperation was now meaningless. It got worse. The tip about where to find the knife came from Tony Scarlotta. Scarlotta and his attorney went to the prosecutor and offered up his cooperation against D'Albote. Since Scarlotta was cooperating against a dangerous, cold-blooded killer, he was accepted in to the Witness Protection Program. He would disappear courtesy of the government. He would be safe.

"Wow, that's something. Sorry guys, I know how hard you worked. That's how things go in this business. Let's move forward; there is a never ending drug war out there and plenty of work to do," was Dinella's answer when we went to tell him about this development. Actually, we knew he already knew; we wanted to see his reaction. He had no reaction. He was smooth.

Epilogue

Zucarelli and I had licked our wounds from the Scarlotta investigation and tried to move on. So many deaths and so little, actually nothing accomplished. What were these drug wars really about? We were fighting it on so many fronts, how could we ever hope to win? Did anybody really care? Did we still care?

In our car on surveillance as usual, we found ourselves on the northwestern tip of Brooklyn. Zucarelli and I talked about the things we always talked about. He planned on moving out of his house next year when his youngest kid graduated from college. Then, he would start planning his retirement in a couple of years. His stories of sexual exploits never waned.

I had a new girlfriend. Zucarelli was surprised that I had met her at a singles' bar. "I didn't think you had the moves to pick up a babe at a bar," he told me. As we know, necessity leads to creativity.

"Can you believe how fast the year is going Zook? The millennium came and we're still here. The summer is gone and winter is around the corner."

"Yeah, but it is a beautiful day today; let's enjoy it."

"Absolutely, as a matter…wait, what's that?"

"What's what, Bob?"

"Right there." I pointed out the windshield facing west, across the East River. "Look at all that smoke."

"Fuck. Whatta ya think, they finally tried nuking Jersey, but missed?" Zucarelli dumped on New Jersey the same way he dumped on the FBI.

"Maybe; that looks bad."

"That's some friggin fire, huh?"

"Sure is." I had never seen smoke like that before.

"What the fuck, you see that?"

"Holy shit, what was that? What's going on?"

"Attention all units, attention all units. Report back to the office ASAP. Repeating, report back to the office ASAP. Keep radio traffic to emergencies only." We rarely heard that on the FBI radio.

As we listened to a briefing of what had just happened, the meeting room, filled with FBI Agents and NYPD Detectives was silent. No jokes, no bantering and no discussion. Nothing but blank faces of experienced law enforcement officers who thought they had seen everything. The reality that we had just suffered a massive, unprecedented terrorist attack sunk in. It had to sink in fast; there was no time to ponder what this meant. We all packed our gear and headed to the World Trade Center to do whatever the NYPD and NYFD needed done.

Weeks were spent at what had become known as Ground Zero. The loss of life and the damage to our national psyche was overwhelming. There was no time and no place to escape the anxiety and depression that was overtaking each of us. Zucarelli and I worked side by side, never finding much to say about anything. Work to home and work again. Nothing seemed to matter; nothing had any significance any more. Eventually, ADIC Gunn held a briefing at our Queens office to bring us up to date on the investigation.

This time, in the meeting room, there was a buzz, not the

silence of the last meeting. We were hoping for some new development – we did not know what we wanted to hear, but we wanted to hear something. Unfortunately, the news was disappointing. There was nothing new to report.

"We will continue to pursue every bit of information, no matter how small or how insignificant it may seem, no stone will be…" ADIC Gunn said what we expected he would say. The war on terrorism had begun and the FBI had its marching orders.

"…according to the intelligence from our Osama Bin Laden Unit," Gunn finished his sentence.

Those words caught my attention and jolted me to speak during an office conference – something I've never done.

"Excuse me, sir," I meekly called out, half-raising my hand.

"Yes, a question?" Gunn seemed pleased to get a response from his audience.

"Excuse me sir, did you just say the Osama Bin Laden Unit?"

"Yes, I did."

"You mean, we, uhh, we have an Osama Bin Laden Unit?"

"Yes, we do. Is that your question?"

"Umm, no sir, I mean, I, I, just had never even heard of Osama Bin Laden before this whole thing, and finding out that we had an entire unit dedicated just to watching him is a little surprising, that's all."

"Well, Agent Douglas, you will be learning a lot about Osama Bin Laden and other terrorist groups in a short time. Terrorism is our number one priority and we expect every agent to understand this threat. Does that answer your question, agent?" Gunn's tone was hostile; he clearly did not appreciate my question, which was not really a question,

"Yes, sir." I sat down quickly as I felt the eyes of everyone in the room upon me.

"The director will join me tomorrow at a press conference at 26 Federal Plaza. We want to assure all New Yorkers and all of America of the FBI's continued commitment to leading the war on terror and thwarting any attempt to harm our country again. All agents are expected to attend, and we invite, even encourage our task force member to attend as well."

"There he goes again. He's good, Bob. He's running for something," Zucarelli whispered to me.

The next day, the director and Gunn held the press conference. I and most of the New York agents were there, as directed. The FBI wanted to assure that we showed a united front. Zucarelli was off to one of his meetings at 1PP.

"These terrorists pose the greatest threat ever to the American way of life. Fighting terrorism at every turn, we will seek them out in every nook and cranny, anywhere in the world. Terrorism is the FBI's highest priority." That message was not only for the public. FBI Agents had to accept that the FBI, as they knew it, had changed as soon as that first plane struck.

*****

"The director is on the line."

"Thanks." ADIC Gunn walked from his favorite spot looking out the window overlooking the Manhattan streets and went to his desk to talk to the director.

"Hello, Bill."

"Hi Pete. That press conference went great the other day;

thanks for your help."

"Yes, it did go well."

"How is every else going?"

"Everything is fine, but clearly there is something on your mind, Bill. What's up?"

"I have to give a briefing on the Hill soon. As you know, there's a lot of talk about taking terrorism away from the FBI and giving it to a new agency, something like the Brits have."

"Oh, we can't have that."

"No, we can't. Not under my watch. That's not going to be my legacy. If we intend to keep the FBI the way you and I want it to be, we have to have a lot of support behind us. How's the Joint Terrorism Task Force working?"

"We're good in New York. How are things in the other field offices?"

"Very good actually. Think about it, all over the country we got small town sheriffs who can say they have a seat on the FBI Joint Terrorism Task Force; they love it."

"Well, Bill that's important support to have."

"It is, Pete. If we can dodge this bullet, we will come out on top. You know, the president has plans for new departments and agencies. Your name is being kicked around for a top spot somewhere."

"Okay, keep me in the loop and we'll get around Congress. Nobody is taking anything away from our FBI."

*****

"Good to hear your voice, Ramon. It has been so hard to get hold of you."

"Yes, El Tigre. It has been very difficult up here. I am sure you have seen all the news."

"We have. It is hard to believe that anyone would be bold enough to wage that kind of war against the Americans. They will only bring hell upon themselves."

"So true, El Tigre. I cannot imagine what they thought this would accomplish."

"As you and I have discussed, Ramon, you can only push so far. We have seen that. That is why we do things the way we do things. We give Americans what they want and they pay us handsomely for it, don't they?"

"Hah, they certainly do."

"As long as we stay under the radar, we should be okay. That is why we had to be so careful after that unfortunate mishap in Manhattan. We would never kill their police intentionally."

"No, that would not be good for business. But I think we got lucky. We should be clean."

"We are. They are back home and safe. All is well."

"What should we do now, El Tigre? When people are afraid, anything can happen."

"Ramon, we are better off now, than ever before."

"We are?"

"Of course. The Americans will be completely focused on those crazy Arabs. They will forget all about us. Once you can, set up a new network and get right back to business."

"You really believe it is safe for us?"

"Yes I do. After all, we are just businessmen, not terrorists."

"No we are not."

Rojas and Ramon shared a laugh.

*****

"Hey, how'd it go?   Got your new marching orders?"   I asked Zucarelli as he came back from another in a series of meetings he'd been having at 1 PP.

"Yes, I do. Let's take a walk."

As we made our way out of the office, Zucarelli was quiet, waiting till we were outside to tell me his news.

"So, I get the feeling this is our last walk down Queens Boulevard."

"I guess things had to change sooner or later, huh, partner," Zucarelli said playfully punching my shoulder.

"They sure did; but what a way to learn a lesson."

"Amen."

"So where are you heading?"

"Bob, I got assigned to the commissioner's new Special Anti-Terrorism Unit."

"That sounds great."

"It is and it gets better. I'm going to Israel."

"Israel? Whatta ya mean you're going to Israel."

"On assignment. I'm going to Jerusalem and I'm getting embedded with the Mossad. We're working directly with them."

"Wow, I didn't know the NYPD did that."

"We do now. It's not just me. We got detectives going all over the world – England, Australia, everywhere they'll take us."

"Isn't that really FBI and CIA jurisdiction?"

"I'll tell you Bob, the commissioner doesn't give a damn about jurisdiction. To put it in his words, New York will never get FBI'd again."

"FBI'd?"

"Yeah, fucked by incompetence. We were relying on the FBI for this counter-terrorism stuff and look what happened. He's not counting on anybody else ever again. It's a new world, Bob."

"Obviously. So the Mossad, huh? They're supposedly the best."

"Oh yeah. They probably got more agents running around the U.S. than the FBI."

"I don't doubt it. You'll learn a lot. How long you gonna be there?"

"Two year assignment with a few paid trips home. It's all good. How about you?"

"Nothing that exciting for me. I'll be working in Manhattan, helping out on PenttBom, as this case is being called and then I imagine I'll be working terrorism for my final years. I think drug work has seen its end of days in the FBI."

"So, all this time and effort we've put in to fighting this massive drug war was all for naught? Not to mention getting cops and agents killed, innocent citizens, even a little baby? We're just gonna walk away?"

"Well, it looks like we have to. Besides, DEA is there; they'll gladly pick up where we leave off. And of course, there's always the NYPD; I can't imagine you guys will stop working the streets. You know the feds can't work the streets like the NYPD, right?"

"I guess. Who knows what's gonna happen? The only thing I do know is that the last couple of years have probably been the worst of my life, Bob."

"Me too, Zook. And while we're all running around trying

to stop the next terrorist attack, Tony Scarlotta gets to live in peace under the protection of Uncle Sam."

"Not forever. His day is gonna come."

"Really?"

"Yeah really. When I get back, I'll have enough contacts and sources to find that fuck. I will find him and when I do...well, I'll find him."

"Okay, and then what, Zook? What are you gonna do if you find Scarlotta, kill him?"

"I don't have to do anything but find him. Once I do, he'll get his. The mob has a long memory."

"Zook, the Witness Protection Program is one of the few places in the government that actually keeps a secret. They take that shit really seriously. What makes you think you're gonna be able to find Scarlotta?"

"Because, I'm Detective Mark Zucarelli."

I should have seen that coming.

About the Author

Author Michael Tabman was born and raised in New York City. He graduated from John Jay College of Criminal Justice in Manhattan, NY. After serving as a police officer for three years with the Fairfax County VA police department he joined the FBI. Michael, Λ 24 year FBI veteran, investigated crimes ranging from white collar to bank robberies, organized crime, drug trafficking and money laundering. He rose through the ranks reaching the level of Special Agent in Charge. His professional travels took him to Israel, Russia, Vietnam, Singapore, Malaysia and Thailand. After retiring, Michael founded and still works at SPIRIT Asset Protection, LLC as a security and risk management consultant and public speaker. He is a crime and security analyst for local news stations.

Michael's book Walking the Corporate Beat: Police School for Business People, is based upon his 27 years of law enforcement experience to draw amusing parallels between the police world, business world and everyday life decisions.

Walking the Corporate Beat: Police School for Business People

- Paperback: 316 pages
- Publisher: BookSurge Publishing
- November 17, 2009
- Language: English
- ISBN-10: 1439255601
- ISBN-13: 978-1439255605
- Product Dimensions: 8 x 5.2 x 0.7 inches

Walking the Corporate Beat: Police School for Business People is former FBI Special Agent in Charge and businessman Michael Tabman's gift to all executives and business professionals seeking new and effective ways to recognize and prevent problems. Readers will be intrigued by parallels between police work and business, and how basic law enforcement concepts resolve management problems. Whether the focus is managing risk or team building, defining company objectives or discussing ethics, the parallels are compelling.

Tabman explains the similarities with candid descriptions and dramatic, and often humorous, vignettes from his days on the force. In an approach that captivates the reader, he juxtaposes such challenges of law enforcement and business as multitasking, conferences, relationships, and strategizing. The concept that rushing into a melee without stopping to think is as dangerous in police work as it is in business is one example of how this book will open new and energizing doors.

Review

This is an awesome book! It is filled with great stories written by a seasoned and very accomplished Law Enforcement Officer and Executive. Agent Tabman shares with the reader plenty of examples of problem and crisis solving which he learned in his many years of service to both the FBI and the Police Department and how one can apply them to those problems encountered everyday in the business world. This book is a "must read" by all upcoming executives and those who face critical and important management decisions on a daily basis. Agent Tabman teaches executives how to safely go "Walking the Corporate Beat" by avoiding problems and embarrassing and tough situations. Thank you for your service to our country Agent Tabman!

Midnight Sin

- Paperback: 340 pages
- Publisher: TotalRecall Publications, Inc.
- Hard Cover ISBN: 9781590956854
- Paperback ISBN: 9781590956861
- Ebook ISBN: 9781590956878
- Language: English

Becoming a cop changes everything you thought you knew about life. *Midnight Sin* is an inside look at the dark and mysterious world behind the cop's badge. Rookie cop Gary Hollings quickly learns that wrestling street thugs and arresting drug dealers while trying to track down a serial rapist is nowhere near as tough as watching his back from his fellow cops. He must also fight his inner demons – ones that he never knew he had until he put on that police uniform.

The police world is one of long hours and split-second decisions. The choices are not always clear. *Midnight Sin* is a gritty cop novel that explores the complexities of the cop psyche.

Review

Midnight Sin is the ultimate cop novel. Michael Tabman blends mystery, suspense and action while exploring both the human side along with the dark side of the police world."

-- *Joaquin "Jack" Garcia, author of New York Times Bestseller, Making Jack Falcone: An Undercover FBI Agent Takes Down a Mafia Family*

"Buckle up; *Midnight Sin* is an exhilarating ride on that dangerously thin line separating cop and criminal. Michael Tabman, a former cop and FBI Agent hits his stride with this spellbinding crime thriller."

<TAB><I>-- *Richard Kline, Television Producer*

"After reading Tabman's first book, *Walking the Corporate Beat: Police School for Business People,* I could not wait to read Midnight Sin. Again, I could not put the book down. *Midnight Sin* is a crime novel that leaves you thinking about your hidden dark side."

-- *Steve Schussler, Founder of Rainforest Cafe, Yak and Yetti's and T-Rex at Walt Disney World, Orlando, Florida.*

www.ingramcontent.com/pod-product-compliance
Lightning Source LLC
Chambersburg PA
CBHW020329120726
47904CB00002B/336